Virtually Forever

ANTHONY EAMES

Copyright © 2013 Anthony Eames

All rights reserved.

ISBN: 978-0-646-59071-4

Cover Design: Anita Williams

Editorial Services: Patricia Cummings

DEDICATION

To the immortal Louise Brooks

CONTENTS

1	The Call	p. 1
2	Take it to the Line	p. 7
3	What a Pity She's Dead	p. 16
4	Kovalevsky's Twin	p. 26
5	We Know What You're Thinking	p. 30
6	Back From the Brink	p. 35
7	Lulu	p. 43
8	A Breath of Life	p. 48
9	Maker of Worlds	p. 52
10	The Toolkit	p. 60
11	Unseen Sentinel	p. 65
12	Hello, Miss Brooks…	p. 73
13	Smell the Roses!	p. 75
14	Someone Else, Somewhere…	p. 86

15	The Only Girl in My Life	p. 92
16	Could I Ever be Sure?	p. 102
17	The Interloper	p. 108
18	Meet My New Friends	p. 116
19	Magic Crucible	p. 124
20	Someone's in Our Sector	p. 136
21	The Wrong Sort	p. 141
22	Some Coincidence	p. 150
23	You Knew, Didn't You?	p. 160
24	The Breach	p. 165
25	Countdown	p. 167
26	Mr Scooter	p. 176
27	Getting the Fix	p. 182
28	Alter Ego	p. 187
29	Stay a Moment	p. 192
30	There's No Other Way	p. 200
31	The Lure	p. 211
32	No Promises	p. 218
33	Give Her My Love…	p. 226

What is this Life?

Only the Dream of a Butterfly...

Old Zen Saying

1. THE CALL

'Wake up, Sunshine! It's your big day! You're going to meet the Divine Caesar!'

Turning slowly in his straw-filled cot, Micalus squinted up at the hulking figure peering into his cramped stall. Galba's bony cheekbones and sideways-slewed, broken nose were thrown into distorted relief by the flickering play of light from his torch. He leered at Micalus and lurched past, pausing at the next stall to yank hard on a leg-iron.

'Stir yourself, you black loafer, or they'll start without you!' he roared hoarsely, violently rattling the chain. 'They'll drag you back on a hook soon enough — and then you can doze away for all eternity!'

He threw back his head and guffawed at his joke.

In truth, few of the gladiators chained in that musty labyrinth had slept that night. Of his companions, Micalus could barely see only one, Salarus, who lay shackled in the opposite stall. But the whisperings, the urgent incantations to unknown gods in strange tongues, the patient scraping of a manacle clasp inscribing a forlorn epitaph on a wall, all told of an unbroken watch through the long, dark hours.

But who could have envied those who did slip into fitful slumber? Their despairing moans and startling cries told of dreams stalked by the very same torments that kept their fellows in numb wakefulness.

Galba passed by Micalus' cell and paused.

'All alive and kicking — and just as well, too,' he proclaimed as he checked the numbers on a wax tablet hanging at the entrance.

'Hey, did you hear? One of today's fighters — a myrmillo next door — thought he'd pass up on the Emperor's invitation. Stabbed himself in the throat. You'll never guess how?'

Galba paused for effect.

'That stick with the sponge on the end you've all been using to wipe your backsides? He rammed it right down his throat and bled to death. Now THAT is what I call balls! Big, yellow-haired German... imagine...'

Slowly shaking his head at the thought, he slammed the heavy door and hauled back the bolt.

After a serve of porridge and bread dipped in olive oil, the gladiators were escorted under guard through the vast network of passageways, cages and alcove-like rooms below the floor of the arena. They assembled before the gladiator trainer who barked out the names of the adversaries drawn by lot to face each other in the arena.

Each announcement was accompanied by groans or cheers, depending on how individual gladiators saw their chances of walking back alive from their encounter. They were quickly hushed as others strained to hear their own names.

'Fracus — a myrmillo — fights with Clavus, scythian,' the trainer called out in carefully-measured tones. 'Micalus, a thracian, you fight Xala... Xala...' He scrutinized the writing on the wax-covered board.

'Xalaphaxus,' intoned a deep voice from the back.

'Xalaphaxus, a retiarius.'

To his relief, Micalus realized that his opponent was not one of the comrades with whom some sort of friendship had developed over the months. Instead, it was to be Xalaphaxus — the tall, thin-shanked Macedonian who hardly spoke a word to anyone. A tricky retiarius, too. But Micalus had carefully studied how to deal with the flailing net and the stabbing trident. And they said a thracian with his shield and short sword was a match for a fisherman — any day!

Micalus looked around at the other gladiators. They all stood apart, oiled skin glistening and with the intense, brooding expressions of those whose world was now the stark simplicity of life and death. Some checked weapons, others loosened up supple muscles — and, with strange gestures, one prayed for his god's protection. From time to time, everyone looked up to take in the sounds of the arena above... the blare of trumpets, the groans and laughter of the spectators, the shrieks and roars of terrified animals being dispatched by the venatores.

Grimly efficient, Galba, the trainer's assistant, checked his charges, tightening a leather strap here, adjusting a helmet, instructing the retiarius to unfold and refold his deadly net.

Finally, this stomach-churning wait was broken by a shouted order for the gladiators to fall into two lines and, weapons to the ready, to assemble at the iron-barred gate. Each gladiator clipped on a purple, gold-embroidered cloak and climbed into a waiting chariot. At last a piercing fanfare sounded and the great iron gate was winched up.

At measured intervals, each chariot carried a gladiator out into the arena. Micalus felt, rather than heard, the rumble of his chariot's wheels: all sound was overwhelmed by the crowd's ecstatic roar, rising and abating like distant, rolling thunder.

In a dignified procession, the chariots completed a circuit of the area and then the charioteers deftly pulled over in a line facing the imperial box. Micalus and the other gladiators dismounted and marched in step once more around the arena.

Although they had been instructed to fix their gaze in front, Micalus furtively glanced up at the tiers of spectators that seemed to rise up to the sky. He could make out a group of giggling girls. One of them threw a little bunch of posies towards the gladiators, but it fell short and hit a spectator two rows from the front. At every step he heard the pleadings and threats of those whose wagers rested on who would live and who would die in the sand over the next two hours.

'Gladiators, halt! Left, wheel!'

In two ranks before the emperor's podium, the gladiators looked up, blinking in the afternoon sun's glare. Then, for the first time in his life, Micalus saw the Divine Caesar, Claudius, under the shade of a richly woven awning. On either side was a sea of white togas — the senators — and close by the box, also shaded, were the Vestal Virgins, haughty and showing scant interest in the proceedings.

At a sign from the trainer, the gladiators cried out in a strong, unwavering voice: 'Ave, Imperator, morituri te salutant' — 'Hail, Emperor, we who are about to die salute thee.'

The emperor, politely attentive during this formal dedication, then turned to make a joke to a dark-skinned prince in a green caftan seated beside him.

'Ah, Caesar!' murmured Micalus to himself. 'I'd tickle your chin with my little sword to hear how loudly you can laugh! If the gods gave me but the least chance!'

Another fanfare and the gladiators descended back down the stairs, leaving Micalus completely alone with Xalaphaxus. His oiled skin already beaded with sweat, the retiarius began a hypnotic, weaving dance around Micalus, the net slowly circling and trident poised. His head was tilted back in an exaggerated show of arrogance. Now the Emperor had finished his anecdote and was watching, intently...

Each adversary took the measure of his opponent with quick, short feints. To the left. Then to the right. A jabbing thrust to gauge a reaction. A pace forward... and back again.

Soon whistles and shouts of derision began to roll in from the edges of the arena, but the gladiators remained heedless of the impatient spectators' temper.

This was to be the last drama for one of them — and they both knew how it was to be played. Here it was they alone who set the play.

Circle and pause, a step forward, probe — and back again. Always with eyes on your opponent.

Suddenly, everything exploded into savage action.

Thrust... a leap sideways to escape the sweeping net... The trident clanged against the small, circular shield. Cut... parry... and Micalus caught the net. Xalaphaxus crouched low to regain his balance.

Micalus sliced deep across the top of his unprotected shoulder. Through his sword handle Micalus felt metal grating against bone. You have him! Within seconds a web of red rivulets coursed down the Macedonian's arm and his every movement sent a spattering rain of blood flying from his fingertips. Yes, you have him... now finish him! For the first time, Micalus became aware of a massive roar filling his senses, omnipresent and unlocated, like the booming surf.

'Habet! Habet!' chanted the crowd. 'He's had it! He's had it!'

Micalus' eyes darted up to see the spectators all around him, in serried tiers rising up to the distant heights. A single voice, a ravening hunger for death.

Then the Macedonian sprang up — and his net whipped Micalus across the face. Sharpened weights at the edge of the net slipped past the helmet's narrow visor and, in a scalding flash of pain, flayed soft tissue. As he spat out a piece of broken tooth, Micalus sensed that the net had snagged the inside of his helmet. A wrenching tug — and the Macedonian pulled him off balance. Micalus rose to his knees, weakly lifting his small shield. Too late.

The trident jarred into his breast armor with such force that he reeled... half recovered... slipped and fell onto his back. Blinded by blood from his torn face and from the cascade from Xalaphaxus' own wound, Micalus felt the trident bite into his neck, pushing his head hard against the arena's sandy floor.

The crowd groaned. Micalus could only see a red mist, but he knew that the Macedonian was even now looking over his shoulder up to the Emperor's box, ready to act on his sign. Ready to put his full weight behind the barbed prongs that cut so deep into Micalus' throat that he could hardly gasp for air.

With mock deference, Claudius studiously scanned the masses around him to gauge the popular will.

Then the Divine Caesar extended his arm — and teasingly slowly, he turned his thumb downwards...

At that moment Micalus heard a sharp, insistent tapping on the left side of his helmet.

'Hey, Michael — Mike! Sorry, buddy, but this is important...'

The virtual reality visor swung up and for several seconds Michael stared uncomprehendingly around him. His wide-eyed gaze settled on the thin, dark-bearded man with the slightly concerned expression.

'Sorry... I'm sorry, Pearson... You caught me just in time,' he smiled weakly, his chest still heaving. 'I was just about to be stabbed in the throat! Phew... Here, hold this a second. Now what can I do for you?'

'There's a call for you. Some heavy in the Defense Department...'

2. TAKE IT TO THE LINE

The limousine drew up at the army compound entrance. The driver's tinted window glided down and the duty sergeant peered inside. His eyes settled on Michael who sat, incongruous in his slacks and jacket, between two crisply uniformed officers in the back seat.

'Visitor. General O'Keefe is expecting us,' an officer said quietly.

The sergeant scrutinized the paper and handed it back. 'You're clear, sir. You can park at the entrance to the Richter Annex.'

He waved the vehicle on and a sentry clicked to attention.

Moments later, Michael and the two officers were briskly pacing down long corridors, past offices and doors so featureless that Michael wondered if they were retracing their steps around an imperceptibly-curved circle. At last he was steered through several doors and into a waiting room which was sparsely fitted out with expensive leather furniture. Wall lights drew attention to nondescript prints in gilt frames. There was a closed set of double doors at one end.

'Wait here, please. General O'Keefe'll be ready for you shortly.'

Michael sank into a black leather chair facing the doors. He chose not to disturb the meticulous fan of magazines on the low table in front of him.

Long minutes passed. His mind went back to the strange phone call he had received three weeks earlier.

A Paul Henderson, who said he was from the Department of Defense's Special Projects Section, had invited him to discuss over dinner an important new development that might be of interest to Michael. At 'Aldo's' — an impressively expensive restaurant — he was greeted by a dark-suited, stocky man in his early forties. Henderson introduced Dr Maria Havas, a small, albino woman with dark glasses who said very little the whole evening.

Speaking in a hushed monologue, punctuated at intervals by a distracting grunt, Henderson described a major government virtual reality project — 'leading edge, over the horizon stuff'. Aware of Michael's expertise in advanced VR design, he would like him in on the project.

'You'd head your own team. All the technical resources you'd dream about. Salary? Forget government grades, we're talking real-world dollars,' Henderson had promised. 'Interested?'

Lost in the recollection of that strange evening, Michael did not notice the conference room door swing silently open.

'Mr Stanton?'

A young woman motioned Michael inside where he stood at the back of a large, dimly-lit conference room.

From a suspended neon ring, a pool of soft light fell onto a large horseshoe-shaped table, around which stood several officers drinking coffee — four men and two women.

Almost immediately, a tall man in his early sixties came through a small door, walked to the table and placed his hands on the back of a chair. His tailored uniform defined a lean and athletic figure and his thick, steel-gray hair was trimmed to a crew cut. He fixed his pale blue eyes on Michael and raised his hand for attention. The other officers broke off their conversations and took their seats around the table.

'O'Keefe,' he said, his open palm motioning Michael to sit down. He then pointed to the others. 'Mr Stanton, this is General Lorenz, Colonel Ericsson... Colonel Walter and... er... Captains Mackenzie and Spanauf. We'll be joined shortly by Mr Henderson and Dr Havas, whom you've met already. OK, Lieutenant?'

The sidelights dimmed as General O'Keefe approached the lectern. Perfunctorily, he thanked Michael for attending the meeting. The project to be discussed was strategically important and highly classified, he said, reminding Michael that he had signed a formal undertaking to respect its complete confidentiality. He appreciated that Michael had been told nothing beyond that the project centered on advanced virtual reality applications.

Turning to the others, O'Keefe said: 'Mr Stanton's expertise and experience in this very area is exceptional — and that is why the project executive has invited him here. His full credentials are contained in the back of your folders, but I'll read you this summary.'

O'Keefe pointed out that after graduating with Computer Science honors, Michael Stanton had joined Zeta-Bando Software Inc. as a software writer developing a three-dimensional animation program. Two years later, he had been invited to join Warp-Play Corporation, where he headed the design team that produced 'Battlechief', 'Death Race' and 'Galactic Crusaders': computer games using advanced virtual reality technology to create remarkably realistic environments for players.

O'Keefe paused and looked up from his paper.

'Now I am not personally familiar with "Galactic Crusaders" — but I believe it was a major advance in... (he slowly read from his notes)... in total immersion virtual reality, making pioneering use of dynamic fractal geometry to create highly realistic environments within real-time.'

O'Keefe looked up at his audience and gave a quick smile.

'Well, whatever that might mean, it kicked up the value of Warp-Play stock eleven-fold. All within a year. Impressive! And most recently, there was "Arena Combat"... We have a video here — a story aired on the 'World Week' program last February. It shows something of Mr Stanton's work and what made "Arena Combat" such a success.'

'Along the way, you'll get a good idea of some of the directions this technology is taking us.'

The lights dimmed and the wall screen lit up. Michael smiled at the TV report's breathlessly hyperbolic treatment of what he and the Warp-Play team had achieved.

'Arena Combat', said the reporter, was an interactive, immersive computer game in which players fought as gladiators in the Roman Coliseum. Exhaustively researched and meticulously crafted, it recreated the world of the Roman *ludii* in exact detail. In their various roles — a German war captive, another a Greek pirate, or an insolent Italian slave — players were sent to gladiatorial school. Their skills were assessed and the 'gladiators' were selected to confront death in the arena as a net-wielding retiarius or heavily armed samnite, as a thracian with his curved short sword or myrmillo with the fish-shaped crest. Over several computer sessions, participants were trained in the special techniques that went with their weapons and armor.

Within two months of release, said the commentary, 'Arena Combat' was the biggest-selling computer game. It had redefined virtual reality gaming and given Warp-Play an incontestable lead in a mercilessly competitive industry (it had won the computer industry's 'Top Innovator' Award for the year 2027). Already a minor legend in VR circles, Michael had featured in newspaper and magazine interviews, even a Time Magazine cover article ('The Man Who Creates New Worlds').

The 'Arena Combat' cult had spawned hundreds of gladiatorial schools in which young men and women undertook rigorous training for their roles in 'Arena Combat'. Supporters' clubs sprang up around gladiators whose VR clashes were avidly attended by pay-view spectators who sat in a virtual Coliseum, decked out in Roman attire. Formal leagues soon followed, modeled on the Green and Blue teams which had attracted such passionate allegiance two millennia ago.

In a world that had become perhaps too soft and comfortable, said the reporter, 'Arena Combat's' realistic, yet physically safe, combat provided an outlet for young people's primal hunger for physical danger and competition.

At last the wall screen dimmed and the lights rose.

'We — and you, I'm sure — are interested in what you might be able to do for us,' said O'Keefe. 'Captain Mackenzie will introduce Project... er... the Project.'

An officer walked to the podium and looking straight at Michael, who now felt even more uncomfortable about the casual clothes he was wearing. Mackenzie began slowly and deliberately.

'In peace and in war, our priority is always the same. We need to understand the psychology of the political and military leadership of adversaries, potential adversaries and... our own allies.'

'In the last decade, particularly, we've seen significant advances in our information-gathering and profiling. But the fact remains that we're still well short of getting really accurate feedback on the other side. Likely reactions to unfolding events, for example. Our tactical and strategic moves and countermoves still hang on scrappy, uncollated data and old-fashioned hunch work.'

Mackenzie looked up from his notes.

'Before I go any further — and for the benefit of those of you who are not computer specialists — I would like to retrace some recent developments in computer technology. This may be familiar ground to several of you, but please bear with me.'

'Seven years ago,' he continued, 'a paper was published by Dr Ernesto Califrani of MIT and Dr Nigel Cummings of Cambridge University, England. It laid down the theoretical basis for a radically different, revolutionary approach to computer architecture. In turn, that opened the way to the latest generation of computers which now promise true heuristic and algorithmic processing in an integrated, seamless functionality!'

At this, General O'Keefe looked to the ceiling and pointedly cleared his throat. Mackenzie smiled apologetically.

'Yes, General, point taken! Some definitions are in order. The classic computing process is algorithmic or "top-down". It enables a computer to rapidly manipulate vast amounts of hard data according to a set of programmed rules and precise definitions.'

'In this fashion, even first-generation computers could play chess so well that they wiped the board of anyone less than a grand master.'

'The problem, of course, is that not everything in the world works to the on-off, black-white, formal logic of the chessboard — and that's where even the biggest computers have always fallen down. They could never match the human brain when it came to drawing inferences or just using old-style common sense. They were like idiot savants. Remarkably clever within specific areas — but morons outside them.'

'On the other hand, heuristic — or "bottom-up" — processing is what until now made humans different to computers. It's the ability to absorb fuzzy and incomplete information, evaluate it and make a best-guess hypothesis about a situation. It also draws upon relevant, but not always identical, experiences. It's a process that makes inferences and includes a lot of what we usually describe as intuition.'

'And right from the start, this has been the Holy Grail for computer engineers and designers.'

'Even fifty years ago, developers were looking at how computers could cope with ambiguous or indistinct forms, incomplete data expressed in analogue form. Boolean algebra — a method of expressing ideas in a quantifiable or computable way — could only take them so far. Then, by the turn of the century, it was obvious we'd find our best clues in the one computer that's always been able to handle all that.'

Mackenzie tapped his forehead.

'Thanks to Califrani and Cummings — Dr Cummings, interestingly, holds Phds in both computer engineering and clinical psychology — we're starting to produce hardware and software which come much closer to the way the human brain works and, therefore, thinks. As you know, prototypes of such computers have already been built and are being tested.'

'And, as predicted, they work comfortably with a set of "givens" or assumptions drawn from a mixture of logic, insight, similarity with earlier patterns and experience. Just like we do!'

'Naturally, this technology will have many military and political applications — including, we believe, compiling highly-accurate computer profiles of foreign leaders. Of course, the technology is only part of it: we have to feed in a considerable database of biographical information, psychoprofiles, physical data, newsreel footage — you name it. We would also factor in the individual's conditioning and total environment, including political, social, cultural, religious and economic elements. Everything and anything, until you've captured whatever it is that makes our subject who he or she is.'

'The result should be a virtual reality model which is, for all practical purposes, the exact clone of the original subject. It will look the same — and move and sound the same, right down to the smallest mannerism.

More importantly, our VR model thinks and acts the same. In fact, it's a simulacrum, a mirror image, that even a wife or husband wouldn't know wasn't the real thing!'

At this point General O'Keefe cut in.

'We're well past the whiteboard phase. Our working model's been in the lab for about eight months. So, we know the concept is feasible. Less than a fortnight ago I got the go-ahead — and the money — to take the project up to full operational status.'

He turned around and addressed Michael directly.

'Mr Stanton, if we can turn this into a workable, reliable tool, our country will hold an enormous strategic advantage. For the first time, we'll have a better than fair idea of how the guys on the other side are going to move. We can use it for writing up our "what-if" contingency planning scenarios — and as a real-time tool for whenever we face the real thing.'

O'Keefe thanked Mackenzie. He slowly scanned everyone in the room (including Henderson and Dr Havas, who had quietly slipped in through a door at the back).

'We're committed to getting this system up and running as fast as humanly — or if you like, inhumanly — possible. I made that promise personally to the President.'

'Our first priority is a working model. To accomplish this, the CyberProfile Group — that's how they'll be known — will operate five task teams. First, the Profile Data Acquisition people will pull together, collate and process all the data that will help create individual profiles.'

'The Profile Modeling team uses this information to build up a cyberprofile model of the target subject. The third team, Environmental Modeling, then creates an environment to mirror the subject's physical world. Both the modeling teams would report directly to the CyberProfile Group Leader.'

He nodded towards Michael.

'The Situational Dynamics people script the scenarios we'll be trying out on our cyberprofile replicates. At the end of the process, the Evaluation team will test the final model in which all these elements have been integrated. Working with the modelers, they'll keep tweaking it until we have an exact replicate of the person we're looking at and the world they live in. Our goal is better than 99% predictive accuracy.'

O'Keefe faced Michael directly.

'To make this happen we'll bring together the best design team in the land... in the world. We know that the sort of unconventional creativity and innovation we're looking for is not likely to be found among our own computer people. They're second to none in systems engineering and standard architecture, but this is an area well outside conventional applications. That's a fact of life and we accept it.'

'Mr Stanton, we believe you have the expertise and ingenuity to lead the two modeling teams and to work with the other groups to reach our goals. I'm inviting you to pick up the ball and take it to the line!'

Captain Mackenzie broke the silence that followed.

'You would report to General O'Keefe through Paul Henderson. We've organized a full facility and we're already putting together the core team to run it. Mr Henderson will describe these resources.'

General O'Keefe continued to study Michael's reactions.

'I'd like to preface Henderson's remarks by saying that if you come aboard, we'd welcome your inputs on recruiting key personnel. In fact, we expect them. Give our review committee a convincing case for any additional resources, human or otherwise, and you've got them. We'll listen sympathetically to any representations made on your behalf by Henderson and Dr Havas... Now Paul, can you go over the allocations?'

What followed was a detailed list of equipment and capabilities which, Michael knew, far exceeded anything he would ever encounter in the commercial world. Earlier, he had viewed the whole proposition with skepticism, even unease. Now he felt engulfed by the scale and audacity of this venture. Tingling with exhilaration, he suddenly realized he was being presented with the greatest challenge of his life.

'So, how does all this sound to you, Mr Stanton?' asked O'Keefe.

'Unbelievable, General. Just unbelievable!' said Michael softly, quite unable to summon up a more adequate reply.

'Well, I hope you damn' well make it very believable... and in pretty short order, too!' replied O'Keefe, only half-joking.

'No doubt you have a few questions,' he added, trying to hide a satisfied smile as he noticed Michael leaning forward with both arms stretched forward on the table.

3. WHAT A PITY SHE'S DEAD…

'It's after six-thirty, Michael. How about an early mark?'

He looked up at the two programmers, Slick and Harriett, standing at the door into his office.

'Not this time,' replied Michael, wearily. 'I've got to…. Ah, hell, why not! You know, it was dark when I left last night — and it was dark when I came in this morning. If I don't catch a glimpse of daylight sometime very soon, I'll go stir crazy! Cabin fever.'

He snapped his briefcase shut.

'Anyway, it's Friday night. So, what are you no-hopers up to? Having a beer?'

'What else? Coming along?'

'OK, see you in ten. The Tavern, right?'

Moments later, he was standing by his car in the carpark, looking back at the complex which housed the CyberProfile Group. As the sun dipped below the horizon, the fading light softened the stark chalk-white of the buildings, enveloping them in pastel pink. The complex's lights twinkled in the half-light, making the whole scene seem slightly unreal.

A strange place to end up, Michael mused to himself. And even after three — no, almost four — months, it all still seemed unfamiliar, even alien. Only in the last few weeks had things begun to take on any sort of pattern. Before that, each day had been a blurred round of technical briefings, knuckle-grinding military handshakes, intense conversations peppered with bizarre acronyms, flying visits to workgroups in the bowels of vast concrete blocks. And everywhere, he saw people with expressionless faces hurrying up and down corridors as long as a city street.

He was relieved to begin completing the team recruitment. For security reasons, he could only give the vaguest outline of the project. However, they all knew him, or knew of him, and when he described this as one of the most exciting and important computer projects ever, they listened. Any residual doubts were banished by the lure of big salaries and all the technical resources they could think to ask for. He had already brought together the core of his group and final interviews for the other positions would be rounded off within weeks.

In the meantime, the planning committee headed by Henderson had submitted its detailed program to O'Keefe and, he had heard that morning, it had been authorized with little change. So, we are under way at last, Michael thought.

Slipping behind the wheel of his meticulously restored 1999 Jaguar S Type, he smiled with satisfaction at the V8's roar — and the prospect of the beer waiting for him. He felt like celebrating.

* * *

'Hi, Michael,' called Harriett over the bar-room uproar. 'We thought you'd changed your mind. What's yours?'

'Just a light beer. Thanks, Harry.'

Michael turned around and his eyes lit up in recognition.

'What's this? You didn't tell me Vince Fadowsky was going to be here. Boy, you sure are keeping bad company!'

Half-propped up on a bar stool, Fadowsky was a tall, thin individual, around thirty and with black straggly hair that seemed to extend to a droopy moustache. He lifted his beer in a casual wave.

'How're things, Mike?' said Vince.

With a long, sly grin, Michael leaned back on his stool.

'Well, they could be worse, Vince. They could be a lot worse.'

Michael paused a moment and slowly shook his head.

'You know, guys, you're drinking with one of the all-time VR wizards. Even when we were still at college, Vince was cutting it in the business.'

'Nothing on you, Mike,' replied Vince, turning to the others. 'We worked together when Mike was at Zeta-Bando. Called me in on some projects. Fun times, hey?'

Michael sipped his beer. 'So, how the devil are you going? Heard you'd quit Prancer Tech. Yeah? Now, that did surprise me. I'd have said that place would have been like coming home for you!'

Vince looked embarrassed for a moment.

'Yeah, they were great — and then the big boys took them over. The Parson acquisition, right? In no time we were up to our danglers in the usual old corporate bullshit. Each day a new direction, screw-ups no-one ever owned, big promises never delivered. So, one morning I came into work in a cab and kept it waiting for me outside the front, while I went in and told the suits to shove their job.'

The others nodded in vague sympathy.

'Anyway, that was three months ago,' continued Vince. 'Been taking it easy since. Couple of projects and, you know, looking around. Talking to people...'

His voice trailed off and he toyed with a beer coaster. Suddenly brightening up, he turned to Michael.

'Anyway, I bumped into Slick and he said this is where you guys hang out some nights. I hear you're heading up some hush-hush, deep-pocket number for Uncle Sam, yes-no?'

'VR training programs for the military, Vince. Can't say more,' replied Michael, placing his hand over his heart with mock solemnity.

'Don't have to. Arcade games for the baby-killers, right?'

The conversation rolled on, with Vince doing most of the talking. Slick and Harry were obviously impressed by him and he fed this attention with stories about mythic achievements of earlier days.

Saying little except to corroborate some picaresque anecdote, Michael saw that Vince Fadowsky was still the offbeat character he recalled from college days. As ever, Vince left people with two overpowering impressions. First, that he was someone with a real brain. Without trying too hard, Vince quickly revealed an encyclopedic knowledge of computing, both at theoretical and soldering-iron levels. More than that, he had a quirky-curious way of solving problems that was sometimes astonishingly imaginative. His trouble was that he communicated — or, as often, obscured — his ideas in a baffling outpouring of track-jumping logic, technical argot and idiosyncratic metaphors drawn from his own lexicon.

His other characteristic, clearly undiminished by the years, was an engaging disrespect for any type of authority. Although friendly and outgoing, Vince saw every icon and convention as an irresistible target. True, he could be a little wearing over a long session, but Vince was good company — and right now he was in top form.

'Hold it there!' called Harry at last as Vince lined up another heroic saga. 'Guys, I'm running late. No, really. I've got to go.'

She turned to her colleague and, with studied casualness, asked: 'Oh, Slick, do you still want that lift...? Vince, great meeting you. I'm planning to come in on Sunday, Michael. Probably see you then.'

After the other two had gone, Michael ordered another beer.

'They're on together,' said Vince, tilting his head towards The Tavern's door.

'You reckon? I wouldn't know.'

'Look at the body language. The way he topped up her beer. Trying so hard to look like they're not an item. Ah, young love!'

'What about you, Vince? Married? Kids? Or what?'

'I'm into year two of a meaningful relationship, pal. Melissa's a network operations hotshot I met at an industry seminar. Some guru was spouting the usual party line on hypercompression standards, so I called out a few home truths from the floor. Before I could reply to his reply, this dame on the other side of the room treated him to a big-time reality dump. Really pulled the plug on his fog machine. Now that's impressive, I thought.'

He laughed to himself.

'She was so short I couldn't even see her when she was standing up. But I knew I'd found my soul-mate. You should meet her sometime... And you? The ladykiller?'

'Too busy, Vince. The last date I had was over a year ago. I'm fated to end up a crusty old bachelor... Maybe I *am* a crusty old bachelor!'

Uncomfortable with this topic, Michael, swung back to Vince's situation. 'So, got any real projects? Getting by?'

'Yeah, I guess. You know me, always on the edge. Still, Melissa's got a good job, so we pay the bills, eat — and buy a beer or two.'

Vince started flipping the beer coaster between his fingers.

'Well, yeah, Mike, if you really want to know, things are tight,' he continued. 'I didn't want to say anything with the others here. Fact is, we took out a mega-loan for our apartment when I moved to Prancer. One serious overbite. I need money, so I need work.'

He twisted awkwardly in his seat.

'Mike, I was wondering if... maybe you could help. Anything you could kick over to an old buddy, hey?'

Michael nodded sympathetically.

'Vince, I know what you can do,' he said. 'I'd have called you, but I thought you'd be the last guy looking to work for the government. Believe me, it's a culture shock. Someone like you should stick to the real world.'

'I don't have that choice, buddy,' replied Vince, leaning over his beer. 'Those Prancer bastards stitched me up with a contract not to work for any other VR company for two years. I tried to pick up a bit of freelance and I had these guys ready to punch the "go" button. So, what happens? Prancer's lawyer hand-delivers a letter to this outfit threatening the death of the first-born. Suddenly, bingo, I'm back dragging my ass on the sidewalk again. Shit, if you're out of it for two years, you're out of it forever! You know what it's like, Mike...'

There was an awkward pause.

'OK. We are still looking for some people,' said Michael. 'You'd have no trouble on the technical side. But they'd put you through the security wringers before you got an offer. Psych tests, the works. I can tell you, though, the money and conditions are pretty good for a government job. But remember, it IS a government job — and I can't offer you a fancy title!'

Vince slapped his thigh and clinked his beer bottle against Michael's. 'Yeah! Go for it, Mike! Just tell me when and where to front up and I'll get my suit out of hock!'

'Hold on, Vince, it's not that straightforward. Call over to my place. I'll tell you what's on offer and, if you're still interested, we'll go through the job description and your application. How's that sound?'

* * *

An Alfa Romeo coupe drew up outside Michael's apartment building. The driver, a young woman, yanked the handbrake and turned to her partner.

'Vince, are you really sure he won't mind? I really wish you'd told him I'd be coming with you.'

'Don't worry, honey. Mike's OK.'

They went up to the entrance and he buzzed the intercom.

'That you, Vince?,' Michael called down. 'Just push the door. It's open. Turn left for the lift. I'm on the eighth floor, eight-one-two.'

Moments later, Michael answered his apartment's doorbell and his eyes fell on Vince's companion. He saw a petite woman, slightly chunky, with medium length brown hair and penetrating, dark eyes. She was attractive in a slightly tomboyish way.

'Mike, I'd like you to meet Melissa Schneider — she's the gorgeous lady I told you about.'

'Michael Stanton. How do you do? Well, come in... Now, how about a drink? I've just opened a bottle of wine.'

'Yeah, great, man!' said Vince as he and Melissa slowly scanned around the apartment. 'Hey, some place, Mike. They sure looked after you at Warp-Play.'

Michael called back from the kitchen.

'Had to look after myself, Vince. I fought hard to get some stock added to my package before they launched "Arena Combat". That turned out to be worth heaps more than my salary. Now, I've got a bowl of nibbles somewhere here... be with you in a second.'

As they waited, their gaze settled on the large, wall-mounted black and white photograph dominating the room. Illuminated by two spot lights, the image was of a very beautiful young woman. Her heart-shaped face was framed by short-cropped hair, lacquer-black and shiny like a tight-fitting helmet. Dark eyes and a direct gaze spoke of penetrating intelligence and innocence, of fierce independence — and a hint of vulnerability.

'What a babe!' Vince murmured.

Melissa nudged him and directed his eyes to the other part of the L-shaped room.

'Look, Vince,' she whispered. 'More pictures. She's everywhere.'

At that point, Michael returned with a tray. They sank into the lounge chairs and lifted their wineglasses.

'Cheers,' called Vince. He gestured towards the large photograph. 'Who is she, Mike? Looks like an old movie star.'

'Louise Brooks,' replied Michael. 'You could say I'm a fan of hers. Got every film she ever made — and everything written by her — and about her.'

'She must be pretty old, right?'

'That picture's from the 1920s. The silent movie era. Of course, she's long dead — that picture's a century old.'

'Isn't she really beautiful?' observed Melissa with genuine admiration. 'Those big eyes. What's her story, Mike?'

'Louise Brooks grew up in Wichita, Kansas,' replied Michael. 'A gifted dancer, she moved to the Denishawn Dance Academy in Los Angeles, became a chorus girl and was spotted by a studio talent scout, then a string of unremarkable silent movies. A fairly standard career path for starlets back then. I guess most tried to hunt down some old moneybags before they lost their looks and the job offers.'

'That's pretty well all Louise would have amounted to if she hadn't quit Hollywood and gone to Europe. She starred in two German films that became classics — and made her immortal. It's interesting how that happened.'

Michael explained that the director Georg Pabst had bought the film rights for Franz Wedekind's notorious stage play, 'Pandora's Box', and had scoured the continent for an actress to play the fate-crossed temptress, Lulu. One day he visited a cinema to while away an hour watching an American film, 'The Vanishing Canary'. The film itself was quite pedestrian, an amusing trifle. But when he saw Louise Brooks, Pabst was electrified. He knew in that instant that his search was over: he had found his Lulu.

Her ethereal beauty, the earthy smile, the confident physicality so rarely found in a woman from the Old World, the vulnerable naiveté, the innocent wantonness: these were the very attributes of the doomed beauty at the vortex of Wedekind's drama. Here, indeed, was the very incarnation of the woman whose fatal beauty and unworldliness destroyed men — and, ultimately, herself.

Pabst immediately cabled Louise, offering her the part of Lulu. Typically, she ignored it, thinking this was just another frivolous pitch from an unknown director. However, some months later Louise had a falling out with her studio and, short of money and with no other work in the offing, she telegraphed Pabst to say she was on her way.

Pabst was overjoyed — and surprised — by this unheralded message. He had already assumed that the offer to Brooks was a lost cause — and he was on the point of hiring Marlene Dietrich. (A choice, observed Michael, that Pabst and everyone else agreed would have been disastrous miscasting: Dietrich's heavy-lidded vamping would have turned the film into a burlesque!)

Made just as the first talking pictures were being filmed in the United States, 'Pandora's Box' was recognized as a masterpiece, although it was only moderately successful at the box office. Important sales were lost because of the public's preference for the sound films now appearing on both sides of the Atlantic. Another problem was that the film's frank and uncensorious treatment of sexual issues (including Louise's notorious lesbian scene) caused outrage in a comparatively strait-laced America.

'She's fascinating. Just looking at her, I can imagine all that happening,' said Melissa, who inwardly noted how often her host referred to the film star by her first name. 'It seems, Michael, you're a very big fan of hers. What a pity she's dead — and that you never, ever met her!'

Still gazing up at the picture, Michael did not reply. Vince looked pointedly at Melissa and finally cut in.

'Well, I don't want to tie up too much of your time, Michael. I've some references and a showreel to see what you think.'

'Oh, yes,' responded Michael. 'Here's the application form. And the official job description — which is so vague you could read anything or nothing into it...'

Glancing up, he saw Melissa was still absorbed by Louise's portrait.

'Melissa, we'll be working on this for an hour at least,' said Michael. 'I've got some books on the divine Miss Brooks. Would you like to look through them? There's a whole shelf of them in my study.'

'Now that would be very interesting,' she replied.

Then, with the earnest conversation of the two men barely audible through the closed door, Melissa sat alone, turning the pages of a large picture book.

4. KOVALEVSKY'S TWIN

'Ok, settle down, guys. Quiet, please.'

Michael stepped closer to the group in front of him.

'Are we still waiting for anyone? Profile Modeling crew? Environmental Modeling — all present? Good. Now, just before I go to the main business... Not all of you would have met Vince Fadowsky. Vince, kindly reveal yourself! Mr Fadowsky joined us on Monday and he's one of our top guns in the Profile Modeling team. You can introduce yourselves when I take him around this afternoon. Thanks, Vince.'

Michael moved back to the podium.

'I called you here to tell you something you've all been waiting for. We've just got our first assignment...'

The enthusiastic cheering surprised Michael. It was clear that they were as impatient as he was to get down to a real project.

'Well, I'm glad you're not too disappointed!' he replied. 'Anyway, here's our subject... Screen, please, Harry... Yes, folks, it's our old comrade-in-arms, Fyodor Mikhailovich Kovalevsky, President of the Russian Federation and Chairman of the Commonwealth of Independent States... Yes, Henry?'

'Why him? He's one of the good guys, isn't he?' called a voice from the back.

'Possibly. Probably, even. But understand this. When choosing cyberprofile subjects, there are no good guys — or bad guys. As we build up our gallery of cyberprofile replicates you'll see that the only criterion is that each one is a heavy player on the big stage. Someone the White House needs to know and understand.'

Michael stepped to one side and looked up at the screen.

'We're kicking off with Fyodor simply because Profile Data Acquisition have already got a good database on him and that'll help us fast-track the modeling. The other thing is that he speaks idiomatic English, which means his replicate can talk away in a language the Secretary of State should be able to follow in real-time!'

'Any plans to replicate HIM?' a programmer called out.

'That's classified information — and I'm not at liberty to discuss it,' replied Michael with a wink. 'Maybe the Russians have already got their own replicate of him! We could do a trade. Swap replicates at the border!'

When the laughter died down, Michael continued. 'On a more serious note, this is the program plan you'll each receive as you leave here. Read it very carefully. You're scheduled for a full workshop with the PDA folks so you'll know what's coming from them — and can see how to lubricate the profile data flow in a way that gives you your best chances. I've set one day aside each for the Profile Modeling and Environmental Modeling teams — details on page three. As I said, bone up on this document — and if there's anything you need to discuss, talk to Henry or Marge or me. OK, that's it. Get to it!'

The room emptied and Michael smiled as several of the younger modelers gave an impression of Snow White's seven dwarfs, shuffling out in step and singing: 'Heigh-ho! Heigh-ho! It's off to work we go!'

* * *

From that day, the lights in the CyberProfile building blazed around the clock, week after week. At first, there seemed little to show for the long hours, for nothing yet could be seen of the being that was gradually incubating within their computer system.

It was frustrating work. Constructions were painfully plaited together from long streams of data, were tested and, then when they either collapsed or locked solid, everything had to be teased apart and re-assembled in a new way. It seemed that every advance was at the cost of one, two or more setbacks. But each time, something new was learnt; another clue was prized out of their labors which promised to make the task easier next time.

Of course, there were surprises along the way, such as President Kovalevsky's Moscow apartment, for example. An enterprising French journalist had cajoled the Russian authorities into giving her a tour of his living quarters and, very soon, copies of her photographs were being scrutinized by Profile Data Acquisition. To the profilers' delight, the photographs revealed that (as they had predicted) the walls were indeed decorated with Oblatov paintings, possibly some early originals. And, on a bedside table was a signed photograph of Kovalevsky with President Mitchell. With broken shotguns, they stood before a heaped hecatomb of bloodied fur and feathers, the American President looking awkward in an over-large Cossack hat. The bucolic sentimentalism of Kovalevsky's favorite artworks, this passion for hunting, the reassurance that men of achievement find in the company of their peers: these were all evident in this old-fashioned, over-furnished apartment. After all, the Russian President was as faithful to his private tastes and proclivities, and as predictable, as anyone else.

There was a framed photograph of a young Komsomol boy being awarded a pennant by a doddering Leonid Breshnev back in 1979. As Henderson dryly remarked to Michael, this was a somewhat incongruous memento for someone who had built a very successful career upon vehement anti-socialism!

Nonetheless, even this detail was added to the cyberprofile.

Like a ventriloquist's dummy, the silver-haired replicate turned and flexed on the computer screen, making facial expressions of increasing range and subtlety. In long monologues, the replicate worked up its spoken routine in accented English. When that was deemed indistinguishably close to the original's many recorded performances, Kovalevsky's electronic replicate was subjected to questions on all kinds of topics and, once more, the replies were scrutinized, again and again. Meanwhile, all around him, the Byzantine world of the Kremlin took form with images rendered and re-rendered to incorporate every scrap of information.

And so, day by day — and quite unknown to him as he fretted over the affairs of state an ocean away — the Russian leader's other self was becoming ever more human, ever more real.

5. WE KNOW WHAT YOU'RE THINKING

'You will be sitting behind this desk, just here, Mr President,' said General O'Keefe, as he led his guest through the small studio.

'The Russian President will be coming through a live video line — on that monitor. There's a camera just above it, so that'll give you the correct eye-line. This is your prepared agenda sheet for you to talk from. And it's also on these cue cards which will be held up for you over there. It includes a range of current items, supplied by your office, several of which follow on from your meeting with President Kovalevsky in Brussels.'

'Right. Tell me, do I ask the questions? Is it all coming from me?' President Mitchell asked.

'No, sir. He will be participating fully as well. It's very much a two-way dialogue.'

'So, what's he pitching my way?'

O'Keefe shrugged. 'Could be anything at all, sir. The other end hasn't given us a clue — but then we haven't briefed them, either.'

The President straightened his tie. 'Can he see me, too?'

'We assume he can. They've got a feed from our camera...'

The studio floor manager interjected: 'I'm sorry, General. Mr President, the countdown has just started. Now, sir, are you comfortable? Good. Quiet everyone, please... Ten seconds... five... four... three... two...'

The screen faded up to reveal a broadly smiling face, unmistakably Slavic.

'Good morning, Mr President! How are you? Your day is starting and ours is finishing — and you can see I am still busy. They won't let me go home to see my family!'

'Hello, Fyodor,' replied the American President. 'They keep me on a short leash, too! The last real break I got was the couple of days at your hunting lodge. We must get together again soon. You come here and I'll show you how to catch marlin!'

'No press, no advisers — only the cook. We solve the world's problems straight away, like that!' he beamed, clicking his fingers and wheezing with laughter. 'You and I, John!'

'Fyodor,' said the President, his smile subsiding. 'I'm calling because there are a couple of things I want to talk to you about before I fly to Helsinki at the end of the month. As you said, we seem to cover more ground in informal talks like this, one-to-one. I'd like to start with the tough one first. The oil credit deal with the Ukraine. We have some real concerns there.'

Kovalevsky affected a look of surprise. 'Mr President, what can you worry about? This is just a commercial agreement between two sovereign nations. Nothing remarkable...'

'And, normally, we would have no business commenting on that,' said President Mitchell. 'Our worry is the quantity involved — up to 37% a year over and above their normal annual consumption! You know how the oil market is right now. If they on-sell your cut-price oil to the spot markets, the whole structure is going to get a bad shaking. Fyodor, as it is, the Saudis are on the phone every day and...'

The Russian interrupted testily: 'Mr President. Do you realize that when Minister Shaliakin signed that agreement the Ukraine's oil stocks were down to 12 days? They want to build up strategic reserves so they don't get caught out again. They already asked for your help and the US said no. Naturally, they turned to us. We're being good neighbors. Within two, maybe three, years, we will cut back. We'll insist on it — and what Kiev gets from us they have to keep... Now, what's next? I have my own questions for you before I go to bed!'

The two presidents worked through their respective agendas in short order with most items being agreed to with little discussion. Looking increasingly weary, Kovalevsky finally waved his hand.

'The Lunar Base protocols? Mr President, John... I think we are now down to small issues we can leave to others. But I have one question which I asked before — and still no answer. The Russian minorities in the Baltic Republics. The US always talks about human rights for everyone else, but why not our Russian people? Your UN position only encourages their bad treatment. We welcome constructive help. Please consider. That is all.'

The producer leaned over and whispered: 'Anything else, sir? We're eight minutes over schedule...'

'Just one last question,' President Mitchell replied, turning back to the monitor.

'Fyodor,' the President continued in a measured voice. 'I have advice that I haven't been talking to President Kovalevsky at all. That for the last half hour I've been chatting to a computer-generated stand-in. Is that true?'

General O'Keefe, who had been standing at the back of the studio, suddenly froze, his eyes locking onto the monitor carrying the Kremlin feed. Kovalevsky stared uncomprehendingly at the camera. Then he turned sideways and spoke to someone off-vision in his studio. There was a short, mumbled reply and the Russian leader turned and looked straight out from the monitor.

'Mr President, unlike you, I haven't had time for make-up. That is why I don't look my best.' He leaned forward, as if to impart confidential advice. 'But to be honest, John, we here are not too sure if I am talking to the real person, either!'

With that he leaned back and roared with laughter. Still shaking mirthfully, he turned around to talk in Russian to his studio crew. The screen then went blank.

The President sat silently, then suddenly spun around. A low chuckle grew into a roaring guffaw so loud that it startled the studio crew.

'Do you mean to tell me that... Oh, I just can't *believe* it! It really was the real thing — and just as exhausting, I can tell you. Look,' he said, holding up his hands, 'Sweating!'

General O'Keefe stepped up to the President, who was now having his make-up removed. 'There was no actor, no pre-scripting or pre-recording, Mr President,' he explained in a matter-of-fact tone. 'Every single element was generated within our computer — in real-time.'

'Well then, General, I'm impressed. Very impressed. You say this will be used for tactical responses and planning? Well, I could see also some of our trade negotiators benefiting from a real work-out with this gear. Load it up with some of those Chinese and Indian officials they deal with. Then maybe we'll start getting somewhere!'

'Of course, what you saw today was only relayed on a screen,' explained O'Keefe. 'Next time, when we've completed the environmental modeling, it will be a total virtual reality experience. Complete immersion. You'll actually be in the same room as Kovalevsky!'

'I think I'd still prefer to keep that cunning old bear at arm's length!' Mitchell commented as he rose from his chair.

'Thank you, Mr President, for finding the time to come here,' O'Keefe said as he escorted Mitchell out of the studio and down the corridor. 'We felt very strongly that to assess the system's accuracy and power, you really had to experience it first-hand for yourself.'

'Too damned right! Even now, I'm still not sure I believe what I saw and heard! Trouble is, I'm not too confident many folk will believe me when I tell them, either. At the very least, you'll have to run the recording of this before the Appropriations Committee.'

Outside the building, President Mitchell paused at his car's door.

'General,' he said, 'I don't know all the ways we can use this tool — and maybe you don't either. But one thing's for certain: it could give us more clout than any one technology since Harry Truman hit the button at Los Alamos. It's as good as breaking everyone else's codes. Tell your people they have done very well. And keep me briefed.'

Henderson pushed himself forward. 'One last thing, Mr President. It occurs to me that it'd be useful for us to create a profile of yourself. That way we can run through scenarios without involving you directly each time.'

Mitchell looked at O'Keefe. 'Would that make a difference? OK. Let me know if you need anything from me to help you put it together.'

With that, he climbed into the car and his motorcade swung towards the gates of the complex.

General O'Keefe turned to Henderson. 'I'd have appreciated a little prior discussion before running that idea past the President, Henderson.'

'Just occurred to me, General. But with the President this impressed, I'm sure this was the best opportunity to get the nod.'

He leaned towards O'Keefe conspiratorially. 'Knowing with 99.2% accuracy what the Chief is thinking… very useful in protecting our turf.'

O'Keefe nodded slowly. 'Well, there's a thought. Anyway, how long would the President's profile take?'

'Pretty well finished already, General,' Henderson replied. 'Just thought we might as well have his OK if we could get it.'

6. BACK FROM THE BRINK

The call came just after six in the morning.

'Stanton, here. Hello?' Michael sleepily answered. 'Sorry? Who? Oh, yes, Dr Havas…'

'There is a car already coming for you' she said. 'Bring a change of clothes and some overnight things. Better bring several changes.' She would explain everything in the car.

As the long black car sped along with lights flashing, Michael picked up the outline of the story. There had been a long history of hostility, including wars, between the Caucasian republics of Azerbaijan and Armenia over the enclave of Nakhchivan — and now this was boiling up again. The trouble was that, although 99% of Nakhchivan's people were Azeri and officially lived in an autonomous region of Azerbaijan, they were physically isolated from their compatriots, being landlocked between Armenia, Iran and Turkey.

Behind the recent news reports of increasingly hostile exchanges and expulsions of minorities, intelligence had learnt of a sinister turn in the situation. Spy satellites revealed a massive, but carefully-veiled build-up of troops and war materiél on the Azerbaijan side of the border with Armenia.

This was corroborated by ground intelligence which, although sometimes incomplete and confused, nonetheless suggested that something big was about to break, most probably a pre-emptive strike.

On top of that, was evidence that the Iranians were providing logistical support to aid the fellow-Shi'ite Azeris against the Christian Armenians.

That contingency, Havas declared in her soft, emotionless voice, had been computed to carry a 35% risk of drawing in a host of nearby powers. Even if that did not happen, the invasion's aftershocks would still reverberate through the region like a deadly Mexican wave. She cataloged some of the possible outcomes. Islamist militants around the world would likely see the conflict between Armenian Christians and Azerbaijan's Muslims as their own jihadist cause. The Turks and the other dozen or so members of the Turkic Council would be also actively sympathetic to the Azeris as ethnic kinfolk.

On the other hand, the Russians would probably continue to support Armenia, and so might Georgia, as well.

'So, why are we concerned?' asked Havas. 'Well, to begin with, the Caucasus is a strategic crossroads between Europe and Asia that's laced with vital gas and oil pipelines. All the major powers have a big stake in this area — the Russians, Chinese, Europeans.'

'And, of course, so do we,' she added softly, as she looked out the limousine's window with a distracted gaze.

* * *

Two hours later, Henderson was addressing the CyberProfile Group.

'Well, ladies and gentlemen, here it is — the big one,' he said curtly. 'A full, real-life work-out.'

The room fell very quiet.

'This is a matter of the highest urgency. Drop everything we've been doing, effective from right now. Our mission is straightforward. We set up cyberprofile replications of the war cabinets of each of the main players — the Armenians, the Azeris, Georgians, Iranians, Russians, Europeans and Chinese — and in that order of priority.'

He explained that the system would become fully interactive with changing events through a direct and open feed of information from all sources: news agencies, open and eavesdropped diplomatic exchanges, friendly and intercepted military intelligence, and so on. They were also bringing in experts with personal knowledge of the protagonists' leaders.

Henderson then told the Group that the Americans and Europeans saw several strategic options.

'First, NATO could simply use the threat of military and economic muscle to discourage any invasion. This has a slim chance because everyone knows — as we know — that we've no troops anywhere nearby — and our air-strikes would involve over-flying some pretty hostile terrain before we even get close to the action.'

'The other alternative,' he went on, 'would be to supply Armenia with covert support, so the Azeri offensive is quickly capped before it gets too deep into their territory. Trouble then is that either side may break the stalemate with some old Soviet-era atomic weapons we think they've hidden somewhere. For us, it's do-able with little immediate or direct involvement, but very risky. We're looking at all sorts of unpredictable, knock-on consequences, from Istanbul to Islamabad.'

The best option, he said, involved Russia. Supported by his allies, President Kovalevsky was strongly opposed to anything that could inflame Russia's southern neighbors and, indeed, the Muslim communities within its own borders. As the biggest player in the region, with all the logistics to hand, Russia's role would be pivotal to any military or diplomatic initiatives.

'The trouble is that, while we want the Russians to do the heavy lifting, we and the EU certainly don't want to deal ourselves out of the equation and forfeit any leverage in the future.'

'So, there you are,' said Henderson. 'We're in a big-stakes poker game — and our mission is to mark the cards so we give President Mitchell a winnable hand.'

* * *

Four days later, NATO drew up a high-profile 'peace offensive', with Russia invited to play a prominent role. Azerbaijan and Armenia were told that the US and the European Union had placed a cluster of observation satellites over their territories. The movement of any one power, or combination of forces, across a border would mean the invaded nation would receive comprehensive and continuing information on the invader's deployment and other militarily vital intelligence right through to the cessation of hostilities. This was the public announcement.

However, the NATO chiefs of staff were advised to ensure that, if hostilities did seem inevitable, Armenia would be encouraged to first provoke, or even fabricate, an 'incident' which could be accepted by NATO as a credible *casus belli*. This would open the way for overt and covert assistance in knocking out Azerbaijan's military machinery and overrunning their frontline troops within days. As Havas cynically commented during one of the CyberProfile Group's briefing meetings, this was a device that had been used very successfully by Hitler and Stalin to divide up Poland in 1939 and, in 1956, by the British, French and Israelis at Suez. However, time was running very short because the Russians were less than a week from launching a satellite to give them a fixed vantage point above the likely invasion sites that would clearly reveal who would be the real aggressor in any conflict. Once that happened, NATO's options would be very limited, unless it chose to add a hostile Russia to an already worrying equation.

The CyberProfile Group created a model of the conference that had been scheduled to include the NATO and Russian negotiators and, at separate meetings, the Azerbaijani and Armenian representatives. For good measure, the cyber-simulation also included a model of the Russian President and advisors — and the cabinets of the belligerents and their respective allies.

As tense days passed, the cyber-simulations delivered a clear message. The secret alliance between the Azerbaijani leadership and the Iranians was less cohesive than the Western leaders had assumed. The computer model suggested that the Iranians were much more ambivalent than the Azerbaijanis about launching a war. Their likely thinking was: if the Azeris go in then we have a chance to build a useful alliance by supporting them. On the other hand, the simulated model indicated, the Iranians had deep worries about creating an enemy out of Armenia's allies, the Russians.

Another surprise revealed by the modeling was how deeply averse Russia was to going it alone against the Azeris. Of course, as part of an anti-Azerbaijan coalition with NATO, Russia would certainly have a lot of fence-repairing to do later, but this would be much less than if it had acted on its own.

The model also highlighted the fact that both the Armenian and Azeri leaders, and especially their armies' old guard, still had strong and influential contacts with the Russians that went back to the early post-Soviet days. This would be important leverage for Russia in presenting itself as the honest broker willing to engineer a guaranteed regional security pact in which, amongst other things, the American and European strategic interests might be marginalized.

The Russians would relish an opportunity to re-invigorate their Commonwealth of Independent States organization of ex-soviet states. The Iranians, too, would also prefer any deal that kept the West at a comfortable distance.

The message was unambiguous: pull the Russians into the tent, but quickly before they had time to come up with their own, independent plan. Especially, the negotiations had to be concluded before the Russian satellite was in position.

This advice was noted, but for a while it seemed to have little effect on the NATO strategists: it was just one of the many options being looked at. Then came a secret report which hinted that the Azeri government in Tbilsi and Teheran might not, after all, be in full lockstep — just as predicted in the simulations. US negotiators met in Brussels and, with a European team, flew to Moscow. The Russians, who were anxious to be seen as the main peacebrokers, accepted the invitation to talk directly to the Azeris.

The price the Azeris and Armenians would have to pay for this brokered settlement would be the installation of an international peace-keeping force and the identification and removal of any nuclear warheads and delivery systems. There would be the face-saving offer of minor land-swaps negotiated through a UN commission, to be followed by a security pact guaranteeing agreed borders.

This proposal was pushed hard by diplomats jetting between a dozen capitals as, all the while, the hostile armies edged towards full-scale conflict. But piece by piece, the momentum of war slowed and, miraculously, events fell into place, just as had been suggested by the CyberProfile simulator.

At last the dangerous confrontation subsided and the world appeared to have escaped a perilous train of events which could have led anywhere. More particularly, President Mitchell could now see doubts about his shaky prospects in the coming election transform into a ringing endorsement for the hero who had reasserted his country's standing as the foremost player in the game of nations.

* * *

General O'Keefe and Henderson walked into Michael's office. Uncharacteristically informal, O'Keefe perched himself on the edge of Michael's desk.

'Stanton, I think Henderson might have told you, I had a telephone conversation with the President this morning.'

'Er, no, I hadn't heard,' replied Michael, drawing perverse pleasure from Henderson's glowering look.

'Well, you should know that he's very pleased with CyberProfile Group's efforts during the Caucasian crisis. He and the Secretary of State made extensive use of the simulations we set up for them. He asked me to convey his personal thanks to the whole CPG crew.'

He paused and, with a knowing wink, added: 'So, if there's anything you guys are thinking to add to the wish list, now's the time!'

'Thanks, General,' replied Michael. 'It's always good to get unsolicited testimonials from satisfied customers! There's nothing we need right now so much as some sleep.'

Seeming to ignore Michael's comment, the General continued brightly, 'This was a real, nuke-rattling crisis. We coped with all the chaos and crap — and we came out smelling like roses! Just like our trials said we would. That'll blow the critics out the window, eh, Paul?'

Henderson, expressionless as usual, simply nodded.

'This thing is now really going to take off!' enthused O'Keefe. 'We'll have all the goddamn brass — government, defense and security — banging on the door! But if they're impressed now, wait till we've got those generation-eight computers linked up!'

He turned to Henderson.

'Like I said, they'll give us everything we ask for. So, I want a preliminary report outlining our options — what we need and how much — in three weeks. And don't pull any punches. We may never get another chance like this again! But right now, get your asses out of here. Go take a week off... you especially,' he said as he punched Michael rather heavily in the soft of his shoulder.

* * *

Michael leaned back in his chair and, for the first time, noticed the chaos around him. His office's walls were papered over with hand-drawn flow charts, 24-hour rosters, notes and reminders, and photographs of the protagonists in the recent diplomatic poker game. Half-buried under a pile of documents were several crushed pizza cartons. It would be a day's work to bring this back to any sort of order.

But first he had to refocus his team on the projects that had been shunted aside by the events of the past several weeks.

Michael leaned forward and stabbed a button on his videophone. Vince was seated at his desk, clearly talking to someone off-camera. He swung around, so close that his face went out of focus.

'Hi, Mike...'

'Vince, we need to call the team together. We've got to get the show back on the rails. How's everyone for three?'

'Can I get back to you on that?'

At that very instant, Michael looked up to see Vince standing in his doorway.

'Ah, Mr Fadowsky, our omnipresent ideas man. Here, take a look. There's someone I'd like you to meet!'

Vince walked behind the desk and looked over Michael's shoulder. His own image smiled weakly at him from the videophone. Then the screen went blank.

'Sorry, Mike. I scanned myself in so it would work like a... an interactive answering machine. That way people would think we never left the office. Which we haven't anyway lately.'

Exasperated, amused and then impressed, Michael, slowly shook his head and motioned Vince to sit down.

7. LULU

Michael brewed a coffee and took it into his living room. Flopping into his favorite chair, he listlessly scanned through a holiday brochure on his tablet — and then flicked it off. The whole plan was to plan nothing, take it easy and just go from one day to another. He had quite enough structure and deadlines for a while.

His mind still restless, Michael got up and walked over to his videostack. He ruminated for a moment and then selected a film, dimmed the lights and settled back into his chair again, swinging it towards the wall screen.

Michael had long ago lost count of how often he had viewed 'Pandora's Box'. Scratched and scored, the film's grainy images lightened and darkened spasmodically, a reminder of primitive processing by some long-vanished laboratory. But Michael avidly soaked in each familiar scene, each wavering close-up. Miraculously, the flickering play of captured light and shadow reached across to him from another century — and once more give life to Louise and all her heart-aching loveliness…

It had been some five years ago when Michael first saw her.

An ardent movie enthusiast, he was familiar with the films and actors of his favorite era, the 1940s, but he knew little of film's first decades and was curious enough to download an old documentary, 'Goddesses of the Silent Screen.'

What Michael saw fascinated him. Of course, some of the faces, such as Clara Bow, Mary Pickford and Lillian Gish, he recognized instantly. Others he seemed to remember by name only, but most were unfamiliar. Then towards the end of the documentary, there appeared a brief sequence showing a girl with the distinctive, pageboy bob that was an icon of the 1920s Jazz Age.

It was Louise Brooks.

There were several snippets from her various films, but one image especially stayed in his mind: a scene from a German silent, 'Pandora's Box'. Wearing a wedding dress, Louise in the central role of the star-crossed Lulu was dancing with another woman whose gaze smoldered with intense, Sapphic interest in the new bride. Quite careless about the reactions of her wealthy groom, his son (who had also been her lover) or the other guests, Louise's Lulu projected the wide-eyed innocence worn only by the utterly pure and unworldly — or those creatures of instinct to whom nothing is forbidden or to be judged.

Michael was electrified. Here was a woman of exquisite beauty and expressiveness who moved from haunting, almost mystic spirituality to heedlessly gratified sensuality. Virgin and voluptuary!

Louise's most recognizable feature was her short haircut, shiny-black as a raven's wing. The pageboy or bob cut — what the Germans called the *'bubikopf'* — had first emerged in America and soon became known around the world as the fashion motif of the 1920s, along with the short-hemmed, flat-chested dress.

The story, Michael read, was that young women in the First World War munitions factories soon found that long hair was both impractical and hazardous when operating drills and lathes. In a way, the short hair cut also symbolized the release of the new generation of young women from Edwardian notions of femininity. It went with the flapper's long-limbed, boyish look which denied matronly virtue, but instead, spoke of late-night parties, bootleg gin and being 'fast' — or worse!

True, there were other Hollywood stars who sported this distinctive haircut, Colleen Moore and Anna May Wong, for example.

But although these actresses were better-known in their heyday than Louise, it was the gorgeous Miss Brooks who made the bob cut her own for all time.

After all, her persona (which was pretty well the same thing on- and off-screen) most closely matched everything that this look represented. More than that, no-one else who ever wore their hair in this way looked so incomparably beautiful.

Captivated, Michael then set out to learn more about this long-dead actor. His persistent search over the following years was well-rewarded. He built up a library of all writings about, and by, Louise Brooks, including her own 'Lulu in Hollywood', the acclaimed biography by Barry Parsons written in the 1980s, filmographies and essays. There were the long dialogues with film historians and others from the time of her 'rediscovery' in the 1960s through to her death in 1987. Among these were those of the English theater critic, Kenneth Tynan (whose famous New Yorker essay helped propel the 'Lost Star' back into recognition in 1979), and the film historian, John Kobal. Needless to say, both became bewitched by Louise and their friendship with her was sustained by a lively correspondence.

Having seen so many of her silent films, Michael was teased by curiosity about what this beautiful creature sounded like. He was braced for disappointment, remembering the horrified reactions of studio executives to the voice tests of many leading stars at the dawn of the new talkies. Eventually Michael located a video of her first sound film, the French language 'Prix de Beauté' and rushed home with great anticipation. To his great disappointment he discovered that her voice had been dubbed throughout. (However, the one consolation was that when Louise 'sang' it was with the beautiful voice of the youthful Edith Piaf!)

Her last movie was 'Overland Stage Riders', with John Wayne: a simple potboiler western in which Louise played a chirpy, young heroine. Wearing long, pinned-back hair and jodhpurs, she could hardly have been less like Pabst's Lulu. However, Michael was pleased to note that her voice was clear and well-modulated. If Louise had shown only a little of the flexibility of any ambitious actress, she could have easily made the transition from the silent movies years earlier.

Some time later, Michael acquired copies of interviews filmed when Louise was in her 70s. She now wore her hair tightly drawn back in a complete disavowal of her bob haircut. Louise's voice was emphatic and supported by vigorous gestures. This old woman, racked with emphysema, still projected the same penetrating intelligence, irreverent wit and the sardonic humor of her earlier life.

Relentlessly, Michael hunted even further afield. From time to time, his obsessive efforts were rewarded by an unearthed treasure. There was, for example, the Australian Jen Anderson's quartet score written for Pandora's Box in the 1990s — and an old program of the dance and mime interpretation of Lulu by Neill Gladwin which was scored with classical and popular music of the Twenties.

He was able to locate on-line copies of century-old movie 'fanzines' featuring interviews and photos of his idol. In two 1926 interviews, the young, somewhat gauche Louise already displayed a fierce independence. No pliable — and modest — offering from the studio publicity machine, she was casually dismissive of the whole star business. In one interview, she airily exclaimed that while she was expected to appear in a film — the studio had already announced the part she would play — she had no intention of complying! In their write-ups, her interviewers clearly dismissed this as the posturing of a Kansas ingénue hiding behind a mask of world-weary sophistication.

If only they had known! As her troubled career unfurled, Louise would demonstrate again and again how little regard she had for the Hollywood machine.

* * *

Michael had checked his wallet, his tickets and other documents. The suitcase was carefully packed from the night before and everything was in order. The cab was due any minute to pick him up for the airport.

The mantra kept rattling around in his head: relax, relax you are on holiday! A week in Hawaii to recharge the batteries and unwind, by order of the General, no less! Still, Michael paced up and down, checking his watch and running through a mental inventory. Yes, he had briefed people on what to do while he was away, wrapped up all the loose ends — and had made the appointments for the week following his return. He had called his hotel, confirming arrangements. He had canceled deliveries, asked the Parsons next door to collect his mail.

Relax. Just relax!

Suddenly he heard the cab's horn blast. He grabbed his bags and made for the door. He checked his ticket in his pocket and looked around the lounge room. Michael's eyes lit on the large framed photograph.

'See you soon, sweetheart!'

8. A BREATH OF LIFE

Neither asleep nor quite awake, Michael lay on his side in the soft, warm sand. His heavy-lidded eyes were fixed on the curl of white breakers, half-mesmerized by the easy rhythm with which they caressed the distant reef. Above the low thump of the surf, rose the plangent cry of an unseen gull hovering in the warm breeze.

It was his second day at this quiet resort. Hidden in a small inlet on the north-east of the Hawaiian island of Oahu, as far as could be from that strange world he had left behind. Here at last, Michael was no longer spinning inside a giddying vortex of deadlines, meetings, reports, presentations, late nights and early mornings. Far from the emotional and mental turmoil, here all was quiet.

It must have been three years since his last real holiday, he calculated with a little surprise. Indeed, he was so unused to the very idea of a vacation that he had seriously wondered if it was possible to slip out of his workplace preoccupations in time to enjoy any of this brief interlude before it ended. Yet here he was, already utterly relaxed and serene and lost in dreamy introspection.

Untroubled by anything more demanding than a dinner menu, Michael slowly assessed the facts of his life. He was doing what he most liked — and was successful. He was as financially secure as would ever matter to him (past employers knew that the lure of money — or even the threat of poverty — was a weak lever to work on

Michael.) Looking beyond work and reward, however, it was a different picture. He had, he recognized, quite lost his appetite for anything outside this tight periphery.

It had been like this for as long as he could remember. As a student, Michael spent weekends and evenings tinkering away at a terminal, rather than drinking beer and partying with his fellow students. It was a necessary sacrifice, he had told himself: put in the time now and reap the rewards later. The trouble was that what started as a temporary commitment became an ingrained habit whereby 'later' was always being postponed, *sine die*. One consequence was that it had been at least a year, no, more like two years, since he had taken a woman out for an evening.

And it was seven years since Elaine had broken off with him. Inevitably, the problem had been his growing workload at Warp-Play. As she said — and, of course, she was right — it was always going to be when this project is wrapped up, then we will go away somewhere, then we will talk, then we will start to live a life.

He clearly recalled the night it had all ended. He and some colleagues left the office late at night and decided to have a quick drink on the way home. At that late hour, 'The Barro' was noisy and crowded. Wanting to be able to get away early, Michael went up to the bar to buy the first round of drinks. He had to shout several times to make himself heard and then waited several minutes before he was able to load up his tray with his order of drinks.

Returning to the table his friends had secured, he noticed Elaine, seated in a corner. Her head was nuzzled into the shoulder of a tall man with black hair, swept back. That was all Michael would ever recall of him. Saying nothing, he rejoined his party and positioned himself so he could keep Elaine in his line of sight.

She stroked and groomed her friend and pouted in his ear. Every so often, she drew him close and kissed him.

At last, they rose from their seats and made to leave the bar. Suddenly, Elaine noticed Michael. Without breaking her stride — or moving her arm from around her friend's waist, she gave Michael a long look and shrugged helplessly.

Michael smiled softly. He never saw her again.

Still, he missed Elaine. She had a pert and lively face, but it was her sleepy, hazel eyes that most beguiled him, especially when she smiled. She was adventurous, sensual and had a sharp, playful intelligence. Elaine was fun and, Michael had assumed, infinitely patient. His friends had warned him, saying he would be crazy to let her go. And they, too, were right... of course.

Afterwards, friends arranged meetings with ladies they knew, but all Michael drew from each awkward encounter was yet another aching reminder of what he had so thoughtlessly lost.

Now, it all seemed such a very long time ago.

Yet, there was another great love in Michael's life. Louise. From the first instant he saw her, some five years ago, she had held him in a thralldom he had never known before, not even with Elaine. It was she who always appeared at the centre of his daydreams, the fantasy sprite who quietly glided in and out of his thoughts.

The trouble was that the woman he was so much in love with was dead. Long dead. In fact, she had died in her old age a good half a century ago — many years before he was even born!

What a ludicrous, hopeless preoccupation!

He turned from this melancholy thought and strayed over recent events. For the first time, he began to reflect on the underlying significance of his group's achievement. Like the others, he had been so dominated by the frenetic quest to create a new tool (as if it were an end sufficient in itself), that he had hardly considered what it might *really* mean. Now he began to see that this remarkably powerful capability must soon find other purposes. It would, inevitably, be used in ways that neither he nor anyone else in the CyberProfile Group or the Department of Defense or the government itself could even begin to imagine.

What might all this hold for the world? For those who controlled this awesome technology — and for him?

The more he rolled these speculations around his mind, the more opaque the future appeared. All he knew was that something had opened up which could lead anywhere. Mankind could now play God and replicate existing worlds. He could even create unimaginable realities that could have no existence outside the cybersphere. Worlds designed to host anyone and any situation or event.

One could fill these worlds with imaginary beings, or faithful replicates of living people. Or even recreate, with absolute fidelity, the vanished world and the lives of people long since dead.

With these thoughts racing through his brain, Michael sat upright so suddenly that he raised a small cloud of sand. Louise! Yes, Louise! I could even breathe life into you, too! And place you in your own virtual world... I could meet you at long last...

He toyed with this bewitching, delicious fantasy. He imagined how it would be to see her, to talk to her. He saw those large, dark eyes teasing him, laughing at him. Inviting him to hold her. Could he even grasp just one, fleeting moment with his Louise?

Michael's eyes fixed on the distant surf for several long minutes. Then, quite abruptly, he rose to his feet, shook his towel and strode towards the resort complex.

9. MAKER OF WORLDS

Michael pulled out his computer pad and brushed away dark grains of sand from the beach that was now already 38,000 feet below and fast trailing behind. Checking again that the man beside him was still dozing, his fingers weaved impatiently and once more he scanned through the strategy sketched out over the past several days.

Michael's first priority was to find a sure way to mask his clandestine activity. To re-create a dead person and her lost world would be a daring and impudent task, certainly, but above all, there could not be the least danger of any interloper ever entering his domain. To be discovered operating a large-scale cyberprofile environment would mean real trouble, and not just because he had signed a thick contract specifically forbidding unauthorized projects. He would be answerable for a serious, high-level security crime.

Of course, it was not unusual for programmers to tinker around on the system with their own little experiments — and they were able to do so without any interference. If such little diversions were noticed (as some had suspected) the authorities did nothing to discourage what was seen as one of the job's perquisites — and, often, a source of some good ideas. However, what he was contemplating was in an entirely different league and he would certainly lose access to the system. Worse, both Louise and the world he had carefully assembled for her would immediately be consigned to oblivion.

If there were the least danger of that happening, he must let the whole idea remain no more than an intriguing fantasy.

It would be no easy thing to camouflage this scheme. Cyberprofiling consumed enormous power and memory, so he could hardly tuck away his little extramural enterprise into some inconspicuous corner of the system. Michael could often tell when one of his colleagues was turning out a new replicate. You could almost see the lights in Washington flicker and dim, he had once joked to a workmate. Michael knew too well that unless he moved with great care and cunning the alarm bells would soon be ringing.

When the plane touched down, Michael already had a broad idea of how to set things up. He would draw upon the vast amount of virtual memory that was always available on the world network, piggybacking his clandestine activities onto legitimate projects, always making sure that this was undertaken with small, discrete and irregularly spaced segments that no-one would notice. His project would be invisible, located in no one place, floating. Once each package of data had been processed, he would update the file and replace it with the original version, stripped of his own work. Meanwhile he would gather his own processed material and quickly park it away from scrutiny in his secure sector.

Michael would use as his hosts major off-site servers with no working links with one another and whose security classifications — or sheer obscurity or unlikeliness — would make any casual scrutiny very difficult. The list of possibilities pulled from his directory included an aerospace establishment that researched heat-resistant ceramic compounds, an ocean-current mapping facility for submarines, a Forestry Commission employee roster management resource and an off-shore claims processing service tied directly to a consortium of American insurance companies. As well, he would make sure that Louise's cyberprofile environment was entombed within a locked-off sector that he would make absolutely impenetrable to anyone but himself.

This sector would lie behind protocols that closely mimicked those protecting ultra-secret military projects. Anyone who came close to it would stumble into a maze of hidden electronic tripwires that would trigger severely-worded warnings about the consequences of breaching protected government sectors and violating various anti-espionage acts and so forth.

Michael knew only too well that, while this might deter most people, especially those already working within Government agencies, such notices would only dangle an irresistible challenge to serious computer hackers. He would deal with these with his 'slingshot bypass'. Anyone probing past the warning notices would be automatically diverted right past his sector and into the field of a genuine military closed sector. The intruder would discover enough to satisfy his curiosity and never once suspect that he had been neatly shuttled past a giant entity in the bowels of the CyberProfile network.

While at university, Michael had been intrigued by cryptology and had devised the 'Dynamic Encrypted Security System' which he then tried (without success) to sell to software developers to protect their products from illegal copying. He was sure he could use this to ensure that only he could ever penetrate his secret domain in the host system. The pass number was arrived at by applying a complex equation to a set of numbers that varied randomly from day to day. Michael's wry sense of humor called for one of these volatile numbers to be the daily price for pork belly futures on the Chicago exchange.

Every day, his sector's 'sentry' would draw upon the daily stock market reports and other readily-available reports, including amongst other items the daytime maximum temperature forecast for Cork City in Ireland. To open up his sector, Michael would have to draw up the same sets of data, apply the formula and key in the result to match the day's pass number already held in the sector. For additional safety, the master equation would be changed weekly.

If the world he was to create for Louise were to float over to the far side of the universe, it could hardly be more remote from the eyes of others.

* * *

Henderson was impressed with Michael's report on reprogramming for the new hardware configurations. In fact, he had already sent it on to General O'Keefe with a covering letter endorsing its key recommendations. The word was that the Group's capabilities would be massively increased by the new hardware, to be called 'CYPROSIM'. Michael's open excitement at this prospect was lifted even higher by the knowledge that summoning Louise back from eternity would now more realizable than ever.

By the time the new facilities were commissioned some months later, Michael had a confident grasp of its impressive operational capabilities. The CyberProfile Group had already used CYPROSIM to create several particularly complex new profiles and both the system's ease of use and the results had surprised even the most optimistic in his team. He now had the crucible for his great undertaking — and it was ready. It was time to bring Louise to life.

First, he selected a basic configuration from the considerable range of shell profiles and characteristic variables already resident in the CYPROSIM memory banks. The program had been so designed that any new profile would be built around a selected, 'best fit' template or 'platform' model that most closely resembled the real-life subject. This would then be progressively modified by personal data subsequently loaded into the program. And so Michael called up a set of physical characteristics: female, Caucasian, 25 years of age, five feet six inches tall, mesomorphic shape, medium-slim body build, average musculature and athletic tone, black hair, dark-brown eyes, heart-shaped face, wide-set eyes, white skin, and so forth. Then the broad parameters that set the personality profile: estimated IQ of 138, Myers Briggs psychological rating of INTJ, English as a first language, American nationality, unmarried, and so forth.

Like an artist who first limns a basic outline of his subject, Michael modeled Louise's 'essential disposition'. Then, drawing upon his vast bank of data, Michael began the great task of defining the precise dimensions of Louise's heart, mind and body.

He downloaded every scrap of information about Louise and her world, starting with every film she had made, both silent titles and the sound movies she had appeared in after returning from Europe.

These and all the biographies, articles and profiles on Louise, her own prolific writings, and still photographs were all scanned in. Especially useful were his copies of the audio-taped interviews conducted by the British critic and Brooks admirer, Kenneth Tynan.

Indeed, Michael was sure that no one person in the world had ever done so much to faithfully preserve the words, the images and all the other small things that might give life to the memory of a dead being. But who else could have been entrusted with her reincarnation? Who else had his expertise — and passion?

Used to lingering well into the evening, he was now transfixed by his glowing screen all through the night hours and into the morning, sometimes managing only a few hours' sleep on his office divan before his colleagues arrived. They joked that Michael was stopping at nothing to ensure another presidential handshake.

Months passed in which he juggled ever-increasing workday commitments with the demands of his own lonely quest. Painstakingly, Michael supplied every detail of Louise, refusing to fill in any gap with a guess unless he had to. Most information came from his own resources, but if that was inadequate he went to almost any length to secure the data he needed. He was lost to any concern except his labors... and Louise. Inevitably, in this seamless continuum of work, Michael no longer could easily separate the Group's priorities from his own, for, almost always, solving a problem for one project advanced the progress of the other.

Certainly, the new system made a significant difference. The CyberProfile Group marveled at the speed and accuracy with which they could now replicate target subjects nominated by the intelligence and military agencies. With that, the list of new profiles expanded: leaders of hostile powers, neutral states and then friendly states and allies were all swept into the system. Soon the CPG was being asked to profile the nation's industrialists, union leaders, influential journalists and commentators. Coyly at first, but less self-consciously with time, members of the Group were asked for discreet 'favors' — never conveyed in writing — which involved running up a little profile on a known political opponent of the President or a troublesome critic. Michael's colleagues whispered about their reluctance to see their skills diverted away from legitimate targets. But Michael, protective of his own mission, found ways to avoid attending protest meetings or signing letters. For this he was singled out by Henderson, O'Keefe and others as the man in CPG who could always be relied upon, as 'one of us'.

Michael decided to use this trust to his advantage. He took the chance to request approval for what he described as 'off-line experimentation' to be conducted in his own time. With such pressing and expanding commitments, he had reasoned, it was becoming difficult to tie up the CYPROSIM system with fairly speculative, but promising, investigations into modeling logic. However, he was prepared to undertake this in his own time, particularly during weekends. Could he count on their assent? Of course, came the grateful reply — and so Michael acquired yet another means of covering his tracks and investing more time on his own quest.

So, like a developing infant's brain, in which neuronal pathways are explored, built up and reinforced in a cloud of unceasing activity, a new being was slowly incubated in the computer's warm innards. Louise's nascent form was laboriously modified and refined until at last Michael began to see her tentative outlines resolve into a surer existence. All the while, he kept moving ever closer to his Louise, and with that prospect Michael's excitement, uncertainty and apprehension made his stomach heave and churn.

But the questions he had only turned over in the vaguest way now became urgent.

The Louise he was creating would be far, far more complex and far more real than any of the gray manikins that CYPROSIM had so far crafted. All that anyone had sought from the *doppelgangers* manufactured by CPG — selected politicians, military commanders and the like — were faithful facsimiles that gave reliable responses covering a narrow range of fairly predictable situations. The number of possible variables was, if numerous, at least limited. It had never occurred to anyone that the cyberprofile of the Chinese leader, Chung, for example, should be able to offer any insights into his aesthetic sensibilities or the romantic side to his soul.

However, with Louise it would be very different. The awesome power of the new CYPROSIM system would be taken to its unknown limits if Michael was to invest in his lovely creature a being far deeper than those shallow avatars.

As he rested briefly late one night, Michael had a troubling thought. What if his creation were indeed the perfect replication of the dead movie star, exact in every look and mannerism; in every thought, word and gesture the precise reincarnation of Louise Brooks? Even if this new Louise responded to him in every way just like a real person, would she truly be a *real* person? With all his technical art and artifice, could he really bestow upon her a self-aware, human mind — even if it were cradled, not within a living brain, but instead deep amid the humming interstices of a massively powerful computer? Would she be an authentic, sentient creature with a unique and aware existence, a sense of autonomy as real as his own? Or would she be but an illusion, enchanting, beguiling and completely convincing, but an illusion nonetheless? And, at the end of it all, how would it be for him if he found, finally, that he had created no more than an artificial shell, a ghost — and that he had invested the yearning of so many lonely years in what, after all, was only a phantom conjured up by the ghostly dance of evanescent electrons?

If this new Louise were a real person, as Michael so fervently hoped, then he surely faced a fearful responsibility. Having once summoned her back into existence, could he ever dispose of her? That would be murder, as surely as if he had stabbed her. No, he had to sustain and care for Louise, always. Her world could be no mere limbo haunted by half-shadows and incomplete echoes of her earlier life: it had to be as rich and real as the one she had once known.

Many years earlier, Michael had read Mary Shelley's novel, 'Frankenstein'. He had been powerfully affected by the pitiful torment of Baron Frankenstein's monster. This abandoned creature had been doomed to roam the earth, self-aware and articulate and obsessed by the fact that it was a hideous outcast without a soul and, worst of all, disowned by a maker repelled by his own blasphemous artifact.

In our time, had not each advance of computer technology only brought closer the prospect of mankind having to share his planet with a very different and, eventually, vastly superior intelligence? The debate this created now enfolded not only philosophers and ethicists, but even pragmatic computer professionals as hard-boiled as Michael's own colleagues.

If the prospect of interacting with a thinking box posed difficulties, he mused, then how would he deal with the reincarnation of a woman as beautiful and bewitching as Louise?

Would an Almighty have pondered such thoughts before he broke the darkness on the morning of creation? Suddenly Michael realized that to the beings in the world he was already creating, he himself would be God — even if, as he hoped, Louise could never suspect that she was not inhabiting a 'real' existence.

Perhaps, for all we knew, OUR universe is no more than a virtual reality game played by some being on another plane, all quite unknown to us. In turn, this Master of the Cosmos, might be the unwitting actor in an illusory world set up by yet another unseen playmaster. And so on, like an infinite succession of Chinese boxes.

With these unsettling ideas kneading his brain, he at last fell into deep sleep.

10. THE TOOLKIT

'Hey, Mike! Just get a load of this!'

Michael swung around from his screen. Before him, a small group of profilers grinned conspiratorially. In the middle stood Vince Fadowsky, wearing an unusual-looking, metallic blue helmet.

'Know what this is?' asked Vince.

'Why, Mr Fadowsky, I do believe you're taking up speed cycling,' Michael teased.

Ignoring this unhelpful guess, Vince paused for effect. 'Mr Stanton, you're privileged to be looking at one of the first, pre-release models of the all-new... (he sounded an imitation drum roll)... Sensator.'

'Look well,' he continued, 'for it won't even be into full production for two months, at least.'

'Sensator?' queried Michael. 'Tell me.'

'It's a virtual reality helmet. That you can see — and you get wrap-around sound and vision, like all the others. But here's the big difference. You also get all the other sensory feeds as well. Touch, balance, hot and cold, skin sensations. In a word, everything for totally immersive virtual reality — except for smell and taste.'

'With just that?' asked Michael skeptically. 'Just a VR helmet?'

Vince took off the helmet and passed it over to Michael, who closely examined the Sensator, slowly turning it over in his hands.

'You've the usual audio and video components,' said Vince. 'What's new are these four beam transmitters inside — see, there... and there. Your computer tells these to focus weak pulses directly into the brain. They converge at a single, precise point to create a combined hit strong enough to stimulate the neurons responsible for a specific sensation or response.'

'I remember reading something about this,' said Michael. 'I'd no idea anyone was close to a real application.'

One of the profilers, Georgina, cut in.

'In a way, it's just picking up on what brain surgeons have known for years. They'd put a patient under a local anesthetic and stimulate specific parts of the brain. That would evoke all sorts of things, like smells, tactile sensations, long forgotten memories. I think that's how they first began mapping the brain's functions.'

'Exactly,' said Vince triumphantly. 'This works the same way, too, but with a lot more finesse than the cattle-prods they were using!'

Michael put the helmet on and adjusted the chin strap.

'How's that?' asked Vince.

'Comfortable,' replied Michael. 'And surprisingly light... A question: how can it tell exactly where to focus those pulses? Wouldn't the slightest helmet movement be enough to throw it off the right spot?'

'OK,' replied Vince. 'Here's how they do it. First, you get three very small metal studs fixed into various parts of your skull. It's no big deal: they're just a millimeter long and it's all done in five minutes under a local. The helmet constantly scans these to lock onto an exact set of co-ordinates. So, even if the helmet flops around, the beams are constantly monitored and adjusted so they're always hitting exactly the right spots.'

'Fine, but how do you know where the right spots are to begin with? I mean, these locations must be absolutely microscopic — and they would be different for each person, wouldn't they?' queried Michael.

'Right,' answered Vince. 'You get the reference studs in and then tutor the Sensator gear through a whole series of exercises. It checks precisely where the old gray matter lights up when you get your back tickled or you hear a blues riff. It's quite a process.'

'I'll bet it is,' replied Michael, holding the Sensator out at arm's length.

Vince leaned over and, in a whisper loud enough for everyone to hear, added: 'And, Mike, one more thing. You can calibrate the strength of the evoked responses to your own exact preferences.'

He turned around and winked salaciously at the others.

'Yes folks, orgasms of unbearable strength and duration. You just set the dial and let it happen — so they tell me, on very good authority, that is!'

Michael waited for the giggles and whistling to subside.

'OK, what about your body movement, how does it read that?'

'From the torso up,' explained Vince. 'You just make normal movements and the Sensator reads the brain signals and reproduces them in the VR environment. Leg movements are easy. You wear sole pads...'

He removed a shoe.

'See? You press the ball of each foot in turn to take a pace forward. Press the heel and you walk backwards. Press either one twice and you turn around 45 degrees. Oh, and the harder you press, the longer the stride. All this is beamed directly to the helmet and from there to the computer you're working with. Smart, hey?'

'And it really works? I mean, the general concept,' Michael asked.

'Mike,' said Vince earnestly, 'this is going to blow the Sensoot right out of the water. You've felt how easy it is to wear this helmet.

Now ask yourself — why would you still want to climb in and out of a pair of wired-up long-johns every time you go VR? They're launching this at a press conference on Tuesday and after that Sensoot shares won't be worth diddly! Just watch!'

Michael gave a slow smile. 'Clicketty-click! Now I know why you kept stalling me on the Sensoot procurement. You knew about this all along. Tell the truth, Vince...'

Fadowsky arched his eyebrows to feign a look of blameless innocence.

'What could I do, man? Sure, I had the inside run with the Bancroft guys — we go back a long way. But they made me promise — I mean, swear — to keep it quiet. Yet I couldn't let you order up Sensoots, not when this stuff was hanging around the corner. Hey, what would *you* have done?'

Michael shook his head. Closely scrutinizing the inside of the Sensator, he asked: 'So, how do we get hold of one of these for evaluation?'

'You're holding it right there, Mike. It's on permanent loan. Gratis. They've written it off as a beta model, although it's really identical to what they'll be shipping out. They said they want government endorsement, so they'll bend over backwards to persuade you to give it a full work-out. Bancroft will organize the configuring to match your personal specifications. Everything. No problemo.'

'Including the... implants?,' asked Michael, wincing.

'Including the implants.'

'You've got me, Vince. Call Bancroft and tell them we're interested!'

* * *

Michael could hardly believe his luck!

From his very first tutoring session at Bancroft Taktek Inc, he knew that he now had the means to meet Louise with all the attributes of a real person.

Because it used exactly the same mechanisms and pathways within his brain, the Sensator helmet provided a flow of feedback that was as subtle — and authentic — as anything he received from his own senses of taste, touch and smell.

Now, it would be nothing to quickly slip on the Sensator helmet and plug it into the computer. And what if someone surprised him before he had a chance to take it off? Well, he had undertaken to personally evaluate this new technology, hadn't he?

11. UNSEEN SENTINAL

Michael had now become a creature of the night, tirelessly working at his electronic alchemy. With meticulous patience, he crafted each feature and gesture, each inflection of the dead actress. Then he carefully assembled these myriad, little attributes — pieces of the most exquisite mosaic — and fused them into the unique being that would soon become Louise.

He had given her a mind, quick and perceptive, complete with reflexes and instincts. But to make her a complete person, he would now invest Louise with the memories of her past life. He trawled through all the biographical sources, notes, letters and minutiae at his disposal — and what was wanting he created himself. His purpose was simply to discreetly fill in gaps, to join events seamlessly: he had no wish to fashion experiences that might shape Louise's character in any different way.

Michael then turned to filling out the world she would live in. Scouring great databases, the computer began enveloping Louise in the physical reality of the 1920s. To merely sketch in the best-remembered icons of those times would have been demanding enough, but Michael knew it would be the detail that would turn an impressionistic backdrop into a universe of rounded authenticity.

Nothing less would do.

Starting from a canvas of flat tones and smooth planes (much like those of a hurriedly-built stage set, Michael thought), this microcosm was now transformed into a place of irregular features, texture and all the variegated colors and tones, reflections, highlights and shadows of life itself. And the denizens of this cyberworld, who had earlier worn the blank masks of window mannequins, moved about their business with expressive vitality.

Michael added a soundscape of voices and sounds. Unseen people could be heard talking, laughing and shouting; cars honked and clattered; children's squeals floated over from a park, along with the slow music of swings and bird song; wind-rustled leaves and all the unsourced bangs, knocks, scrapes, squeaks and muffled noises that swathe our lives.

Every cell in Michael's brain and every fiber of his body was dull with fatigue. Yet, still, he was drawn on by the exhilarating thought that no other human had ever commanded such unfettered power and creativity — or had undertaken such an audacious task. He was intoxicated by his journey of discovery into another world, where even the smallest detail or incident seemed magical. He laughed with surprise at brand names that were still familiar a century later. Especially, he examined automobile radiators to see what names he might recognize and the many more that were unfamiliar.

Next, he sifted through a vast lode of information about the society of that era, including its fads and fashions, attitudes and politics, the personalities and the gossip, modes of behavior and address. He scanned in pages of novels, newspapers and magazines, even advertisements. Nothing was inconsequential.

He read all the novels of Scott Fitzgerald, that preeminent chronicler of the Jazz Age, meticulously noting the slang, turns of phrase and incidental detail. He was particularly taken by 'The Great Gatsby' and could see in the mysterious, lovelorn Jay Gatsby something of the person he would soon incarnate for himself.

Then, as Michael saw his goal looming closer, he faced a new crop of apprehensions and uncertainties. What was once an interesting speculation, even a pleasing reverie, now became a disturbing preoccupation: when should he approach Louise — and how? What would happen when he finally met her? How would he react? Supposing he said — or did — something that made him appear strange or ridiculous? What if, after all this, she dismissed him (her creator!) as just another importuning young man from among every film star's line-up of eager suitors?

It was true that he could undo any awkwardness, retrace an action or re-script events so they conformed more easily to his own plans. (After all, he could move through this little cosmos and mold events and people, Louise included, just as he wished.)

For here was the savage paradox! The only way Michael could guarantee Louise was his would also ensure that she was no longer Louise. Stripped of her free will and with her fierce independence curtailed, what would be left of her for him? Of what value would be her love, if not freely given? What if all he could see was merely the programmed response of an automaton? Now, at last, Michael understood why a divine creator would have fashioned sentient creatures capable of defying him... and, of their own volition, of loving him.

Thus, Michael resolved that when he entered her world he would move quietly and unobtrusively, invisibly at first, listening and watching and learning. He would wait until he was ready — and then seize the right moment to reveal himself.

* * *

The first moving screen images of Louise were indistinct and jumpy, as if the torn sprocket-holes of a much-used film strip were causing it to intermittently race past the projector lens. At other times, her image would suddenly freeze before jerking into action again. Michael watched her as she left her apartment — suite 12, number 26 Bellevue Court — and walked across a street to talk to some almost featureless man. Her voice was clear, yet stilted, somehow not quite natural. It was disconcerting that her two-piece outfit and matching louche hat appeared to have changed from a vague apricot color to a light green hue in the interval between crossing from one side of the street and reappearing from behind a parked car. Her movements had an odd uncertainty about them and sometimes were out of sync, with her responses lagging behind the stimulus by a full second.

It seemed a deeply disappointing reward for all the inhuman toil.

Intently staring at the screen, Michael took several slow, deep breaths. Easy now... This was all to be expected. There was always a settling-in time after the initial formatting of a cyberprofile. Operating within a completely new environment, the computer had to shape everything afresh, referring to rough templates and scanning millions of scraps of often unconnected data each second as it strove to sustain so many animated images in real-time.

Once in a while, the system's resources were just not enough to keep refreshing every minute detail dozens of times a second. The result was momentary pauses and sudden jumps as the computer tried to catch up.

However, even within hours, Michael saw rapid improvements. Each time the computer dug into its memory to fashion a gesture or inflection, it added the result to its rapidly growing repertoire. Through a system of self-tutoring and feedback, the rendition of the computer subjects became more naturalistic and their actions ever more fluid and life-like. Sometimes, when Louise's toss of the head or sly smile seemed to have a strange familiarity about it, Michael recalled seeing just such a gesture in one of her films. But more and more, the marionette movements were giving way to the natural grace and assurance of a beautiful, *living* woman.

For now, Michael was content to see and hear all this played out on the screen. He was not yet ready to don the virtual reality helmet and enter into Louise's domain. Of course, the computer still had some way to go before it could present its subjects and their settings in their final, polished form. But more than that, he had much more to learn about Louise and her milieu before he could confidently introduce himself. And besides, he was still uncertain, perhaps afraid. What happens when one confronts a fantasy? What *can* happen?

* * *

Invisibly, soundlessly, Michael observed Louise. At first he had followed her gradual incarnation with the artificer's dispassionate eye, coolly assessing each modification as he reached to perfect his handiwork. But the ceaseless weaving of electronic pulses worked their magic and the tantalizing wraith resolved itself into the transcendent loveliness he had dreamt of. Moving through her world, trailing surprises, playfulness, little acts of willfulness and pique, Louise was becoming as real to Michael as anyone he had ever known.

From another universe, he tracked her every move and mood, tirelessly and with hungry eyes...

Once, Michael visited Louise while she was sleeping. An unseen sentinel, he stood at the foot of her bed, gazing down at the head buried in a white satin pillow. Her hair was tousled and spiky like an urchin's mop and she seemed touchingly guileless and vulnerable. Rising and falling, Louise's breath whispered sleep's light rhythm, only broken by a weary sigh as a white hand traced over the pillow. Marveling at his lovely creation, Michael patiently kept his invisible vigil until the morning light played on her face and stirred her into wakefulness.

Louise arose and glided across the bedroom, humming happily to herself. Pausing before a full-length mirror, she turned a graceful little pirouette, innocently unaware that these intimate moments were shared with a discarnate lover.

Looking around her room, Michael noted how surprisingly sparse it was: almost austere. Its few contents revealed individuality and discernment and, as well, a wry sense of humor (like the large teddy bear wearing one of her hats). For a film star, Louise's wardrobe seemed surprisingly modest, although the clothes — usually dark-hued — were well-cut and understated in a classic way.

A man's bedroom always looks like that of every other man, thought Michael. Always functional and predictable. Yet each woman's bedroom was uniquely her own and, whether neat or carelessly untidy, entirely faithful to her special mystery.

Preparing herself for the day, Louise moved briskly and soon sauntered out the door after only a bare moment's pause at the mirror.

She laughed a lot in company — and on her own — and seemed happily self-sufficient. She was a person who could be gay and boisterous among friends, even noisy and, usually after a few drinks, bawdy. Yet there were other times when she shunned people and sought refuge in more introvert pastimes, especially reading.

All the time, unaware that her every move, her private moments, were followed assiduously.

Michael had never before played the voyeur and he was uncomfortable about violating Louise's solitude, even though his presence was so completely invisible. When she was with her small circle of close friends, raucously laughing in a restaurant, or bantering with her agent or the film crew on the studio lot, that was different: in fact, Louise cared little who overheard these exchanges. And neither had Michael felt any unease earlier, before Louise had assumed her present form, for then she was still an artificial, incomplete entity.

But now she was truly a real, living person — so Michael thought — and entitled to the rights and the respect due to any self-aware individual. His memory turned to when his mother told him about his guardian angel. For a long time he felt uncomfortable that whenever he picked his nose, went to the toilet or stole the last slice of chocolate cake, this was all observed and grimly recorded by his unseen 'guardian'.

The *physical* closeness of his divine Louise tormented Michael. Each glimpse of her clear white skin, the penetrating and lively dark eyes, the smooth shoulders and elegant neck was like a fresh discovery. His curiosity was insatiable and the more he fed this ravening, shameful appetite, the more it craved.

* * *

Michael's first impression was that crossing the interval of only four generations had revealed an America as exotic as the remotest corner of his own, contemporary world. Shadowing people through the streets and shops, he listened to the light-hearted exchanges and earnest deliberation of a people complacently confident that their values and habits, their way of doing things, were eternal, never-to-be-disturbed verities. Nowhere was there the slightest notion that great changes could so soon again rock their lives. But was this any different to his own time, the early twenty-first century? No, for we are all provincials in our own little era, Michael realized. How else could we cope with a life as inconstant as the rolling clouds?

But in time, Louise and the world she lived in grew more familiar to Michael. Indeed, this self-contained microcosm seemed almost as immediate, coherent and comfortable to him as the narrow and reclusive half-world of his other existence. As he became less distracted by the more obvious, superficial differences, he noticed that people themselves were the same at their core. The interplay of love and hate, happiness and despair, yearning to belong, yearning to be free: all the elements of the human drama were there, quite unalloyed by time or fashion.

Michael wondered how true this cybernetic fantasy he had conjured up might be to the real world that Louise had once lived in? Different in numberless small details, to be sure. But he knew that if Louise could recall her former existence she would not find this new life completely strange and unfamiliar.

* * *

Michael watched Louise carefully arranging flowers in a glass vase whose etched surface broke up the afternoon sunlight into diamantine spangles. Deftly she moved a flower one way, bent a leaf this way. Then, impatiently, she reordered the blooms and stood back apace to study the effect.

If this creature is not real and authentic, then, mused Michael, *who is real?* Could it be the grazing multitudes who shuffle through their days without turning over one single original thought; who are content to perceive life with the unchallenging detachment of a bird? The graveyards are full of people who were once real and yet have left no imprint on posterity other than a barely legible inscription and, perhaps, a name that flits briefly across the pages of an unread family chronicle. Are these shadows more real than the creations of Tolstoy or Joyce? Or the screen character whose vitality and authenticity lives on for millions, long after the actor's death?

Yes, this Louise owed her new existence to him. But in Michael's mind, that fact could never rob her of her authenticity. He had worked so hard so that almost everything about her mirrored her own previous life. All he had done was simply to cloak her soul with a new vitality. For that matter, surely everyone he had ever known was as much a creation of his own mind as was Louise. The world we 'live in', Michael thought, is but an internal construction of the mind. The brain's only contact with the world is through the nerve impulses fed by our sensory organs. These sensations (which only reflect a narrow spectrum of sound and light) are then processed into a model that offers us a useful part-view, or rough simulacrum, of the world. The point is that this model is assembled within the brain, not 'out there'.

This, Michael remembered, was what Plato referred to when he described us all as like prisoners in a cave whose apprehension of the world was built upon the passing shadows from the outside world!

Perhaps, after all, the only certainty anyone could ever count on was the reality of their own consciousness. But what gave him the vantage point of his own conscious mind? That he existed was no mystery, but why, thought Michael, am I me — and not someone else? Indeed, why am I anyone at all? Could not a Michael have existed, identical in every way to me, down to every trait and gesture, thought and memory, and yet be inhabited by a self that has that not-me otherness possessed by every other being? And, immediately, he thought of Louise again. Could this new Louise, no matter how authentic a facsimile of the original, ever be truly the same person as the long dead actress?

12. HELLO, MISS BROOKS...

'Ah, darling, you really look so divine,' purred Betty Packham. Louise turned to the plump lady with the tight blonde permanent wave and returned a languid half-smile.

'With that gorgeous dark hair and white skin, you just look so *dramatic* in black! Mind you, your velvet dress at Henry's on Friday was spectacular. Everyone, but everyone, simply *raved* about it!'

Barely listening to her gushing table companion, Louise slowly swept her eyes around the room, eager to pick out any sort of diversion.

'And do tell me, Louise, how long have you known Boris Wahlstein? You must know he is such a talented producer. Set to become another Irving Thalberg, I'm told. They say he is already worth a quarter million — and he's only just turned thirty...'

'Truth to tell, I hardly know him at all,' said Louise drumming the top of her empty glass with a bread stick. 'When he asked me to come here I was too lazy or slow to think of a plausible excuse. Because Boris is one of the few front office powerbrokers I haven't offended — and I need work — here I am... in my usual condition.'

'Why, Louise, you're not tipsy, surely?'

'Unfortunately, no. Bored. Anyway, where is Boris the Wunderkind? I want to go home as soon as I've paid my respects.'

'Oh, Louise, you can't go yet,' insisted Betty, slightly alarmed. 'I've just seen someone you must meet. Wait and I'll get Freddie to introduce us. I'm sure you'll be quite taken with him. His name's Michael — I'm not sure of his surname. Anyway, he's very, very clever with the stock market.'

Betty leaned over and half-whispered into Louise's ear.

'What I hear is that he has some serious money behind him. I mean really serious money. And he's also very attractive — and *very* single...'

She winked slowly at Louise and covered her mouth as she broke into a conspiratorial giggle.

'Well, it will have to be another time,' said Louise as she snapped her cocktail bag closed and reached for her wrap.

'Look, Freddie has already agreed to talk to him. He's sure to want to meet you... a film star and only just back from the Continent. Just wait... do wait!'

Louise resignedly sank back into her chair and impatiently picked up the breadstick once more. At last Freddie finished his rambling story and, hurried on by a little elbowing from Betty, left the table and shambled into the crowd. Nearly ten minutes later, he re-emerged, steering by his arm a youngish, serious-looking man. With an expansive sweep of his arm, the visibly tipsy Freddie beckoned towards the table.

'Mr Michael Stanton... I would like to introduce you to, well, Betty Packham whom you've already met, Bill and Clare Delahunty and Miss (he sibilantly emphasized Louise's unmarried status)... Miss Louise Brooks, the well-known — I mean, famous — film star who has just returned from making several flicks in Europe. All lead roles, of course.'

'Pleased to meet you,' said Michael, nodding to the company at the table. He turned to look straight into Louise's dark eyes.

'Hello, Miss Brooks. I've been looking forward to meeting you at long last...'

13. SMELL THE ROSES!

The open convertible coursed along the coast road and the balmy night air washed over them, laden with the gentle perfumes of early summer.

'Why, isn't that lovely!' said Louise. 'I adore the scent of frangipani — it's so tropical. Exotic... We never had this where I come from.'

'So, where are you from?' asked Michael, pretending not to know.

'Wichita, Kansas.'

'Ah, cow country. They'd have a different perfume there, I guess!' Michael jibed.

'Why, there are a lot of things there besides cattle. You'd be surprised. But there sure isn't much frangipani, I do admit.'

Michael pulled off the road and drove along a sandy track to an elevated point that overlooked the moonlit ocean. For several wordless minutes they stared out at the crashing breakers and the ever-changing lacework of foam on the dark water.

'I was quite old when I saw the sea for the first time,' said Louise. 'I found it quite fascinating — and indeed I still do.' She paused for a few moments' reflection. 'All that movement and energy. Isn't it hypnotic?'

Michael nodded slowly. 'Those same waves washed the shores during the age of the great dinosaurs. And before that, through the long ages before any living creature was there to witness it, there was this same great ocean.'

'I guess the sea's a metaphor for life,' said Louise. 'Each individual existence rises up like one of those waves, builds and ends in a spray of surf, only to be followed by new generations. All this movement, all this constant change — and yet everything remains the same. It certainly puts our own little lives into perspective... don't you think?'

Michael said nothing. Oh, Louise, he thought, if you knew how short our time really is! In the world I come from, your life has already passed long ago. You blossomed into beautiful womanhood, lived a life, you grew old and died — all many years before I was born. Louise, if you only knew.

She suddenly swung around and her hand lightly stroked the chrysanthemum in his buttonhole.

'God, I hate parties like that one,' exclaimed Louise. 'People hanging around pretending to have fun — and all the while desperately toadying their way towards the next career move. I was just about to leave when you rolled in.'

'Glad you didn't.'

'I'm glad, too. Right now, I don't think there's anywhere else I'd rather be. Isn't that just a spectacular sight?'

'Oh, I thought for a moment it was my company you found so entrancing!' Michael teased.

'Why, I don't know you. In fact, I've forgotten your surname already. But, yes, I think you *are* sweet. You certainly seemed a much more interesting prospect than the crowd at the Packhams. You know, I hate the movie business circuit. So much insecurity and arrogance. Superficial.'

She slowly shook her head. The snapping sea wind had blown her hair away to reveal a high forehead and she now looked more reflective.

Louise turned to Michael and gave him a gentle nudge.

'And tell me, Mr Michael Whoever, what do you do that rewards you with a handsome car like this?'

'It's Michael Bowes Stanton, if you want to know... So, you like my chariot? You're in a Stutz Black Hawk Speedster, with a single-overhead camshaft and a straight eight under the bonnet. Ninety-two horses, hydraulic brakes on all wheels, the works. Came second in the 1928 Le Mans, you know.'

Louise smiled. 'Right, now I know all about your pride and joy. But you haven't told me about you!'

'Well, I guess I'm a bit of a capitalist,' answered Michael. 'Started with a little family money and built up a few assets back East. Property developments to begin with. A little factory. That sort of thing. Lately, with the market the way that it is, I've become something of a speculator — for the time being, anyway.'

'And what are you doing here?'

'Thought I'd get some sun and fresh orange juice, so I came to California. Well, to look into the movie picture business, actually.'

'Oh, Christ! Michael, you're really too nice. Believe me, you should try the juice canning business instead!'

Michael laughed. 'Thanks for the compliment! No, I don't want to make movies. I'm developing equipment for the people who do. I've a precision instruments business outside New York and one day I came across an interesting patent and saw the possibility of a new type of camera crane. The more I looked into it, the better the idea seemed. So I bought the patent — and here I am! Just another Hollywood hopeful.'

'That's why you were at the Packham's? But no wife?'

'No wife. I'm fancy free and exceedingly available — just as Betty probably described me!'

'Well, that IS a pleasant change! Actually, that's just what she did say... now how *did* you guess?' Louise joked.

Louise's hearty laugh carried far into the night air. Abruptly, she turned around and seized Michael's arm.

'But we'll have to continue this interesting topic another time, I'm afraid. It must be well after midnight and this waning movie star is auditioning for yet another stellar comeback at eight in the morning. I don't want to look too dissipated. Home, James, if you don't mind.'

As they drove back along the coast road, Louise buried her head into Michael's shoulder and fell asleep. Eventually, the Stutz pulled up outside her apartment block and Michael stirred Louise with a gentle shake and escorted her to the door. She turned around and gave a sleepy little yawn.

'Well, Mr Michael Bowes Stanton, thank you for rescuing me this evening.' With that she gave him a warm, soft kiss on the lips that sent an unexpected shiver down Michael's spine.

'Miss Brooks. I would deem it a great pleasure and privilege if you would have dinner with me,' said Michael with mock formality.

'Well, you just don't know your luck!' Louise replied with mock haughtiness. 'Call me at the studio tomorrow.' And then, without turning around, she disappeared inside.

Michael sat in his car in the dark for several minutes. He struggled to absorb the reality that he had met his beloved Louise at long last. And he was pleased that he had deported himself so well, that he had played to near perfection the role of a wealthy young man of the world, accustomed to achieving his goals, not least the interest of a beautiful movie actress. He had not hidden his keen attraction to Louise, he thought, but neither had he overplayed it. Certainly, she could never have guessed that this self-assured suitor, so attractively diffident about the things most important to others, had for so long planned and worked towards this chance meeting with a cold passion that even he found frightening.

He turned the motor of the Stutz and returned to the lonely promontory overlooking the beach. Already he could see the first light of dawn on the gray horizon. Michael slowly raised his hands to his face, removed his VR eyepiece, leaned forward and turned off the computer. It was too late to return to his apartment, he thought.

Besides he had promised to have a new routine to show O'Keefe in the afternoon.

* * *

Later that week, Michael picked up Louise and took her to Barrault's on Caldwell Avenue. She wore a wine-red, crushed velvet dress and black gloves and black shoes and a cloche hat pulled low so that only a hint of her fringe showed. He had never seen her look so beautiful in any of her photographs.

'Monsieur?'

As if woken from a dream, Michael lifted his eyes from Louise. 'Sorry…? Oh, yes, Paul. Wine… I think we'll have a Saint Galvyse 2023. I had it here last time, Louise, and let me tell you, it was a revelation!'

'2023, sir?'

Flustered by his anachronistic slip, Michael quickly corrected himself. 'Sorry, I meant 1923.'

Louise giggled at what she took to be a quirky little joke.

The wine waiter returned moments later and placed a bottle of blackcurrant cordial and two beakers on the table. Then, with a perfunctory look around the room, he produced a dusty wine bottle and after Michael had pronounced it good, he half-filled Louise's beaker.

'My apologies, Madame. A precaution in case we have some uniformed visitors. We would not want any of our law-abiding guests to be… ah… embarrassed.'

Louise's eyes darted with annoyance. 'God, isn't Prohibition so damned… *barbaric!*'

Michael smiled. 'Well, it's an experiment that will soon be over. You mark my words, the Volstead Act will be repealed shortly.'

'I really hope so.'

'It will,' continued Michael confidently. 'I've been picking up a few properties that could be converted to bars at short notice. In fact, two of them used to be bars originally!'

'Michael, you seem so very sure. What happens if things don't turn out that way? These aren't settled times.'

He did not answer, but just slowly raised his glass to his face. 'Here's looking at you, kid,' he drawled slowly. Louise smiled and mockingly responded. 'And here's looking at you, Buster!'

Michael grinned broadly, amused by her mimicking of his well-rehearsed delivery of a borrowed line — and by the thought that it would be some twenty years before Louise would have a chance to see 'Casablanca' and hear Humphrey Bogart toast Ingrid Bergman in Rick's Café Americain. He wondered, would she remember when she first heard the expression?

The meal was served — boeuf Chateaubriand — and Michael was surprised at the gusto with which his partner tackled her meal. No sooner had she finished this generous serving than she called for the dessert menu. Michael gently chided her about her appetite and wondered how she managed to stay so slim.

'Easy. I don't nibble between expensive restaurants! Don't forget, I'm a working girl — and right now, I'm not working. It's called the poverty diet.'

'What about the audition?'

'Turned out to be an exercise to prove that the producer's girlfriend got the part in fair and open competition. Happens a lot.'

'But, Louise, you must have some savings from your movies. You can't be broke?'

'I earned the money effortlessly — so I spent it effortlessly.' She tossed her hair defiantly and her eyes turned misty. 'And what the hell, anyway! I'll find something. Trouble is, though, I've a reputation for being a bit, shall we say, difficult. I never played their game and I damned well never will!'

Her raised voice turned several heads at a nearby table. She's tipsy, Michael thought. Or more troubled than she wanted to appear.

Michael leaned forward and took her hands in his. 'Louise, I have a proposition for you...'

Her eyes narrowed, suspiciously — and he felt her hands tighten.

'No,' he smiled. 'It's not another Hollywood proposition. Look, I know for an absolute certainty that a certain stock is going to lift quite spectacularly after a board announcement next Tuesday. I'm going to put some money in — if you have anything, even a little, I'll set aside a few shares in your name: you'll get your money back — and more — within a few days.'

'Michael... I...' Louise shrugged hopelessly.

'Tell you what I'll do. I'll lend you the money — and you can pay me back after you've realized your profit.'

'But I can't afford to pay you back if it doesn't work out.'

'If this number fails to cover itself, I'll carry the shortfall. Now, you can't get a fairer offer than that, can you?'

'I guess not,' Louise said uncertainly. Quickly brightening up, she commanded, 'Come on, get the bill — and we'll come back to my place for a coffee. I've got a bottle of gin, too. I mightn't be able to eat, but I can always find a dollar for some hooch!'

Very soon, Louise was leading Michael into her apartment. He felt strangely awkward as she ushered him from room to room. If she only knew how intimately familiar he was with every corner of this austerely-furnished place! That, as an invisible interloper, he had already studied Louise in her intimate domain, just as a biologist might peer through a microscope at a water nymph: with a dispassionate and remote eye. Again, he felt acutely guilty that he had so callously and unthinkingly violated another being's most private moments.

Louise took him by the hand and walked back into the small hallway, flicked on a switch and peered through a door.

'And this... is my boudoir. Just smell that perfume!'

'Perfume?'

'Why those roses — over there, on the dresser. From one of my anonymous admirers. He sends me a bunch every week, always deep red.' She pulled a stem from the vase and held it under his nose. 'Just smell it. Isn't it heavenly?'

Michael remembered that the one sense he did not have in this virtual world was that of smell. Sight, hearing, touch, yes — but he had decided to save time by not bothering to tutor the Sensator to add the olfactory dimension to his VR expeditions. He would correct this deficiency as soon as he could.

'Louise, I've no sense of smell to talk of. I've had hayfever all day. My nose is pretty well restricted to breathing duties only for the time being.'

'Oh, no. You poor thing.'

Louise narrowed her eyes with suspicion.

'But the way you talked about the wine in the restaurant?'

'Ooops! Well, it tasted fine to me. Paul can be quite dismissive of uninformed hobbledehoys, you know. He's the best sommelier in town — and that was just a little showmanship to impress him.'

'And me, too, I suppose.'

'Naturally.'

They sat outside on the balcony and drank coffee. The talk ranged over the movie business, Louise's experiences as a professional dancer and the theater. But it was the topic of reading that most animated Louise.

'Aren't books the most wonderful invention ever? Open a book and you can look into the intimate thoughts and the insights of so many great minds. Whether they are alive or dead, you can still converse with them. And there are no distractions such as personality, mannerisms or appearances to get in the way.'

'So, Louise, what do you read?'

'Most things. Some novels, but mostly non-fiction. I'm fascinated by the German philosophers, you know.'

'Oh yes, I'd heard that,' noted Michael. 'You're quite notorious as the lady who reads Schopenhauer on the set between takes.'

'Amongst other things.'

'Mmmm... Schopenhauer. Bit of a miseryguts, don't you think? What was it he said? *Die Schadenfreude ist die Reisenfreude?* The only true joy is that derived from the misery of others.'

Louise laughed incredulously. 'You've actually read Schopenhauer?'

'Just a little,' replied Michael candidly.

'Well, you and I must be the only folks in this town who can make that claim. By the way, have you ever seen his portrait? Hardly the life and soul of the party!' observed Louise, laughing heartily.

'Definitely not,' agreed Michael. 'But he was one of the very first European thinkers to understand Hinduism and Buddhism.'

'I'm not quite sure he was always right in the way he interpreted all their concepts, though,' she replied. 'Take the Buddhists' goal of Nirvana, for example. Schopenhauer saw this only as complete and utter extinction. If I understand the Buddhist belief, they strive to merge the individual into a universal self. They talk about a drop of water falling into the sea and then ask: is the ocean absorbing the droplet — or is it the droplet absorbing the ocean?'

Louise nodded slowly. 'Then there's the good doctor's suggestion about how to deal with the question of an afterlife. After death you'll be what you were before your birth. Simple!'

She explained that Schopenhauer's view was that the will-to-live, or ego, inevitably set itself against all other things — and so made suffering unavoidable.

'Schopenhauer said that the only escape is to deny your will — even try to annihilate your own sense of self.'

'Does sound a bit like Buddhism to me,' observed Michael, adding with a smile, 'And, by the way, what about you repressing your own sense of self? I hope you're making impressive progress!'

There was a pause and the rain began to splatter heavily on the tiled patio and they moved inside. Michael noticed an opened deck of cards on a coffee table.

'What's your favorite game?' he asked.

'Blackjack... and poker, I guess. I really only play when I'm on the set...'

'When you're not boning up on your German philosophers?'

Louise shook her head wearily.

'Michael, you've just no idea how boring it is on a shoot. Those endless intervals between takes! As for actors' conversation, it's just a few basic variations on self-obsession — and after a few minutes I'm at my limit. So I dip out of sight with a few technicians and hands and we open a deck. It was Bill Fields who taught me to play properly...'

'Bill Fields?'

'W. C. Fields. You know, he could make a living just as a poker player. Come to think of it, he probably did in his early days. He was quite well on before he made any money. A real struggle till then, he told me.'

'What was... what is he like?' Michael asked.

'Oh, so sweet. Intelligent — and not just that, but wise. He really relishes the role of the screen cad, but in real life he's a heart of gold and he's just a little shy, too, although he'd hate to think anyone guessed it! And quite the most astonishing juggler you ever saw!'

'Really?'

'He's one of the few amusing or interesting people in the movie business. Like Mr Pabst, who directed me in Germany. Now, he really understood me,' said Louise wistfully.

'Mr Pabst... Funny thing. I always called him Mr Pabst. Even when we were sleeping together, he was still "Mr Pabst". He was the one who showed me that film could be an art form... and that acting really might be something worthwhile after all.'

'Until I left Hollywood, I thought movies were just business. In fact, I never even got around to seeing half the films I was in. I already knew they were rubbish when I was on the set. Until I met Mr Pabst all I learned that was useful were those cardsharping tricks from Bill Fields. He made me believe that I had some talent, that I wasn't just a dancer from Kansas who'd struck it lucky...'

As she talked, Louise's gaze shifted past Michael and seemed fixed on distant faces and events. Her eyes moistened.

'Trouble is, Michael, I don't know if I'll ever get a chance to work with anyone like that again. Somehow, I think it's very unlikely.'

Suddenly, she turned back to Michael and her sad expression was transformed into a wicked grin.

'Here, let me show you some of the four-flushing tricks I learnt at the knee of the great W. C. Fields!' she exclaimed, innocently unaware of the single tear gliding down her cheek.

* * *

Wordlessly, Louise led Michael by the hand into her bedroom. With slow and graceful moves she undressed him and lay on the bed with him, still fully clothed. She gently traced her fingertips over his skin and pressed little butterfly kisses onto his lips.

Utterly passive until now, Michael suddenly lifted himself up and pressed her to him in a fierce embrace. She melted into him, velvet-soft, and gave a little rapturous sigh.

Chest heaving, Michael gazed down at her. Her eyes closed, she looked vulnerable and innocent, almost child-like.

'Oh, Louise! My beautiful Lulu! I've waited so long! So very long...'

14. SOMEONE ELSE, SOMEWHERE...

The next morning Michael quietly let himself out of the apartment, taking care not to wake Louise. He wrote a note on a card, folded and draped it over the top of the dressing table mirror.

> *'Dear Louise,*
>
> *If last night was a foretaste of Heaven — as I think it was — then I'm going to stick firmly to the path of righteousness!*
>
> *I have a commitment tonight, but I would love to see you tomorrow (Friday) night. I'll call you later today.*
>
> *All my love*
>
> *Michael.'*

Minutes later, he switched off the computer and removed the Sensator helmet. How did he let himself get talked into an evening at a VR arcade? Of all things! Vince was always good company, but Melissa's conspiratorial aside about introducing him to a friend had made him apprehensive. *I've always thought that the two of you would really hit it off*, she had said. Recognizing a certain portent of disappointment, he smiled wanly — which Melissa, naturally, immediately read as an attractive, boyish shyness. Damn! A whole evening politely fending off the persistent probing of yet another 'eligible divorcee'! A whole evening that could have been spent with his darling Lulu!

Of course, he could simply change Louise's time zone to fit into his own availability. However, that was something he was reluctant to do. It was disorienting enough slipping from one world to another without the added problem of adjusting to different hours. And if you play around with entry and exit times, he told himself, you will soon trip over yourself. Besides, if his body clock was not synchronized with hers, she might find him nodding off in the middle of the day!

How odd, he reflected with a wry smile. Here he was, skating to and fro, from one century to another, and worrying about a couple of hours' jet-lag!

* * *

Even before Vince tapped the horn, Michael was already bounding over to the car. He opened the rear passenger door and sat down beside a tall lady with long, wavy black hair. Melissa introduced Jessica to him — with embarrassing emphasis — as a 'bachelor girl'. Still, she was attractive enough and, as the evening flowed, Jessica revealed an impressive intelligence. In fact, Michael found he quite enjoyed her company and, if it were not for Louise, this might easily have turned into another of Melissa's little triumphs!

After several unenthusiastic 'shoot 'em up' sessions in the VR arcade, Melissa suggested they try the 'Deathsprint' race, two to a car (another move to throw the unattached couple together!). Jessica insisted that Michael drive and Melissa took the wheel in the other vehicle. The cars were mounted on hydraulic jacks to simulate movement and were encased within a large hemisphere which carried a 360-degree projected image of the entire race course.

At the flagfall, Michael got off to an immediate lead and within seconds Jessica's hair was being flicked behind her by the 'slipstream' blown over the front of the car. Looking behind, they could see that Melissa and the other driver were both drawing up alarmingly close behind. Vince was laughing and smacking the side of their vehicle to encourage it to go faster.

After a long, very fast stretch, they suddenly encountered a sharp corner which began to tighten alarmingly. The third car was very close behind Melissa. Suddenly she hit her brakes and, in almost the same second, accelerated again. This prompted the other driver to instinctively stamp on his brakes, just as he arrived at the sharpest part of the bend. His vehicle spun around twice, slewed right across the road and thumped into the ditch. Now the race was between Melissa and Vince.

The road straightened and then presented a series of tricky chicanes. The two cars negotiated these without any change in their relative positions. Once again the road opened up and Jessica tugged Michael's arm. Melissa had pulled out to overtake! Michael slipped down a gear, but could go no faster. They were in this inconclusive draw when they hit another corner. Without warning, Michael and Jessica were jolted sideways against their safety straps — Melissa had deliberately rammed them!

At that moment a sign flashed up on the screen: 'Deliberate ramming of another vehicle will result in the race being stopped!' Another savage impact and Michael decided to pull over and let Melissa past...

Moments later, their cars drew up one behind the other at the pits. Melissa vaulted out of her vehicle, punching the air triumphantly. Vince smiled apologetically.

'With Melissa, winning's everything' whispered Jessica in Michael's ear. 'Haven't you noticed?'

Since the first stop after the arcade was Michael's place, he invited them in for a few drinks. Vince said that Melissa could drive them home afterwards, since she had demonstrated such prowess at the arcade. In the meantime, he would sample some of Michael's excellent reds!

As the surprisingly agreeable evening wore on, the talk somehow turned to a free-ranging speculation on the nature of time.

'Well, it's easy,' drawled Vince with the ponderous dignity of inebriation. 'Time is inseparable from space because all it is... is the interval during which physical conditions and relative positions change. If there's nothing there, how can you have time? It's all mixed up together. The space-time continuum, Eisenstein called it.'

'*Einstein*,' corrected Melissa, trying to conceal her boredom with the subject. 'You're thinking of the Russian film director.'

There was a small silence as Vince scanned the company to make sure that his profound insight had been absorbed.

'Well, Mike? What do you think?'

'I have often wondered if there is a time outside time,' Michael replied. 'In other words, that there is a dimension beyond time — the fifth dimension, if you like. It's the sphere in which all things that happen, have happened or will happen are all coexistent.'

'I don't get you,' said Melissa, shaking her head slowly.

'It's something outside our normal experience, that's all,' replied Michael. 'But all we need is the right analogy and we can understand almost any concept. Think of it this way...'

Michael rose up and walked to the entertainment system and took a video disk out of its case.

'When you run this disk you see a succession of images that follow a linear progression, right? For you, the viewer, each image or piece of action has a beginning and end, it comes and goes and is replaced by another scene. And that's the way we see and experience life itself. Right?'

The others nodded.

'And yet, each and every image, word, scene, every single detail of this two-hour movie all coexist and are all equally latent on this disk. We humans are limited by being only able to experience temporal events in a linear fashion. Like the head of a video player which reads an individual track without reference to the disk in its entirety.'

Jessica held up her hand. 'OK, so you're suggesting that — let me get this right — that there is a dimension where every single event past, present and future is equally real, equally contemporaneous?'

'That's right. But more than that,' Michael continued. 'Don't forget that we're looking at all the events of time without limit, in which all possibilities will have been played out in countless variations. So, in this other, higher dimension, we will find that all the experiences of our own life will also co-exist with every possible variation of those experiences.'

Melissa started laughing, which annoyed Michael.

'No, don't get me wrong, Mike,' she said. 'I'm just thinking when I had a cold and nearly missed the conference where I bumped into Vince. Who knows? In some other universe I might have stayed home — and ended up marrying that lawyer I had my eye on!'

She nudged Vince in the ribs.

'Well, Mike, what you talk about reminds me of my college reading of Nietzsche,' Melissa continued. 'He had this idea called eternal recurrence. If the universe could happen once, it could have happened an infinite number of times. And in this infinity of universes, all possible events would be played out, again and again.'

'So, there's a world where a fat lawyer gets you, sweetheart — and I'm the one who gets the lucky break!' interjected Vince, ducking as a cushion was swung at his head.

Seeing the levity that had taken over, Michael decided not to push the topic any further. As he toyed with his glass, his thoughts turned to Louise. Could it be true, my dear Louise, that my love for you is being endlessly reincarnated, double-mirrored through all eternity?

* * *

Melissa hung up the phone.

'That was Jessica,' she said to Vince who was tapping away at his laptop computer.

'Oh, yeah?'

'Remember when we got up to go and Michael said he'd drop Jessica back himself?'

'Yeah, looked like they'd clicked!' said Vince, looking up with a lascivious grin. 'So, what's her report card say?'

'Nothing. She said Mike dropped her straight home last night. Said he'd see her around. No phone number, even.'

She shrugged.

'I thought they'd got on pretty well — and Jessica's very... well, you'd think any discerning guy would be interested in her.'

'A real babe,' agreed Vince, without lifting his eyes. 'Anyway, maybe you should ease up on this matchmaking.'

'Vince — you're forgetting *you* are the one who suggested I introduce him to someone.'

Melissa paused reflectively. 'He's strange, but attractive. Jessica thought so, too. But there's something about him that just doesn't add up. I don't think he's gay. Are you sure he doesn't already have someone else somewhere?'

15. THE ONLY GIRL IN MY LIFE

'Miss Brooks? There's a telephone call for you. It's Mr Stanton. Will you take it in the studio manager's office?'

Louise put her script to one side and lightheartedly skipped out of the studio. It had been more than a week since Michael's last call and she was wondering if she was ever to hear from him again. He sounded affectionate and friendly, but to the point. Would she meet him that evening? They could have dinner, but if she had any other engagement, just a few minutes would suffice.

Several hours later, Louise walked past the studio security gate.

'Goodnight, Miss Brooks,' said the commissionaire.

'See you tomorrow, Arnold,' she replied. 'Oh, by the way, I was expecting someone to pick me up...'

'Hey, Brooksie! Over here!'

Louise turned to see the Stutz parked on the other side of the street. The hood was down and Michael was flagging her attention with a slow, exaggerated wave. As she crossed the road, he flung open the car door and started the motor.

'Hop in! I've something special for you,' said Michael, leaning over and kissing her.

Before Louise had even settled into her seat, he threw the car into a dust-raising turn and sped down the road. She started giggling.

'OK, Michael,' Louise shouted above the motor's roar. 'What's with that silly big grin? Come on, tell me! You've been up to some mischief — I know it!'

Michael just chuckled and drove on until he had reached the open road. He gunned the Stutz even faster until it was difficult to speak and impossible to be heard. At last, the car squealed to an abrupt halt outside her apartment. Engaging the handbrake, he turned around to his passenger.

'Well, Louise, I have to tell you that just over a week ago I put you down for a parcel of shares in Silberfeldt Resources. In fact, ten grand's worth — all in your name.'

Louise's grin gave way to an expression of alarm.

'Oh, Jesus! Michael!! I told you, I just don't have anything like that money to play with. What if they go down?' she cried.

'Well, I don't doubt that they will,' said Michael in a matter-of-fact tone. 'So I instructed my broker to sell this morning.'

He leaned over to the glove compartment, took out a large envelope and scanned through various documents.

'Right, here it is. Let's see, where does this leave you? Twenty thousand shares at one dollar and sixteen cents each, less brokerage for purchase and subsequent sale, tax, minus the original ten thousand I put up for you.'

Michael held up an envelope and opened it.

'Here you are, a check in the name of Miss Louise Brooks, payable at the Longueville branch of the Western and Industrial Bank. They know me there and I've asked them to work in with whatever arrangements you want to make...'

Louise snatched the check from his hand and held it up close to her eyes. Without expression, she scanned it several times before finally absorbing the information imparted by the small, neat handwriting. She lowered the check and stared at Michael.

'You know, I really can't take this. This is your money... It's too much.'

'Rubbish! I just loaned you the money to have a little flutter. It's nothing — you should see what I made on that number... a real killing. Take it Louise, it's yours. I truly want you to have it.'

'Twelve thousand dollars! Twelve thousand, six hundred and forty eight dollars?'

'And seventeen cents. Remember the cents, Louise, they count, too. You're really too careless about money!'

With that, Michael kissed her on the cheek and left the car.

'Tomorrow night. 7.30 sharp!'

'Michael,' called Louise after the departing car, 'I love you!'

* * *

In the weeks that followed, Louise saw more and more of Michael. The usual pattern was a call at the studio (if she was working) or to her apartment. He would then drop by and they would drive off on an excursion or to a restaurant, occasionally a show, and they would return to her apartment a few hours later. Sometimes, Louise suggested they eat at her apartment and Michael would bring a bottle of champagne. Only once did he stay the night — and, again, Louise awoke the next morning to find Michael gone and another little note on the breakfast table (*My Darling Louise. Thank you for a beautiful evening. I have an early call coming through and didn't want to disturb you. I'll ring you later today. Love, Michael*).

Protective of her own privacy, Louise was disinclined to probe much into Michael's own life, least of all his history. Like so many true hedonists, she saw little profit in sifting through the past and even less in speculating about tomorrow. And when the endless round of parties and movieland's other glittering, flimsy distractions bored her, she was content to lose herself in the hefty themes of her books.

However, the time did come when Michael's mysterious appearances and disappearances provoked her curiosity.

'Do you know, you have never told me where you live. Where do you slink back to after you've squired me around town?'

'I've a suite in the Alhambra Hotel,' he told her. 'I haven't had time to buy a place yet.'

'Are you ever going to invite me there?'

Michael reflected a moment.

'I'd like to, of course,' he began, awkwardly. 'But... Well, it's the whole thought of the gossip columns. I really don't want to read about us in some rag.'

'Oh, come on!' exclaimed Louise in disbelief.

'Look, the bellhop would be phoning Louella Parsons or whoever before we'd even reached the lifts. I've seen it — and you know it.'

'So?'

'Louise, we both know how salacious gossip lubricates the motion picture scene,' Michael replied defensively. 'But it's definitely something a businessman like me wants to keep well clear of. I just don't belong in it. The people I deal with — you've no idea how stuffy most of them can be. Anyway, that's getting away from the point. There's really nothing to see there — it's just an ordinary hotel suite. That's all.'

Louise narrowed her eyes and gave him a long, knowing smile.

'You're married! Admit it...'

She began to bait him, pretending to believe that he was hiding the existence of an unsuspecting wife and, very probably, a brood of young children as well. Louise's increasingly florid speculations about Michael's betrayals were supported by alternating attitudes of feigned hurt, outrage and jealousy.

'Michael,' she finally announced with mock seriousness, 'the time has come for you to chose. It's me — or it's her!'

But he only smiled mysteriously.

The following day Louise insisted on meeting Michael in the Alhambra's lobby, explaining that one of the studio people would drop her off there, since it was on his way.

Arriving early, she asked the receptionist for Mr Stanton's room number and, saying she wanted to surprise him by calling unannounced, she took the lift and made her way to his room. As she was about to knock, Louise stopped and listened at the door. She could just make out the sound of Michael's indistinct voice inside. His delivery, slow and measured, paused for a few second between sentences. She thought he was practicing phrases of a foreign language. Intrigued, she looked up and down the empty corridor and then pressed her ear to the door.

'....Voice I.D. clearance, please... CyberProfile Group... Stanton, Michael... 5...4...3...2...1... Closed sector 326... Password Lulu...'

Louise then heard a woman speaking in a way that was strangely flat and expressionless.

'Voice I.D. completed, Mr Stanton... You are now cleared for access to closed sector 326... Log-on time is EST 21.48 and thirty-seven seconds. Press the return key for access...'

Then silence.

Louise knocked softly on the door. Almost immediately, Michael opened it. For a second he looked startled, but he quickly caught himself and welcomed her with a wide smile.

'Why, Louise! So, you've run me to ground at last! I wasn't expecting you so early. I was just about to go down to meet you at the lobby... Well, now we've met up, let's hit the road!'

Louise fixed Michael with a long, knowing look. Her tongue played over her lips as she tried to hide a smile. 'But Michael, your lady friend in there. Are you going to leave her to let herself out?'

'Lady friend?'

'Michael, you were talking — to a woman.' She jabbed him in the ribs. 'Oh, come on. Don't be bashful! I'm broadminded. I play around, so why shouldn't you?'

'There's no-one in there... I swear! Here, have a look! No, go on — see for yourself.'

Louise peered past Michael and then entered the suite.

'Look,' said Michael. 'No-one in the closet. Under the bed? Here, the bathroom... behind the shower curtain, see? No-one. I'm completely alone!'

'Michael, it was a woman. She said something about "closed sector Lulu"... *Lulu?*'

'Your imagination, Louise. I was just singing to myself. You're the only girl in my life, believe me. Now, let's go and eat! By the way, what's this about *you* playing around?'

She ignored him and opened her bag.

'It's for you... It's a present,' said Louise coyly.

'For my birthday? How sweet!'

Michael held up the small package. It was daintily wrapped in glossy, seaweed-green paper, tied up with a neat bow of gold ribbon.

'But how did you know?'

Louise smiled mysteriously.

'Well, Mr Stanton, aren't you going to open it?'

Michael carefully unfolded the gift.

He held up an ivory fountain pen with a white gold clip and matching ring on the cap. He held it in his hand, viewing it from different angles.

'How truly lovely' he whispered — and leaning forward, he kissed Louise softly on her brow. Opening his bureau drawer, Michael took out a sheet of paper and tried to write with the pen.

'Michael, it's a fountain pen!' exclaimed Louise, patiently. 'You have to fill it with ink first!'

Of course, thought Michael. Ball point pens are still years away. Silly me. He felt inside the drawer again and located a convenient bottle of ink.

'Here we are. You'd better show me how it's done. I'm a little clumsy and I'd hate to break something so beautiful.'

Shaking her head, a mystified Louise deftly drew the ink into the pen and handed it to him. Michael drew the sheet towards him and inscribed the words, *'To the Beautiful Louise, I love you now and always. Michael.'*

* * *

Over dinner Michael suggested that he would like to visit the studio set where Louise was playing a support role for a western.

'I hear this is a talkie production.'

'Yes,' replied Louise, 'they're all making sound pictures now. The theaters are installing sound systems just as fast as they can.'

'What about the silents? I guess the demand has collapsed.'

'Once an audience has been to a talkie, it just won't settle for a silent flick ever again. That's why the films I made in Europe, "Pandora's Box" and "Diary of a Lost Girl", didn't get much of a run here. In fact, even then Pabst was among the last directors to produce major silent productions in Germany. But then, I don't speak German — so I wouldn't have been able to appear in them if they had been talkies.'

Louise went on to explain that the advent of talkies had ruined many acting careers.

'Not to mention an army of cinema piano players,' quipped Michael.

'Rudy Valentino,' she went on. 'There's someone who would've been a disaster if audiences were able to hear, and not just see, him. Thick accent and thin voice, apparently. One word and you know straight away that Clara Bow hails from the Bronx. She's got a voice like a washboard — and swears like a deckhand, too. But a great gal. Then there are quite a few whose voices turned out to be real assets.'

'Well, you'll have no difficulties in that department, Louise. You've got a good voice. Nicely modulated.'

'Thanks. But aren't you just a little biased, don't you think? It's a real chore working with sound. For one thing, you can't shift around much because you have to stay close to the microphones. Half the time you can only move when you've finished talking — then you position yourself over the next rose bowl hiding a mike and start talking again. The camera is much more restricted, too. All that sound equipment and the sound-proofing they need to hide the camera noise — it really limits what you can do. But do you want to know the worst thing about making sound movies?'

'Tell me,' Michael responded.

'You have to learn your lines the night before. You've got to stay sober and go to bed early. And that really hits me where it hurts most — no time for fun! Such a *bore*!'

'Sign of the times, Louise,' he said, knowingly. 'We're moving into an era of great earnestness. The big party is coming to an end, I fear.'

Squeezing his hand, she lifted her big wide eyes close to his.

'But Michael, you'll make sure life stays fun, won't you,' she pouted. 'I need a playmate. Otherwise, I'll just get completely bound up with those dusty old books.'

'Louise, there are lots of playmates in this town. Guys who are probably a lot more fun than I'll ever be...'

'No, you're much more than a playmate, Michael,' she said, now more serious. 'You understand me. You have an intelligence and sensitivity that's really very rare. And you're strong in your quiet way — that's something I admire.'

She leaned forward.

'Kiss me.'

Michael gently brushed her lips with his. He cradled her face in his hands and playfully blew her bangs away so he could again admire her strong, intelligent forehead.

'Louise, you're someone very special — and very precious — to me. I think you know how very close I feel to you.'

She returned his kiss. Then brightened up.

'Good, then I expect you to provide unquestioning support tomorrow morning at Stage 11. I've got all of six sentences to dispose of, so you could easily miss my performance. Be there at 7.30 sharp. I'll tell security to give you a pass.'

'On the dot — and I'll be the most vocal supporter in the Louise Brooks claque! You can count on me,' responded Michael.

Next morning Michael presented himself at the studio front office and was escorted to the set. There was Louise and the other actors, lounging around in Western attire while the lighting director fidgeted with a troublesome shadow on the set.

'Michael, over here!' Louise called out. 'Now, let me introduce you to some of the rising stars in the Hollywood firmament!'

Michael shook hands with various cowhands, including one strikingly handsome young actor who stood well over six feet tall. 'This is John,' said Louise. 'John Wayne. He's fairly new to town. But you couldn't see this extra staying unnoticed for long, now could you?'

Wayne looked embarrassed.

'Cut it out, Louise! Nice to meet you, sir.'

Louise's familiar and somewhat proprietorial way of presenting the young actor suggested a thought to Michael: here is another one of her conquests! He was sure of it. And that might explain some of Wayne's deferential awkwardness, too.

God, you're a loose little number, Brooksie, he observed to himself. He knew her honesty would never be in doubt, but could he ever count on her to be faithful? Probably not.

In between takes, Louise was playful and teasing with the other actors; indeed, she appeared to dominate the conversation. Despite her small part in the production, she was comfortably confident in discussions with the director. Michael noticed that the crew and stagehands all appeared to know her well and they traded jokes and conspiratorial asides with the ease of old troupers who had put in long hours together over many productions.

However, once the camera was trained on Louise, she became completely focused on her piece. Her movements and lines were all worked out perfectly. And when the director called for a slight variation she was able to recalibrate her performance to match the request exactly. Unlike most of the other actors, she never once fluffed her words and always seemed to possess an almost intuitive physical awareness. To Michael, Louise was not so much playing to the camera in the way (he imagined) that comes to most proficient actors, but was actually using the camera. She had a strangely indefinable, *natural* affinity with the lens, like a virtuoso violinist and his instrument. Once the camera started rolling, this laughing, irreverent young woman transformed herself into a commanding presence. While others merely acted, hers was a transfixing reality.

After a hurried lunch of cut sandwiches and coffee (during which Michael, unlike Louise, declined a draught from a brandy flask proffered by an older actor), the shoot continued through the afternoon till about five o'clock, when the director dismissed most of the actors for the day. Louise explained to Michael that they would be shooting every day for the following week — and that she would need to spend every evening learning her lines. She looked forward to hearing from him the following week.

16. COULD I EVER BE SURE?

Louise appeared without a hat and wearing a loose, dark-blue satin blouse with a sailor's collar framing a white silk kerchief. She spun around for effect and then stopped, looking coyly over her shoulder back at Michael.

'It's called a middy. What do you think?'

'I'd go to sea with you anytime you like,' laughed Michael. 'You look a very mate-able shipmate to my rheumy old eye!'

With that Louise did a quick little hornpipe and warmly kissed Michael on the lips.

'Miss me?'

'Oh, a little...'

Michael sprang up and grabbed her by the elbow.

'Tell you what. Since you're obviously dressed for the part, why don't we hire a boat and go for a spin? There's enough of a breeze to make it worthwhile. I've got a hamper and some bubbly in the car, but I think the water's a better idea than a picnic spot. Get to it, Miss Brooks — let's get some salt in the face!'

Michael swept her up in his arms and ran towards the car. Seeing an elderly couple, Louise pretended to be unconscious, with eyes closed and one arm hanging down limply.

'I've just rescued her from an opium den,' declared Michael solemnly. 'By the look of things, not a moment too soon, either...'

'Oh goodness me,' said the stocky lady, clenching onto her spouse's arm. 'White slavery! There, didn't I tell you it's happening in this very town. Poor young girl...'

Louise giggled all the way to the marina, pausing only to mimic the victims of her joke.

At the jetty, Michael clambered onto the deck and Louise passed things down to him, beginning with the hamper. Finally, she lowered the large, leather bag she had brought with her.

'Good God,' uttered Michael. 'What on earth *is* that dead weight in your bag? A brick?'

'A book,' replied Louise in a matter-of-fact tone. 'Here.'

Michael turned the heavy, moroccan-bound volume over in his hand.

'*Dead Souls*... by Nikolai Gogol. Jesus, Brooksie, are you really hauling this along with you? Why? To escape my oppressive company by delving into this Slavonic levity?'

He flipped through the pages.

'I'm deeply flattered, I really am.'

Louise laughed.

'Michael, you must know that it's only because I feel so comfortable in your company that I brought it along. Besides, there are several passages I wanted to read to you.'

'You're the only person I've ever met who could make that sort of reply sound at all plausible,' replied Michael. 'But, then, you're probably the only person who'd ever dream of bringing *Dead Souls* to a picnic!'

* * *

They had both been silent for some while and Louise was dreamily trailing her toes in the water. As she leaned over the side of the boat to examine the effect, her wind-blown hair (which, earlier, had been such a neat bob!) tumbled around her face. To Michael, Louise looked enchantingly innocent and playful — so different from the self-possessed screen star on his arm, trailing glamor behind every shimmering step through Hollywood's nightlife.

Michael realized why he had always found Louise's bob cut — and, indeed, short hair on any female — so attractive. Of course, it highlighted a woman's face and the bangs, especially, drew attention to the eyes. But above all, this gamine look lured one's admiring eye to a woman's neck, that most vulnerable, loveliest portion of a woman's body. If her neck was of ordinary length, such a cut made it look long and where her neck was already long, she would take on the beauty of a swan.

Now he understood why he had been disappointed by films of the French actress, Brigitte Bardot, which showed her generous mane spilling over her shoulders — and not swept up into the delicious pile that transformed her from the back of her head right down to her pert bottom! Yes, and this was the true Japanese aesthetic for the female form. When did it ever matter to Utamaro and eighteenth-century Edo's other painters that a maid's bosom was strapped down and smothered to the point of invisibility? Their art was amply inspired by the gracile neck emerging from the robe's artfully draped shoulder-line, with the hair ornately arranged to transfix a man's gaze upon the object of his desire...

Suddenly, Louise let out a shriek. The wash from a motorboat that had passed some minutes ago had thrown a mass of chilly water right onto her lap. The transformation from idyllic repose to drenched horror was so complete and immediate that Michael could not help burst out laughing.

'You pig! You saw that coming, I'm sure you did! Look at me, I'm drowned!'

Still grinning, he tossed a towel over and watched as she furiously rubbed her hair and alternately flicked it in the brisk wind. My Louise, he thought, you are so alive, more real, than anyone I have ever known! But when I am not with you, are you really living and experiencing life in the same way as now? Or is the computer simply compiling a plausible narrative for you to recite when you chatter to me about your busy day? Does it implant a false memory which you, quite unaware, draw upon as your own first-hand experience?

Perhaps, Michael pondered, Louise is only ever truly 'alive' when she is with me and at other times is just a frozen specter, lying ready to compliantly take form when I am beside her?

If Louise, herself could not know the answer, then how could *he* ever be sure?

* * *

'Look after the car, please,' said Michael to the restaurant commissionaire as he opened Louise's door.

'Yes, sir.'

'We'll need it again in about two hours, perhaps just a little longer,' added Michael, pressing a five dollar note into the young man's hand.

'Yessir! Thank you, Mr Stanton.'

As they walked through the open lobby door into the restaurant, Louise jabbed Michael and whispered urgently in his ear. 'Michael, are you crazy? Do you know that was a whole five dollars you tipped?'

'Yes. What of it?' he replied absentmindedly. He smiled to himself, reflecting on how little gratitude five dollars earned in the twenty-first century.

'Now then, how about a little something to drink while we're waiting?' prompted Louise in a conspiratorial whisper. 'Uh-oh — too late!'

'Louise, darling!' shrieked a rather large lady whose jowly face was framed by a very close-cut bob cut that was an appalling caricature of Louise's own style. She insisted they join her table.

Louise was delightful company that night. She chattered incessantly and kept prodding Michael and teasing him. He responded as well as he could and, tried to enter the conversation, launching into an item he had read in the paper, some gossip. But he kept falling back into quiet pensiveness. Again and again, he debated whether he should — or could — do something to prepare Louise for the telegram that he knew she would be reading in the morning.

Michael looked at his watch — and prompted a loud chorus from his table partners, chiding him for being such a bore. He smiled faintly, hardly seeming to notice. Within the hour, he knew, Louise's father would collapse to the floor of his library, clutching his chest.

He looked across the table. Poor Louise! It would be some time before he would see her so cheerful again. There and then, he resolved that in future when he next re-entered his Luluworld he would resist the temptation to look at Louise's biographical notes. Wouldn't we all be frozen in abject misery if we had the least inkling of the train of sorrows heading towards each of us and those we love?

'Come on, Michael! Liven up, do! Tell us a story!'

'No,' he replied with a start. 'I'll tickle the ivories for you instead.'

This drew a burst of applause — and for the twenty minutes Michael sat at the rather beaten upright piano, amusing himself hugely by tapping out a medley of tunes whose composers, if only his little audience realized it, were yet to be born.

'That's catchy, Michael darling! What's it called?'

'Just made it up, Cynthia darling,' he lied. In a later moment, he laughed loudly when Louise said: 'You know, Michael, if you applied yourself, you could write a show... Don't cackle like that, you fool! He could, couldn't he, Lambert?'

* * *

Back in her apartment, Louise accepted Michael's offer to make a jug of coffee. Meanwhile, she disappeared into the bedroom to change into her dressing gown.

A quarter hour later, Michael quietly pushed open the door. There was Louise, still in her evening gown, sleeping on her stomach with her head nestled into a large, red-colored pillow. He drew up a chair beside the divan and watched the gentle rise and fall of her shallow, almost inaudible, breathing. Michael leaned forward and gently stroked the satin-smooth shoulder. His hand moved up and lightly parted her black hair. Louise looked as open and untroubled as a child. And that, thought Michael, was the endowment of a nature that was instinctively honest and frank, that easily recognized, and accommodated itself to, reality. Behind this sweet and unfurrowed face you would find no harbor for lies or evasions, no treacheries to self or others, no cruel dreams or foolish myths.

He quietly retreated from the room. A gentle sadness washed over him as he contemplated what only he knew the next day would bring. Louise would need as much sleep as she could get for, Michael knew, she would be up for much of the following night, reading and re-reading through red-rimmed eyes the curt message of the Western Union telegram.

> *'Dear Miss Brooks, Regret to inform you that your father passed away peacefully last night of a sudden heart attack. Your mother coping reasonably well and expecting your call. Have already advised Ted Brooks. Sincere condolences. Dr Henry Gavin.'*

17. THE INTERLOPER

Michael was exhausted...

The heaviness that weighed him down had nothing to do with any loss of appetite for Louise's company. It was no more than the physical and nervous fatigue exacted by his two demanding lives. In truth, Michael's absorption with Louise was so enveloping that he now knew only to mark his hours as time spent with her or yearning to be with her. From the first moments of each encounter, his mind was turning over how to contrive another visit — or another telephone call — with the least delay. And if Louise explained in her offhand way that she could not see him for a day or two, he felt a despair that was almost physically painful.

Yet, Michael also saw that there was danger in spending so many long hours, night after night, at the computer terminal. Of course, colleagues driving past the CPG building late at night had come to recognize that the solitary light in the dim building meant Michael was trying to unravel a conundrum that had defied the team's best efforts earlier that day. Nonetheless, he felt unsettled whenever anyone else called in at night. On two occasions, something prompted him to turn around and discover Vince standing soundlessly by the office door. He had barely time to hit the escape key and bring up a screen of routine programming.

Michael had fallen behind on the current project and a week's uninterrupted effort would do much to close the gap. Besides, he was afraid that his insatiable hunger for Louise might be the very thing that could lose her. He was overwhelming her, he told himself, and a short respite might be good for both of them. True, Louise was always pleased to see him, but he knew that if she ever sensed that her precious independence and freedom of movement were threatened, she would be lost to him. Now would be the chance to see if she missed him.

The relentless shifting from one era to another, and back again, was taxing. There was the constant strain of adjusting to a world in which everything seemed so different and at times, almost alien. The very look of early twentieth century America — even the unfamiliar noises (and silences) — disoriented him and, in the early days especially, each visit confronted him with a hundred small surprises. It reminded him of when he made his first visit to Tokyo: it was so overwhelming that, for the first three or four days, he had to sleep as much as nine or ten hours a night.

Sometimes, too, his journeys to this cyberworld touched Michael with a vague sense of melancholy. He could not help thinking that in his own time, the twenty-first century, all these people were long dead. The world they lived in had now almost vanished, and any intimate sense of its unique character and essence lost utterly. Likewise, he could understand that his own world, too, would be no more enduring — and that the time would come surely when a future age would also see his era as quaint and unreachably distant.

Michael cast back to his discussion with Vince about the universal contemporaneity of all possible events and experiences within the dimension outside time — the Universal Now. If what the philosophers call 'block time' or 'eternalism' truly describes reality, then it would make him as ephemeral and, yes, as real as Louise, Betty, Freddie and the others.

Along the way, Michael discovered many conventions and idioms unique to the Twenties. The 'fast' movie world that Louise adorned was even more exotic, but outside that microcosm, Michael quickly learnt, there was a profoundly, even startlingly, conservative America.

This point had been deeply impressed upon him during one luncheon with some business friends of a producer. Provocatively, he set out to gauge the liberalism of his acquaintances by introducing the subject of a recently-published work by a young Irish author.

'No, Mr Stanton,' came the emphatic reply. 'I have *not* read "Ulysses"!'

'Maybe you should,' suggested Michael. 'They tell me it's a brilliant novel. A work of real genius that breaks new ground. Someone said he wouldn't be surprised if they're still talking about it a hundred years from now.'

He noticed that Louise had discreetly lowered her gaze and was smiling to herself as she fiddled with her napkin ring.

'With respect, sir, I have to tell you I am frankly surprised that you're acquainted with the scribblings of a degenerate like Joyce. What's more, I am dismayed to learn that a single copy of that blasphemous book has made its way to these shores...'

Michael turned to Louise, whose eyes had widened with lascivious interest, and tried to save himself from further scolding by explaining that, purely out of innocent curiosity, he had merely leafed through the pages of an Olympia Press edition in a Paris bookshop. That was all, he said, feeling a little ashamed of his moral cowardice — and wondering what they would have made of the fact that one day this masterpiece would be prescribed study reading for undergraduates!

People at all levels dealt with one another with a formality that he found intriguing. While this could take the form of a cool and distant rigidity, more often it was manifest as an oddly attractive politeness in speech and behavior, an instinctive deference and consideration for others. The years to the early 21st century were not to be a tale of progress in all areas of life, he mused.

When talking with Louise and others in her circle, Michael was particularly wary about letting the occasional anachronism slip out. This would have been a sufficient challenge for anyone from his time, but Michael also had to constantly filter out the argot of computer programmers and cyberfreaks — and some of the military vernacular that had crept into his workaday speech). Yet, despite his best efforts, the odd egregious expression still caught Louise's attention.

'There you go again!' she once upbraided him. 'Feedback... *feedback*? What does that mean, Michael? And there was something you said yesterday about including someone in the loop. You do really come up with the oddest expressions! Tell me, do other people over East speak like you? I never heard such talk when I was in New York...'

On the other hand, back in his own world Michael felt quite free to use expressions from the Roaring Twenties. First of all, this was his authentic domain and there was no sense of being an alien interloper. Again, his colleagues and friends vied with each other in coining neologisms and novel imagery. Eager to affirm their own solidarity within the alien government-military environment, they had created a patois that was intentionally incomprehensible to outsiders. And so Michael felt quite free to pepper his talk with 'Old Sport', 'jitterbug', 'jalopy' and the like.

Then there were the different attitudes between the two centuries.

For example, Michael discovered that, in the world before powerful antibiotics, the fear of syphilis and other venereal infections had been as widespread as the horror of contracting AIDS was towards the end of the 20th century.

In contrast with his own times, people in this cyberworld had an absolute horror of marijuana. One puff of Indian hemp, it was universally believed, and a promising young man was ruined for life — and a woman was sure to wake up from her stupor to find herself a white slaver's helpless commodity. Yet by contrast, there was little self-consciousness about the use of cocaine to pep up a cocktail party. It was deemed a smart drug and completely free of any serious side effects: any dependence on it was ascribed, not to a physical addiction, but rather to an inherent moral weakness.

Michael limited himself to a very modest intake of champagne, mostly to provide company for Louise — an enthusiastic drinker. Still, at the many cocktail parties they attended together, Michael was much in demand behind the bar, where he 'invented' cocktails which (if they only knew it) were not to appear outside Louise's privileged coterie for years to come. Michael's Bloody Mary was a particular favorite — and his Irish Coffee, they said, would make him a legend!

Sometimes he engineered such diversions as relief from the tiresome preoccupations often dominating the small talk at these gatherings, particularly on the subjects of hypnotism and Freud and psychoanalysis. More than once he felt like proclaiming his opinion that future generations would be *sure* to discount many of Freud's assertions and would likely discover much more of value in his then little-known student, Carl Jung. For all that, in his more generous moments, he had to concede to himself that if these people moved forward several generations, they would still have plenty to feed on. Exchange Madame Blavatsky for any one of California's New Age gurus — and what difference would there be? The power of 'animal magnetism' and the power of crystals, the spiritualist seance and the out-of-body experience? Verily, as the man said, *plus ça change...*

While amused to see the fixations of his generation thrown into sharp relief by the fads of their great-great grandparents, he was startled by the universal assumption that nothing was better for an asthma or bronchitis than to smoke. Nor could he overcome his unease about driving around in a car without a seat belt or collision bag, especially given the (to his mind) utterly inadequate road-holding and braking in these early days of the automobile age!

Each time Michael crossed over between Louise's world and his own, he had to adjust his senses to a world whose form, as well as content, seemed disorienting. From his first visit, Michael was struck by the odd effect of so many smooth lines, so unlike the chaotic discontinuities of his own world. In this computer-shaped world, tones were precisely graduated, with little of the dappled play of shadow, light and shade he knew. The clouds had an odd regularity and tidiness about them — and, he noticed, even the waves he and Louise looked out upon in the moonlit bay had moved with an almost mathematical periodicity. Michael saw that they processed in sets of six or seven, repeating each sequence over and over again. And, he observed, there was no dust or dirt anywhere. The cars always sparkled with immaculate paintwork and his Stutz inevitably returned from an afternoon's drive with unblemished whitewall tires. If Louise wore a snow-white or cream dress to a picnic, it remained as pristine at the end of the day as when she started — like Michael's own spats!

In designing the cyberworld environment, Michael and his colleagues realized that they could considerably reduce the massive demands on the computer by only constructing in full detail a selected portion of the image field: 'dynamic floating focal point', it was called. In this way they mimicked the mechanism of normal vision, but they accentuated the difference between the central area of focus and the peripheral field of vision. It took a little getting used to, of course, but the eye (or, more properly, the brain) quickly made the appropriate adjustments. Nonetheless, it all had the effect of making the central image stand out much more than the surrounding background — as if a scene were bathed in a spotlight. As disconcerting was that when the visor was lifted after a long session, objects in the real world seemed poorly differentiated from one other and the overall impression was that everything had become pallid and surprisingly flat.

At first, before he adjusted to it, Michael imagined that Louise lived in a brightly-lit, fastidiously-painted stage set. Her domain had a dreamy quality that somehow seemed to match the magical powers Michael brought with him. Yet, upon returning to his own 'real' existence, he often felt a vague sense of unreality that was both troubling and confusing. It took time — at least an hour — to adjust back again, and even then he was often left feeling weary and strained.

In the days since Michael last visited Louise, he sensed a vague frustration with the people and the world. He — and those around him — did not fail to notice an uncharacteristic impatience, frequently revealed in a prickly irritation over trivialities that had once been accepted with unmurmuring stoicism. Michael had attributed this to his missing Louise's company. At first that seemed a readily acceptable explanation and, while it must have been true to an extent, there was something else.

Finally, it came to him. One afternoon, he walked into the office feeling particularly disgruntled: his car's air conditioning had broken down on a particularly hot day and, to crown it all, he found that his parking space had been taken and he was forced to hunt around for an empty visitor's spot. As he sat in this bad humor he remembered that when he was with Louise, nothing of this sort ever happened to him! Then everything was orderly and functioning. All-powerful and all-knowing, he was always in perfect, effortless control of his environment and the events that unfolded there. The direction of great events or the groundward spiraling of a leaf: all lay comfortably within his masterful purview. THAT was what he missed — and it was the temporary deprivation of this far-reaching power that made him so peevish!

This was something he had to watch out for, he realized. It would be all too easy to find the real world so limiting and unsatisfactory — and the other existence so accommodating — that he might become reluctant ever to leave his self-made little universe. He had often appeared in forums and TV debates where sociologists and educators debated their concerns about young people disengaging themselves from the world around them and spending too much time in the Virtual Reality arcades (and playing the games that he himself had helped develop). If there were the least grounds for their fears, then how more easily could he lose himself to a self-fashioned world inhabited by the woman he loved?

A world in which one moved with all-knowing omnipotence.

An almost-forgotten incident came to mind. Years earlier, when Warp-Play launched his 'Arena Combat' game, Michael received sackfuls of suggestions for all sorts of future VR games. Most were bizarre and usually centered around a highly-individual sexual fantasy.

But one letter hooked into his mind.

Why not, this correspondent suggested, recreate the Galilee of two millennia ago and devise a scenario whereby a player could act out the life of Christ — right up to the crucifixion?

The letter was followed by several phone calls until Michael finally explained to this middle-aged man (whom he was never to meet) that such a proposal was not commercially feasible. Few would care to take on this role — and, besides, Warp-Play would be unwilling to take on the ire of all those offended by such blasphemy.

Yet here he was, playing God to the manikins of his very own little world!

But, it was not a perfect deification, after all. Daily, he was obliged to descend from Olympia to share the feeble capabilities — and all the privations — that make up the daily round of mere mortals! Little wonder, then, that his CyberProfile Group colleagues were whispering about how tetchy Michael had become lately...

18. MEET MY NEW FRIENDS

'Where IS she? Sam Hiller's asked twice about when he's going to meet her. We've looked everywhere!'

Michael assured his hostess that he would bring Louise directly to her.

'Oh, thank you, Mr Stanton! Would you please? I can't understand her at all. You know, Mr Hiller is very big in the movie business — and I know she's been looking for work since her vacation in Europe. To tell the truth, that's why we made a point of asking him along. And she does know he's here!'

'I'll be back shortly, Helen. She can't be far.'

Moving from room to room, Michael eventually found himself in the kitchen. He asked several of the hands if they had seen a young lady with a black bob and wearing a deep blue dress. No, they said, and one of them called over an elderly black waiter who was passing by. With his silver hair and impeccably-cut uniform, he struck Michael as more impressively dignified than any of the guests he was serving.

'Why, yessir. Miss Brooks? She's down at the bottom of the garden, near the main entrance gates. She took a tray of vol-au-vents from me. I do believe she's still there.'

Walking under a continuous rose arch that led from the lawn to the front gate, Michael could see nothing but the narrow path ahead.

As he approached what appeared to be the main entrance, he began to pick out the sound of lively conversation, then Louise's voice and laughter.

'Why, Michael! Come here and meet these lovely people!'

Louise beckoned him over with an impatient wave. She was sitting on a stone balustrade with the heaped tray perched precariously in front of her. At her feet a bottle of champagne peered over the top of a silver ice bucket.

'This is Michael... Mr Stanton. He's the most loveliest man I've ever met in my whole life,' she slurred as she rose to her feet. She threw both arms around his neck and kissed him wetly. Michael smiled awkwardly at Louise's three new-found friends. They were a plainly-dressed young couple, fresh-faced and polite, and a thin, older man, perhaps in his late fifties, whose constant grin revealed a disconcerting gap in his front teeth.

'They were looking in, so I invited them to our party, explained Louise. 'We're having a drink and some nibbles. Here, don't be so stand-offish, Mr Stanton. Pull up a stone and join us!'

She broke into a fit of giggles and spilled champagne from her glass.

Sensing Michael's embarrassment, the young man cut in.

'We didn't mean to intrude, sir. My Dad here, he's the gardener at the Bothwell's, two houses up. Well, Mary and me, we'd never seen any movie stars before and he said with the party and all we might just peep through the gates here.'

Mary and he looked at each another. She took her boyfriend's arm and said firmly: 'Well, Dan, don't you think we'd better be going now?'

'Why, there's no need for you folk to be going anywhere,' interrupted Louise. 'Michael, tell them to have some champers. You'll never guess. Mr Wilson here...'

'Williams,' the older man interrupted quietly.

'Worked in a fire station' she continued. 'Imagine that!'

Michael curtly nodded in Williams' direction and noticed with some exasperation that Louise had poured the champagne and deftly popped a strawberry into each glass.

'Only way to drink champagne,' she declared, passing the glasses.

Laughing lightly, she added: 'And the only way to eat strawberries! That's what Bill Fields says. W. C. Fields? Know him? He's in movies, you know.'

'Do *you* know Mr Fields, Miss Brooks?' asked Mary. 'Personal?'

'Indeedie, I do!' replied Louise. 'One of nature's gentlemen. And has an encyclopedic knowledge of alcohol in its many forms. Here's to Bill Fields and to each and every one of us. Cheers!'

As she took a draft of champagne, Michael cut in.

'Louise, do you know Helen Dennis is looking around for you everywhere? She's anxious for you to talk to Sam Hiller. She sent me for you. I'm sorry, but we really do have to go.'

'Tell him to come down here,' Louise replied, defiantly flicking her hair.

'Come on. We've got to go.'

'Then I'm bringing my friends with me!'

'Miss Brooks, honest, we'd better go home,' interjected Mary anxiously. 'Been real nice to...'

'Stay right here,' commanded Louise, picking up the champagne bottle and pouting sulkily. 'You don't come, I don't come. Plain as that.'

'Louise...' Michael looked at the three reluctant visitors and smiled wearily. 'Sorry, but you'd really oblige me if you'd walk with us to the house.'

Mr Williams, Dan and Mary conferred silently. Michael felt their apprehension about venturing into the domain of glamorous people — *stars!* — whose lives were an impossibly remote fantasy that they, mere mortals, knew only through fan magazines or the screen's flickering images. Yet, here and now, was the one chance in their lives to catch even the briefest glimpse inside this magical world — and wasn't Louise Brooks herself insisting that they be her guests?

Uncertainly, they edged forward. Michael thanked them for their help and the group made its way towards the house, with Louise leaning heavily on his arm. He asked them to wait by the veranda while he slipped past the French windows to seek out the hostess.

'Mrs Dennis, I've Louise here. She found some fans at the gate and didn't think you'd mind if she brought them to the house for a moment.'

As she looked over his shoulder, Helen Dennis' thin eyebrows momentarily arched with disapproval.

'Of course, Mr Stanton, I'm quite sure they won't be any trouble. I'll ask Clarice to bring them some sandwiches and soda. Now, could you ask Louise to join me? Mr Hiller is in the library, I do believe.'

Michael stayed on with the other three whose discomfiture had been overtaken by a wide-eyed absorption of everything around them. Picking tentatively at the sandwiches, they sipped their sodas and stood conspicuously still and silent at the edge of the revelry. From time to time, a recognized face moved past and Mary would shyly whisper a famous name into Dan's ear.

Dan cleared his throat.

'Er... Mr Stanton. It's real strange being so close by folks like this when you've only seen them in the movies before. You kind of feel you know them well — and yet you don't, if you know what I mean.'

Mary smiled up at Dan and squeezed his arm.

'When I seen them in the pictures I just never thought that one day I'd meet them face to face. Real movie stars.' Almost regretfully, she added, 'Trouble is, no-one's going to believe me!'

With that she shook her head as if she scarcely believed it all herself.

'And Miss Brooks, such a lady! Beautiful — and so friendly.'

The other two nodded vigorously.

At last Louise appeared. Clutching his hand, she dragged a bulky and bemused man behind her.

'This is Mr Sam Hiller. He's a very important executive with Animascope Studios. I told him that to make movies that ordinary people want to see, he's got to start meeting the folk who stand in line outside a picture theater. Sam, this is Mr Wilson, this is his son, Dan — and Dan's fiancée, er... Mary. They're getting married at the end of the month.'

'Why, congratulations,' exclaimed Hiller with cool formality. 'I'm sure you'll make each other very happy.'

What followed was excruciating for everyone in the group, except Louise, of course. Vehemently propounding her views on the artificiality of movies and the people who made them, she goaded Hiller and then her three guests into a most reluctant debate. Despite relentless pressure from Louise, the best they could muster was an exchange of weak platitudes.

After several tormented minutes, Hiller turned around to Helen Dennis, who had positioned herself several paces back, and wordlessly implored her to rescue him. Her eyes were ablaze with furious embarrassment.

Michael cut in. 'Mr Hiller, Louise. If you like, I'll escort our friends back now. I know they were anxious to get home.'

As he led them out the front gate, Michael slipped a five-dollar note into Dan's hand. 'For your help,' he said.

Inside the house, Michael found Louise in a deep armchair, fast asleep. Slowly prizing the champagne bottle from her tight clasp, he gently lifted her in his arms. Then he discreetly crept through the back of the house and, hugging the shadowy bushes, made his way around the house to his parked car. Delicately, he opened the door and laid Louise on the back seat with a pillow under her head. He pressed the electric starter and swiveled around to reverse the Stutz off the grass and onto the driveway. Looking over his shoulder, Michael's eyes fell on the dozing Louise. Her head was turned to one side, exposing an impossibly beautiful neck and shoulders. Caught by a shaft of bright moonlight, her serene face was the shade of purest alabaster.

'You bad, bad, beautiful bitch,' Michael said to himself.

Moments later, the car drove through the gates. The headlights arched around, momentarily catching three figures on the other side of the road. Two men and a small, slight young woman in a dowdy frock were still gazing up the long drive to the rambling house covered in fairy lights and ringing with music and the laughter of the denizens of another world.

* * *

At about three the following afternoon, Michael called in to Louise's apartment. Hearing his tap on the door, she shouted out to let himself in, the door was unlocked. He peered inside and saw Louise talking to a young woman whose back was turned to him.

'Won't be a moment, Michael,' she said as she pecked her visitor on the cheek. Carrying a large paper bag, the girl was taken to the door and, as she passed, Michael caught a flash of recognition. The young woman smiled shyly and disappeared.

'Louise, she looks familiar, haven't I...?'

'God, you're hopeless, Stanton! That's Mary. Don't you remember? Mr Williams, Dan and Mary — last night. We introduced them to Sam Hiller. I was drunk, yet *I* remember!'

'Please. It was *you* who introduced them to Hiller,' admonished Michael. 'Don't think that went over too well, by the way. What's she doing here? Want to get into movies?' asked Michael cynically.

'Are you kidding? Why would a nice kid like that want anything to do with this shitty business?' replied Louise as she dabbed some perfume behind her ear. 'No, she was here to choose a frock for herself.'

She sat down on the bed and drew a deep red lipstick across her full lips, studying the effect in a hand mirror.

'I promised it to her as a wedding present, that's all.'

'That was very thoughtful,' said Michael, gently. 'You are a generous soul, Louise.'

'I don't think so.'

'Well, I think you are.'

'Michael, material things have never much mattered to me, so it's really quite easy to give them away. It's as much indifference or, perhaps, carelessness as anything else. And, anyway, I like to surprise people.'

She paused and reflected for a moment and put the cap on the lipstick which she then absentmindedly turned around in her fingers.

'Do you know what real generosity is Michael?' she said, still looking down at the lipstick. 'It's being prepared to give something of your own self. Willingly compromising or even surrendering part of your existence for the sake of someone or something else. I have to tell you I don't recall ever doing that — and I'm not even sure I ever will. If you don't believe me, go talk to my former husbands.'

Michael nodded.

'I guess every one of us is driven by one dominant impulse,' he said, balancing the shaft of his walking stick on his finger tips. 'For some people it's money, for others it's fame or recognition. Power, security, sensual gratification, novelty, the quest for beauty, whatever. But the odd thing, Louise, is that you have enough of all these things to satisfy anyone. What you treasure most of all is independence. It's an appetite for freedom so strong that I think you'd let it put just about everything else at risk. In fact, I know you would.'

'But isn't freedom what any aware person seeks?'

'No, I don't believe so. On the contrary, very few people can handle it — and fewer still would put themselves out to protect their independence. They're too lazy or insecure. They don't want to stand against the tide. Besides, they wouldn't really know what to do with it. You can only be free when you learn not to cling onto things — and most of us have scrambled too hard for our baubles to ever think of disowning them.'

'And what about you, Michael?' asked Louise. 'Are *you* free?'

'Perhaps. I value freedom a great deal — and I think that's a big reason why we understand each other. But for me there's an impulse that's even more powerful.'

'What's that?'

'Curiosity. The urge to explore and learn. That's what I would make the most sacrifices for. You know, if I were offered the chance to travel on a rocket to another planet, I'd probably go. Even if there was no possibility of returning to Earth, I think I would take the opportunity to see and experience what no other human being had ever encountered. Naturally, I'd insist you come with me!'

Louise nodded her head slowly and gazed into his eyes for what seemed a long time.

'Why, I believe you would... you screwball!'

She reflected for a moment.

'But you're right about me. Take away my independence — my freedom — and I'd suffocate. You won't find many people who understand that and so they think I'm giddy and strange because I won't do the little it takes to make things safe. I can tell you Michael, what they're offering me is nothing against what they want to take from me. Nothing!'

Louise looked up at him.

'The fact is, Michael, that at heart I'm a profoundly selfish person. Really. I like you enough to warn you that I don't usually bring much happiness to those who care about me.'

She smiled mischievously. 'I'd think about that, if I were you!'

Michael stroked her hand, reassuringly. 'Well, Louise, you may be quite impossible, but at least you're the most honest person I've ever met.'

'Honest? Yes, I'm honest alright, brutally honest. And just see how many friends that makes you — and where it gets you! Ask Sam Hiller...'

19. MAGIC CRUCIBLE

High in the hills, they had wandered away from the car to enjoy a late summer breeze. Wordlessly, Michael and Louise sat down on a large smooth rock and gazed at the city lights twinkling in the far distance like glistening beads of dew on a cobweb. Above the horizon's faint glow, the sky merged into black velvet.

'Oh, my! There's a shooting star! Michael, did you see it?' cried Louise with girlish delight. 'Never mind. You're sure to catch another one shortly… Have you ever in your life seen so many stars? There must be millions of them, if you could only count them. Millions and millions of stars — and all so clear and so very far away.'

Her voice trailed away in soft wonder as she lay back and gazed upward, gently tugging Michael's sleeve for him to join her. For several silent minutes they contemplated the silver-dusted canopy that arched above them, all the while soaking up the gentle warmth the rock still retained from the day-long sun.

'Do you know,' observed Michael, 'The light from those stars set out on their journey to meet our eyes centuries or even thousands of years ago. For all we know, some of the stars we are looking at right now might have disappeared ages ago and no-one will know about it until we're long forgotten.'

Louise slowly shook her head as she contemplated this mystery. 'I wonder what life will be like in the future. Automobiles, airplanes, telephones, radio — no-one would have thought such things possible a hundred years ago. Just imagine what the world will be up to a century from now. Have you ever thought about that?'

When her question sank into his mind, Michael's skin tingled as he realized that he was the only being in her universe who could give a truthful answer. He raised himself up on one elbow and looked into her eyes.

'Well, Louise, do you really want to know what the world will be like? Let me tell you. Yes, science will certainly have crafted quite a few more marvels to surprise us — like this television thing, sending moving pictures by radio that some papers have written about — and who knows what else. But it is people, not technology that ultimately shape our world. So, the real question is: will we, in ourselves, be different in any significant way? Will we be happier — or better? Well, let me tell you, in the next century we'll still be the same hopeless creatures we are today. There'll be just as much folly and wisdom, vice, virtue, cruelty and compassion as we see around us now.'

'What an old pessimist you are,' laughed Louise. 'Surely, as the world becomes smaller and people know more about each other, we'll be a bit more tolerant and understanding? I can't imagine anyone would want to see anything like the Great War again. Too many people know how dreadful it all was. They just wouldn't let it happen.'

Michael did not reply. Ah, Louise, he reflected, if you only knew that there is in Germany a man whose dark, hypnotic eyes are even now fixed on a mad dream... and who is already plotting catastrophe.

* * *

That night, as Michael listened to the dreamy murmurings breaking through her sleep, a strange train of thought ran through his mind. He slowly lifted her cupped hand from his shoulder and, once again, he quietly left her room... and her world.

Back in his own apartment, Michael poured himself a scotch and slumped deep into an armchair. He kept turning over the awfulness of knowing so much of what lay ahead for Louise and the creatures of her world. This must be why the Gods kept our fates hidden from us, for who could bear to know of so much inescapable pain and disappointment, the slow robbing of our years and dreams? Often, the greatest part of hurt is its anticipation and, for the condemned man, the executioner often brought merciful release from the torments of the last, awful vigil.

Michael slipped into a fretful sleep and found himself in some gray and grimy city whose streets were filled with somber people of all ages, all moving in the one direction, like silent sleepwalkers. They wore an expression of weary resignation and ineffable melancholy and Michael somehow sensed that their shuffling steps led to some dreadful destination. Running from one to another, he enquired where they were going and why. Eventually he came upon a beautiful young woman resting against a wall and holding a little boy and girl to her. Please stay, he implored, don't go. She looked at him with eyes dark and moist with sadness and wordlessly turned away. Taking her children tenderly by the hand, she followed after the thickening procession.

Michael woke in a cold sweat with this vision still real in his eyes. The thought seared through his mind: he had created a universe in which millions of innocents were already set on a path towards unspeakable horrors. And he alone had the knowledge and power to avert such a calamity.

Or had he?

* * *

Louise had telephoned him to say she was calling over to the Alhambra to pay an impromptu visit. Michael had arranged for such calls to be routed right through to him without his having to access 'Luluworld' (as he called her domain).

Louise, he had pleaded, I am very busy. I'd love to get over to you in, say, two hours' time. No, she couldn't wait.

At the appointed hour, Michael slipped on his Sensator helmet. This was not unusual: CyberProfile Group members frequently donned a helmet to check out new profiles — or simply to pass a few minutes 'de-stressing' with some game. However, he still felt reluctant to be logging onto his secret site during working hours.

'Come in,' he whispered, as he opened the door to his suite and kissed Louise quickly on her cheek.

'What's the secret,' she mockingly whispered back. 'Or is it a cold?'

Michael nodded, pleased that she had already supplied him with a plausible excuse for keeping his voice so low that none of his CPG colleagues would hear his conversation.

'You should be in bed,' Louise suggested. 'Anyway, seeing you're out of sorts, I won't be long. I just wanted to ask your advice on a contract I've been offered. This time they've inserted some additional restrictions I'm not happy about.'

Louise's eyebrows rose as she pleaded, 'Could you have a look at them? I'm desperate — they want this copy signed and returned by this afternoon's deadline! Please...'

'Sure,' said Michael, picking up the document. As he leafed through it, he jotted down some notes on a sheet.

'Glad to see you're using the pen I gave you!' interjected Louise. 'Oops! Sorry, no more interruptions.' She continued to sit primly in front of him, like a schoolgirl trying hard to be on her best behavior.

Michael was suddenly startled to feel a firm hand grasp his shoulder and begin to shake it with increasing vigor.

'Mike, back to reality, pal!' It was Vince's voice. 'Henderson's waiting for you. Forgot our review meeting?'

'I won't be a minute,' said Michael, flustered that he was simultaneously addressing both Vince and Louise.

In her world, Louise watched Michael suddenly leave his desk, open the door and stride out of his suite.

One and a half agonizing hours' later, the meeting with Henderson ended. By now the office floor was almost empty and Michael donned his Sensator helmet and quickly entered Luluworld.

Opening the door of his suite, he found it quite empty. He walked to his desk to find the contract had gone with Louise. His sheet of paper, with only a few of his notes on it, carried a message in Louise's handwriting:

'I waited a whole hour, hoping you'd be back to help me with my contract. Don't you ever take me for granted!!'

Beside it lay his ivory fountain pen. A long, thin trail of white dust curved across the desk's lacquered surface and ended at the pen's twisted gold nib.

* * *

'Louise. My peace offering.'

Still pouting with annoyance, Louise, tore open the gift wrapping.

'What's this? Chanel No. 5? Oh, Michael, it smells just divine! Here, you... oh, sorry, I forgot...'

'Well, I do have just a slight vestigial sense of smell again. I can just pick it out. They tell me this is all the rage in Europe ever since it was launched in '22. Do you think you'll wear it?'

'Oh, yes.' She gave Michael a lingering kiss on his cheek.

'Don't worry, the pen's repaired,' said Michael. 'All forgiven?'

As he sipped his champagne, Michael thought over the lesson learnt from that day's incident. He could not slip in and out of this world without great risk — or, at least, the chance of embarrassment. This time he had been lucky. But there would surely come a time when he would not be so fortunate. And then what would happen?

*   *   *

At his home terminal, Michael downloaded a complete biography of Arthur Schopenhauer and a selection of his written works. These included his great opus of 1818, *'The World as Will and Idea'*, as well as *'Parega and Paralipomena'* and an edition of his essays and aphorisms.

When he searched a photograph of the philosopher, he saw an image of an ancient with wispy silver hair and deep-etched features that proclaimed a profound pessimism, if not sour misanthropy. But this is not the man who wrote the seminal *'The World as Will and Idea'*, thought Michael. He was all of thirty years old when he delivered this exposition of a philosophy that remained almost unmodified over his long life. Michael called up 'schopenhauer, arthur+:portrait' and within seconds he was gazing at an oil painting in the archives of the Universitätsbibliothek in Frankfurt am Main. The work by a Ludwig Sigismund Ruhl showed an intense, handsome young man with wild, curly hair and deep-set eyes, at once both passionate and profoundly introspective.

Yes, this is the person who is addressing us, Michael reflected. It occurred to him that when we consider the life of a living person, we almost invariably perceive them in their current condition, usually in their declining years, often doddery and decrepit (for it often takes a full lifetime to become a legend). On the other hand, after such a hero has passed on, the residual image we choose to retain is most often taken from when he or she was in their prime. A picture editor preparing an obituary will discard the most recent photo of a baggy-eyed actor leaning on a stick and staring uncomprehendingly into the lens and will choose instead the still of a handsome young lead with raven hair taken from the film that won him an Oscar. Yes, one of Death's consolations is that all your years become equally current and you have a chance of being presented at your best!

It was many years since Michael had read anything of Schopenhauer — and that, he was certain, must have been very little. Probably a section in an anthology of the great philosophers. But as he read on, he discovered much that seemed to resonate with his own thoughts and unformulated perceptions.

When the opportunity came, he was sure he would have much to discuss with Louise about her favorite philosopher.

* * *

'Connecting you now, caller,' said the operator.

'Hello, Louise, how are you?' enquired Michael. 'Good... Tell me, how did the interview go?'

Louise sounded weary. 'Madge Delahunty? The "Confidante of the Stars"? Oh, the interview went without a hitch. She was all sugar and sweetness — and I was under strict orders from my agent to be as nice and accommodating as possible... which I was.'

'Now I'm most impressed!' Michael observed.

'And, my dear Louise,' she mimicked, 'After having been away from Hollywood, I suppose you must know it will be a real struggle to pick up your motion picture career again?'

Louise paused for effect.

'Yes, Madge, I told her, my voice tutor and I have been working hard together and I'm really looking forward to getting down to some demanding roles in the talkies. I want your readers to know that I'm being very realistic — and I'm willing to look seriously at any part that's offered me, no matter what it is...'

'You really said that?'

'God forgive me for my lying ways, but I did! And you'll see it all there under a big headline: "Louise Plans to Raise Her Fallen Star"... You know, Michael, I could spit. When I was in Europe was the only time in my working life that I did any work that I'm actually proud of. Georg Pabst was the only real director worthy of the name I've yet encountered. And the only one who saw I had talent and knew how to bring it out... And this was the holiday I took from my movie career, as that Madge Dela-hawkface described it. The bitch!'

'Too bad,' sympathized Michael. 'But if that's what she writes it'll go down well with the studio bosses. You gave them a pretty hard time before and they'd like to read that headstrong Brooksie's been brought down a peg.'

Louise laughed. 'Christ, Michael, why do I need an agent? What little work I get I pull in myself — and I can get the same rotten advice from you for free!'

'Well, my Lulu, I think I know a little place where I could help you feel like the star that you really are! What say I pick you up this evening?'

'Not tonight, I've got lines to learn. I could be shortlisted for a part tomorrow. Nothing big, but it's work. Rent money.'

'Friday?'

'I've already agreed to go out.'

The buoyancy in Michael's voice dropped noticeably.

'Oh, anyone I know?'

'No, he's from out of state. Sam and I go back a long way.'

'Well, it's not too serious, I hope.'

'Michael, why don't you call me... after the weekend?'

'Yes, I'll ring then,' said Michael quietly.

After he hung up, Michael stared at the computer screen. He was accustomed to phoning Louise without donning the Sensator helmet, content simply to hear her voice. He lingered on, watching her move around her apartment, picking up a script and listlessly fanning through its pages.

Right, let's check out this Sam character, Michael thought to himself. He scanned though his 'LULU' database and came up with nothing. But then, Louise had had quite a collection of one-time lovers.

The screen reverted back to Louise, the time having moved to Friday evening. There was a knock on her apartment door. She opened it to reveal a tall, burly man, not handsome particularly, but strong-featured. He gathered Louise in his arms and gave her a long kiss. Michael leaned forward and angrily punched the 'off' key.

* * *

Michael and Louise had just finished their alfresco lunch. Under the shade of a large oak, they lay back on the rug, enjoying the refreshing breeze and lulled by the droning of unseen creatures. Yet, although everything was so peaceful and relaxing, there was an edge to Michael's conversation. He was still piqued that Louise had put him to one side to give time to her 'old friend' from the East.

'I take it that your weekend went well?' he enquired.

'Not too bad,' she replied with studied casualness. 'And yours?'

Michael ignored her question and looked up at the rustling leaves high above them.

'Well, you're quite a mystery-woman, Louise. I wonder what other surprises you have in store for me.'

She said nothing for several moments, seemingly preoccupied with tearing up bread and throwing it at the birds hopping around nearby. At last, she turned to Michael.

'I'd like to think that I'll always keep surprising you... and everyone else. If I ever became an open book — obvious and predictable — then I'd have lost my independence, my soul, everything. Anyway, it's not a conscious thing at all. You'd be surprised how often I baffle myself!'

'Well, that's reassuring... I think,' said Michael with an ironical laugh. 'You could have also mentioned that a carefully cultivated air of mystery serves very well to stoke up the interest of a woman's many admirers.'

'Cuts both ways, Michael. I'm certain you've told me a lot less about yourself than you know about me.'

'Well, what can we really know about anyone?' asked Michael, evading the point of her comment. 'We can only get so close to another person's true, inner personality. Beyond that it's always going to be elusive.'

'Or illusory?'

'Or illusory.' Pursuing a path of irony that only he could appreciate, he continued, 'You know, Louise, you couldn't prove to me that you and everything around me has its own independent existence. Why, for all I know, you might just been a creation of my own mind. As soon as I drop you home, you might cease to be until I come back again!'

'Well, that's funny. I was just thinking that about you, too!,' countered Louise puckishly. 'Tell you what, if you maintain the fiction that I'm real, I'll return the favor. There's really no need at all for our friends to ever suspect that we're mere figments of each other's disordered imaginations!'

'Agreed,' chuckled Michael. 'Let's keep them in their ignorance!'

'Including Madge Delahunty,' Louise added. 'Now I wonder whose fancy conjured her into existence?'

Louise threw the remainder of the bread at the birds and giggled at the noisy fight that this provoked.

'But the question is still a valid one,' continued Michael. 'The Louise that I know and recognize, the Louise that lives in my own mind, will always reflect how I think and view things. So, my Louise will always be different to the Louise that others know. And none of these versions will be quite the same as the person you are to yourself.'

'That's true for everyone,' replied Louise. 'Everyone has their own reality. That's why I've always thought that we best describe ourselves when we describe everyone and everything around us. Don't you think?'

'Absolutely. What our senses collect about the world is translated into a facsimile, a reality which is constructed *within* our minds. This view of things is shaped and limited by our individual ability to see, hear, feel and smell.'

Michael reflected on this thought and then continued: 'Just think about it. There must be as many universes as there are observers.'

'Including every type of creature.'

'Absolutely,' continued Michael. 'Take a dog, for example. Compared to us, it has poor eyesight and is pretty well color-blind. Yet its world is a tapestry of subtle scents and odors far richer and more diverse than we humans could ever know. Contrast that with the bat flying through an intricate web of echoes as it stalks a weaving moth — all in complete darkness! There's just no way for us to imagine how they subjectively experience all this: it's just so different. Yet, each of these creatures lives in a world as authentic as our own.'

'But aren't our own perceptions shaped by more than by our senses alone?' interrupted Louise. 'Aren't they also interpreted according to our psychology, experiences, memories and all sorts of conditioning?'

'Nonetheless, you know I am real simply because my actions and the things I express are entirely consistent with what you would expect from a being that has an existence like yours,' she continued.

'That sounds very much like what Turing suggested as a way to recognize consciousness in a computer,' Michael commented.

'Turing?' asked Louise.

'Oh, yes. Allan Turing. Wrote a speculative essay on how we might deal with thinking machines, if they were ever invented. Friend of mine,' Michael fibbed. He wondered how old the father of computer theory might be at this time. Still a boy, probably.

'Isn't it such a mystery, the human mind?' pondered Louise. 'Brain specialists, psychologists, philosophers — none of them have the first clue as to how all this works.'

She tapped her beautiful forehead and turned to Michael, who was staring off into the distance. She leaned over and tickled his nose with a leaf.

'Why, I really don't think you're paying me the slightest attention. Now I'm boring you.'

'Oh, no. Not at all, Louise. It's just that what you said set my thoughts running ahead.'

They loaded the folding table into the car and then strolled along, hand in hand.

* * *

Again, Michael found his mind taken over by the question that now obsessed him. Was this beautiful and unpredictable spirit really just a phantom? Her memories, mannerisms, her mischievous teasing and wry jokes, the special way she played with the ends of her hair — was all this, her whole being and her very soul, a mere illusion? No! Now, more than ever, he knew that *this* Louise was real! After all, if a kilogram of soft brain tissue — small enough to be cradled in two hands — could contain the makings of a symphony, a great scientific idea or an elaborate and rich world of fantasy, then a globe-spanning cybernetic structure could also summon up an unimaginable range of creation. Surely, it could once more animate this beautiful creature with life's warm breath!

And if Louise and her world were contained within this electronic crucible, need that make her any less real? And, as she herself had asked that day, whose is the right reality, anyway?

20. SOMEONE'S IN OUR SECTOR

'Hi, honey!' called Vince.

Melissa ate her breakfast without lifting her eyes from a journal. From the nervy way she bit the toast, he realized she was in a bad humor. He knew the signs.

'So, what's happening in the world?' he enquired as he stood right behind her, enveloping her shoulders with his arms. This gesture was answered with a sharp jab in the ribs from her elbow.

'I'll tell you what's NOT happening,' came the grating reply. 'We're not happening, my friend.'

'Ah, Jesus, Melissa! Look, I was working late and I took the team for a beer just so we could run over next week's strategy. We don't get the time during the day. Was that so unreasonable?'

Melissa got out of her seat and stood in front of Vince, arms folded uncompromisingly.

'Well, Vince, I just happen to think it WAS unreasonable. You see, while you were regaling your friends through the night, I was waiting patiently in my office... Waiting for you to turn up to show Bill Bannister and I how to unclog that damned diagnostic routine you talked him into setting up — as *you* arranged!'

'Oh, shit! Mel, I really am sorry. I forgot. I really did.'

'Of course, Vince. Just like always,' said Melissa sarcastically. 'You're overworked and have just so much on your mind. That's what I told Bill when he drove me home. Too tired to even turn on your phone! He said he understood — and not to feel embarrassed.'

She walked over to the window and looked out wordlessly. Vince slid into a chair and sighed.

'Vince,' said Melissa turning back to him. 'When things didn't suit you, you decided to walk from Prancer Tech. Didn't talk it over with me. Just walked. For how long? Seven months? I kept this whole show on the road. The big mortgage, the bills and your beer money. I lined up contacts and I encouraged you. Never any complaints, right?'

'No, you were great. I appreciate it,' answered Vince softly.

'It's not gratitude I want, Vince. I'm not looking for a pay-back. And I especially hate finding myself in this nagging-female, victim role. All I want is a little support when I need it most. When you let me down — like last night — it hurts and it makes me angry. Very angry.'

She threw the rolled-up journal down on his lap and strode towards the bathroom.

'Vince, stop being so selfish. Think of others just once...'

* * *

Vince stared at the computer screen, transfixed. With one minute rolling into another, he sat quite motionless. His ponderous, snuffled breathing, was always a sure sign he was lost in deep thought.

Suddenly he bent forward and his fingers beat out a rapid staccato on the keyboard, switching the computer over to the vocal exchange mode. Then the dark room, bathed in the low glow of banks of electronic equipment, was sporadically illuminated by the flickering screen as each spoken command summoned a quick succession of images, request fields and information panels.

'Closed sector entry.'

'Closed sector entry. What code, please?' asked the computer in the husky, female tone that Vince favored from the bank of vocal options.

'One... zero... eight,' Fadowsky grunted.

'Password?'

'Over-ride...'

'Over-ride authorization?'

'Over-ride authorization: Battleaxe-oner... zero... three.'

The computer paused an instant, then intoned: 'Over-ride authorization: Battleaxe-oner... zero... three. You now have access to closed sector one zero eight.'

'Cancel,' said Fadowsky softly. 'Right, so now I KNOW there's nothing wrong with the system. Now let's try again.' He adjusted his headset and leaned forward. 'Voice I.D. clearance.'

'Go ahead for voice clearance,' said the computer with the same fresh, welcoming voice.

'CyberProfile Group... Fadowsky, Vince... five... four... three... two... one... Closed sector entry.'

'Closed sector entry. What code, please?'

'Three... two... six...' he called.

'Password?'

'Over-ride...'

'Over-ride authorization?'

'Over-ride authorization: Battleaxe-oner... zero... three.'

'There is no over-ride authorization for this closed sector. Your voice print is not registered for this sector... I am sorry, you may not gain entry to closed sector 326 without a recognized voice print and the correct password. Do you wish to continue?'

'Shit!' exclaimed Fadowsky.

'I am sorry, is that affirmative or negative?' enquired the infinitely polite, infinitely irritating computer.

'Just fuck off!' he groaned wearily as he tapped off the spoken dialogue mode. He had no time to waste and he could type — and read — faster than the vocal exchange. Besides, he could not run the risk of anyone coming up behind him and overhearing what he was uncovering.

At last he stopped and placed his hands behind his head and stared up at the ceiling. He noisily exhaled and slowly shook his head in disbelief.

'Christ....' he intoned softly. 'The bastard's been prowling around in our closed sector for three weeks at least. Tripping through the firewall like it didn't exist! Over a hundred hours logged. A hundred frigging hours — by now he must know the system as well as I do! Holy shit.'

He leaned over to pick up the phone. 'Baby, this is bigger than both of us. Time to call in the US Cavalry...'

The phone rang seven or eight times.

'Oh, come ON! Answer the thing, will you!... Hello, Michael, I... Damn! Message bank!'

He hung up and tapped out a new number.

'Hey, Jodo! Jodo? It's me, Vince... Yeah, yeah... Believe me, I know its frigging late. Hey, I need O'Keefe's home number... Look, man, I KNOW you've got it... Well, that's precisely why I want the number... We've already agreed it's late... I tried Mike Stanton. No answer. Man, this is a Triple A frigging emergency, for Chrissakes! *Will - you - give - me - his - number, goddammit!!,*' he shouted into the mouthpiece.

Vince fell silent and jotted down a number on the cover of a code manual.

'Thank you... right... yeah, got it. No, Jodo, I can't tell you — maybe later. Yeah, and good night to you, too,' he said softly as he hung up. 'You prick!'

Vince stared at the number for several seconds, inhaled deeply, and read the digits into his phone, slowly and deliberately. A full twenty seconds passed before there was an answering click.

'General O'Keefe, my name is Vince Fadowsky. I'm one of the CyberProfile programmers. I know it's very late, sir, but I have to see you personally. Yes, sir, right now. This IS an emergency... No, I haven't. It's something you should hear first... Got it — second left off Martin. I'll be there right away.'

He hauled his lanky frame out of the swivel chair and pulled on a leather jacket. Pausing only to take a savage bite out of the remnants of a cold hamburger, Vince barged out the door, leaving his player pounding out an old rock number to an empty room.

Several minutes later the phone rang. The answering machine recorded a terse message from Melissa.

'Vince, I'm ringing from the 'Toucan' restaurant,' she said. 'I thought you'd be here to meet me. Anyway, if you've left the office, I assume you're already on your way...'

21. THE WRONG SORT

As soon as Michael drew up outside Louise's apartment, she popped out from behind one of the columns at the entrance and purposefully strode towards him. He was out of the car and about to help her in when she impatiently opened the door for herself and plumped down in the seat. The day was going to be eventful.

'It's good to see you! Everything alright?' he called out with forced levity.

'Oh, just dandy!' Louise replied sarcastically.

They drove on wordlessly until they pulled up outside Zeltzer's restaurant. Louise said she only wanted coffee and listlessly played with the sugar bowl while Michael ate breakfast.

'How did your meeting with Cohen go yesterday?'

'He said he had me in mind for some good parts. There might even be a three-year contract at my old salary,' Louise responded.

'Why, that's great news! So, what's next?'

'Nothing. I told him to go to Hell,' she replied coldly.

'Louise, are you out of your mind? A studio big shot like Cohen? Like they say, you'll never work in this town again. He'll see to that!'

'Well, at least that revolting bastard won't be pawing me...'

'Oh, no...'

'It's a standard clause in his contract. Cohen doesn't sleep under the stars, they sleep under him! One of Hollywood's oldest jokes.'

'What did he say?'

'I was completely without talent — and a tramp. Said that everyone knows that I am completely immoral. Mr Cohen, I told him, my bed partners have only ever been men I have liked and admired. If I let you touch me, I *would* be a common prostitute — just like half the women on your payroll.'

'Jesus...'

'So, there you are. Everybody wants something from me.'

'Louise, that's not true! Do you include me, too?'

She looked away and shrugged. After a pause, she turned around and gazed straight at Michael.

'Since you ask, yes, I do, Michael. You've been very kind — and good company. I like you a lot. But you want more than I can give... more than I want to give. I have to be free and no-one owning me. Not you, not Cohen, not any of the others. No-one!'

Her eyes blazed and her chest heaved. She turned away again.

'When you've finished, would you take me home again, please. I don't think you'll find me much company today.'

'OK, Louise. I'm through here. Let's go.'

Moments later, Michael was escorting Louise up the steps of her apartment building. He paused at the top step and gave her a soft, affectionate kiss.

'Louise, tomorrow I'm leaving town on business and I guess I'll be away for ten days, possibly up to a fortnight. I'll call when I get back. Now, keep your chin up — and don't worry about me and my intentions. I refuse to believe a word of what you said about me. All I want is what you wish to give me — freely. I'll call you. Take care, sweetheart!'

Michael drove for a mile or two before pulling the car over at the end of a long, dusty road. He did not know where he might go or what he might do. Everything had taken such an unexpected, sudden turn.

Minutes later, still behind the wheel, he saw a woman in the distance, pushing a pram. She was dragging along a girl of three or four who wore a large, red beret. Every few steps, the child dug in her heels and refused to go any farther. When the mother turned to admonish or entreat her sulky daughter, Michael glimpsed a Madonna face that still wore the fresh bloom of youth. But her thin frame, the cheap, printed frock and the battered pram all told of a life that too soon would etch its cares across her smooth skin. Eventually, she rounded the corner and disappeared, unaware of the silent figure in the large car.

Michael, disengaged from the cyberworld.

As he sat blinking his eyes and adjusting to the startlingly different environment that was his workplace, he contemplated what he would do for the next week or two. His work was making particularly heavy demands on him, with a major project now well behind schedule.

On top of that, several times he detected unsettling half-hints that his movements in the system had been noticed — and, as well, there was the vague water-cooler talk that a 'stranger' might have broken into the sector. Someone even mentioned an unnamed security officer asking for unusual information.

Still, for four days, Michael buried himself in his work. The current project was particularly complex and seemed to roll out one difficulty after another. This would have been taxing at any time, but now, with the uncertainties of his love affair and the difficulties of living in — and maintaining — a parallel life, he felt overwhelmed.

One evening, made restless by unhappy speculation about Louise, he gave in at last to his hunger to see her and, invisibly, slipped into her world.

He found her in the apartment, drinking heavily with the man she called Sam. He was sprawled across one of the easychairs, his jacket off and tie loosened. He was still wearing a high-crowned trilby. From their rambling conversation, Michael picked up that they were raking over past events. Their exchanges were at first loud and abusive and then, later, they subsided into conciliatory reassurances. It was clear that Sam was an old lover who still had an interest in Louise. At one point he sat down beside her and placed his hand around her shoulder. She ignored this move with such studied indifference that he immediately withdrew it and lurched back to his seat.

As Louise droned on, Michael became lividly angry. His first, mad impulse was to close down his whole cyberworld and be done with it all, including its cauldron of personal risks and worries. Almost in the same instant, he recoiled at the idea. Murder Louise — and all the other people he had called into being! How could he even think of snuffing out these thinking, feeling beings, just because *he* was jealous? Unthinkable!

Instead, he returned to his own world.

Another week passed before Michael looked in on Louise again. He decided that, before confronting her directly, he would observe her movements undetected by posing from time to time as a newspaper seller outside her apartment. Michael soon learnt that the large limousine parked outside belonged to Sam — and that he was now a regular visitor. Twice, while keeping this vigil, the newspaper vendor saw Louise leave the building, laughing and with her arm linked with Sam's. When they drove off, Michael made no attempt to follow. He revisited the scene when the early morning sun was already peering through the trees in the park opposite. Still, Louise had not returned.

The next night Michael walked by the apartment and saw the familiar large car. All the lights in Louise's apartment were ablaze and he could hear music wafting from the open windows, only partly masking a loud, but indistinct, conversation. Louise appeared to be doing most of the talking — and her emphatic and emotional tones told him she was drunk again. There was a silence and then a man spoke. Sam, of course. Michael heard breaking glass and Louise shouting.

'You bastard, you cheap, swindling bastard! Get out of here!'

She began to cry and sob and then to shout abusively. There was a sound of furniture being thrown around and a loud scream.

A man's slurred voice called out: 'Cheap? Cheap? What about you? What about you — WHORE!' More noise and he roared out, 'You bitch! Take that... take that... that... and that!'

Between each pause Michael heard the stomach-turning sound of a fist thumping into flesh and bone. Within seconds, Michael had shed his newspaper vendor's attire and was hammering on Louise's apartment door.

'Louise! It's me, Michael. Let me in!'

More crashing sounds.

'Michael! For Christ's sake, Michael! Help me!'

He pulled a key out of his pocket and opened the door. The apartment was a chaos of smashed furniture and broken crockery and overturned bottles. A curtain was half torn off its rail. There was a strong smell of whisky.

Peering inside, Michael saw Louise lying on the kitchen floor with a man sitting on her stomach and with both hands raised in the air. Sam turned around and blearily focused on Michael.

'Well, what do you know? It's lover boy! Push off, Buster. I'm booked in for this shift.'

With that he turned back to Louise and began to slap her on the face, first the left hand, then the right, then the left. This was no display of helpless, frenzied rage. The cool and methodical way he beat her — quite indifferent to Michael's presence — was that of a master whipping a pup into obedience.

Slap.

'Tell him, Louise.'

Slap.

'Tell him you've already got a customer, Louise!'

Slap.

A red mist of anger filled Michael's vision. Moving like an automaton, he sprang across the room, drew his arm right back and smashed his clenched fist into the side of Sam's head. Louise's assailant moaned and fell heavily to one side, banging his forehead against the oven. He lay still.

Michael clasped Louise in his arms.

Her eyes were black and swollen almost shut and her face still wore the scarlet marks of Sam's hand. She buried herself in his chest and convulsed with sobs.

'There, baby. It's OK, it's OK,' said Michael soothingly as his own eyes filled with salty tears. 'It's alright now. My poor Lulu...'

After several minutes, Michael laid Louise on the couch while he went into her room and gathered together whatever clothes and toiletries he could find. Answering a quiet, but persistent, tap on the door, he found the elderly janitor looking in with astonishment at the disorder. Then his eyes fell on Sam's form.

'We were worried about the noise. It sounded like someone was being murdered. I sent my son to telephone the police.'

Michael looked up from Sam. 'There was some trouble, yes. An old boyfriend of Miss Brooks. He got drunk — but he's sleeping now. Could you please tell the police it was a lover's quarrel, but no-one's hurt. Just a bit of a mess in here, I'm afraid.'

Michael slipped several bills into the janitor's hand.

'Miss Brooks wants no publicity. I know you wouldn't want the newspapers nosing around this building. It would be embarrassing for her — and, of course, for your other tenants as well. I'm sure you understand.'

'Of course, sir. Just leave it to me. There'll be no scandal. But Miss Brooks? Is she alright? I think he was beating her pretty bad from the sound of it.'

'She's upset, of course. But no real harm done. Anyway, I'm taking her with me to stay the night with a relative. Everything will be fine. And I'll tell her you wished her well.'

'Thank you, sir.'

'Now, if you don't mind, I'd like to help her get ready. We'll leave quietly and lock up before anyone else calls around.'

The janitor's wife appeared and, and unashamedly strained to look into the other room, where Louise was still moaning quietly to herself. She gestured towards the snoring form propped up against the oven.

'What about him?'

'I'll take him downstairs and put him in the back of his car to sleep things off. It might be an idea if I disconnect the leads in case he tries to drive. He's in no shape to be on the road tonight.'

The janitor helped Michael move Sam downstairs and into the back of his car. Then, after helping Louise wash herself and gather her things into an overnight bag, Michael locked the apartment and the two drove off to his hotel.

* * *

When Michael returned to his suite with some fruit and a newspaper he found Louise was sitting in the lounge room. With half-closed, puffy eyes and wearing a rather extravagant turban, she was barely recognizable.

Without greeting him, she picked up from the internal dialogue she had held with herself while he was out.

'You know, I've always found first-class bastardry the most irresistible quality in a man. The men I respect most — my friends — are the ones I'm least inclined to bed. Don't you think that's strange?'

'Perverse, I'd say,' corrected Michael. As he sat on the bed looking at her, he remembered reading Louise's account of being raped by a 'Mr Feathers' when she was only nine years old. When told, her mother had blamed her daughter, saying she must have led him on. As an adult, Louise was to wonder if this awful event had set a pattern for her future sexual experiences. The theme of physical domination and violence was one she would revisit again and again.

'I suffer two consequences because of this,' she continued. 'First, I've no hope of my sustaining any kind of lengthy relationship — because the bastardry must eventually get through to me. The other is that I have little trouble retaining the loyal friendship of the men with better qualities for the simple reason that it's never complicated by sex or passion.'

'That begs the question about the nature of our relationship,' interjected Michael. 'Which category do I fit in?'

Louise laughed quietly. 'I just *knew* you'd ask that!'

'Well?' asked Michael, unable to hide his irritation.

'Now you *are* a puzzle, Michael. You're a nice guy. I trust you and I feel safe with you. I'm pretty sure I can rely on you. But what keeps me interested in you is that there's something of a mystery about you. I know you haven't revealed everything about yourself — and I'm not really sure you're ever likely to. You keep surprising me and you're...'

She hunted for the words.

'Somehow, and I don't know why, I don't feel entirely secure with you. At the bottom of it all, it's unpredictability that engages my interest.'

Michael said nothing. He was turning over what these revelations could mean for them both.

Louise continued: 'Of course, there are many gentlemen who are just as attracted to the wrong sort of girl, aren't there? Seems they've been pretty thick on the ground in most of the movies I've ever made. Me being the wrong sort of girl, of course!'

'Of course,' agreed Michael with mock resignation.

'Yes, but in real life. You know the type of man I'm talking about. Could easily settle down with an ideal wife, but instead is drawn to a destructive jezebel — like a moth to a flamethrower.'

'Do I know any men like that?' repeated Michael. 'Hadn't you noticed? I AM that type of fool you're talking about!'

22. SOME COINCIDENCE

Michael realized that he had lost Louise.

It was at least fifteen, probably twenty, minutes since she had squeezed his arm reassuringly, mentioned something about catching up with a girlfriend and being back in a moment and then disappeared into a throng of people. Within moments he had lost sight of the shiny black bob.

Michael scanned around the crowded room. He hated cocktail parties — and yet here he was, inhabiting the very era in which they were invented! As usual in such situations, he detached himself from the little chattering knots and pretended to be preoccupied with something or to be waiting for someone. It was always more diverting to be an observer than a participant at parties like this. Another Jay Gatsby, he mused. (And had Scott Fitzgerald already finished writing *The Great Gatsby*?)

Bootleg liquor flowed and the murmuring backdrop gave way to shouted exchanges, laughter and piercing shrieks which rose and fell to let through disjointed snatches of Dixieland. It was a pantomime of exaggerated smiles, postures and frenetic movement. And, yet, Michael reflected, all this pandemonium and manic energy was being conjured up by a computer, with each manikin's phrases and gestures being coldly fashioned just for his eyes.

As usual, in this cyberworld, only the people in the foreground were shaped in any detail. The partygoers at the end of the room were vague, stiffly-articulating caricatures and their conversation an indistinct mumble. Such a strange dream-world!

A sharp tap on his shoulder jolted Michael out of his reverie. He turned around to find a short, fat man standing beside him.

'Ferris... Toby Ferris,' he announced.

Michael stared at him, fascinated by the peculiar cut of his new acquaintance's trousers: the waist was stretched up almost to his armpits by a pair of embroidered braces. The effect was to make his pot belly look even rounder. Michael recalled Tenniel's engravings of Tweedledum and Tweedledee in the original *'Alice in Wonderland'*.

'Mr Ferris... I'm Michael Stanton.'

Ferris held out his hand and looked away while Michael shook it. A gesture which Michael interpreted as a sign of rough shyness, rather than indifference or rudeness.

'Yes, yes. I've heard of you.'

'Indeed,' Michael mused. He was by now well aware that in Hollywood, where opportunity was so elusive and reputation and fortune so evanescent, Ferris' vague, second-hand recognition, even if only feigned, was the least a stranger owed you upon a first introduction.

'Indeed, yes, Mr Stanton,' beamed Toby (as he would insist on being called). 'You gave an investment tip to a friend of mine, Ridgeway. Harry Ridgeway? Yes. He invited me in on it, but I said no. I tell you, if I had followed up on all the sure-fire stocks I've heard of, I'd be an even poorer man than I am today. Yessir, I declare that's the truth.'

The little man sat down on the arm of a lounge chair and leaned forward.

'But, blow me down, if Ridgeway doesn't call by a week or two later to tell me he made a sizeable coup (he pronounced it 'coop') on those South West Oil Corporation shares. Now, I don't mind telling you, Mr Stanton, that I'm not one for this type of socializing. I'm here to find out what I might put some of my modest savings on.'

Michael smiled indulgently.

'Mr Ferris... Toby. We might have to wait a little while to find another performer like South West. But there is one prospect that should deliver a useful return. In fact, I've put a little on it myself just this morning...'

Ferris' eyes glinted and he pulled a little, black leather-covered notebook out of his pocket and a silver propelling pencil.

'Yes, Michael. You can trust me. Strictly just between the two of us. Yes. Not a word...'

'It's a fruit and vegetable canning company, Rosaria. Their shares have been drifting for quite a while, but I suspect — I know — they'll be announcing a big contract with the Army. Any day now. You'll get in at about forty cents a share. Sell as soon as it hits sixty. It may look as if it could go higher, but don't wait — cut out at that figure and you'll still find a buyer for your parcel. You should be in and out within three weeks.'

'Just three weeks?'

'Yes, before their mid-year financials. I suspect they'll be found to be somewhat undercapitalized to handle that size contract. They've a lot to lay out on irrigation equipment.'

'You don't say? Rosaria Canning Company...'

As Ferris scribbled away, Michael looked up to see Louise gazing at him with a wide smile. He winked back at her and, excusing himself from Ferris, moved to join her.

'Michael, this is Henry Ballantyne, he's been doing a little lobbying to persuade me to persuade you...'

'Well, now my subtle diplomacy's been undone, I'll come straight out with it,' said Ballantyne as he firmly shook Michael's hand. 'I'm on the board of the California Commonwealth Bank and we're looking to fill a seat. What we're really after is someone who's pretty knowledgeable about the Eastern stock and bond markets. The word is that you've got a pretty good head for this side of the financial scene. I'd be very pleased if you would have dinner with me soon. I'd like to introduce you to some of my colleagues. What do you say?'

'Be delighted,' replied Michael. 'Here's my card.'

'There you are, Henry,' laughed Louise, 'A bold frontal assault wins the day!'

With a proprietorial air, she linked with Michael's arm and shepherded him out of the room.

'Michael, you should know that Toby Ferris is worth hundreds of thousands, if not more. If he believes you're on to something, he's likely to back it pretty heavily. I hope you were very sure about whatever you told him.'

'Safe as houses, Louise.'

'It wouldn't worry me if he lost his wallet. Probably do him good — and would make a lot of people in this town very happy. It's really you I'm worried about. If his investment went bad, he'd turn on you. And I know he could be dangerous.'

'He'll find out within a fortnight. Just don't tell Toby you saw me jumping on the train to Philadelphia!' he teased her.

Suddenly, Louise's expression froze.

'Well, hello, Louise. It's nice to see a familiar face. Aren't you going to introduce me to your escort?'

Michael turned around to see a rather fleshy, saturnine man in his middle years standing behind him. Louise glowered and said nothing.

'Stanton's the name, Michael Stanton.'

'And I'm Phil Cohen. I thought I knew everyone here, but you're a newcomer to this circle. Just arrived in town?'

'Not really, I've been in California for seven, perhaps eight, months now. I came out from the East to follow up some business interests. I'm not in the motion picture industry — which might explain why we haven't met before.'

'If you were, we'd certainly have run into each another.'

Cohen led the conversation with one question following another, relentlessly probing into every area of Michael's background. Where he was from? What did he do? Who did he know?

Feeling increasingly uncomfortable, Michael was composing an excuse to detach himself from his company (Louise had already quietly slipped away) when Cohen spotted two couples walking through the door.

'Aha! Now here are some latecomers you must meet before they get swallowed up in the crowd,' said Cohen as he led them towards the corner in which Michael was pinned. 'Mr and Mrs Gavin Talbot, Mr and Mrs Adolf Kasselman — please meet Michael Stanton. He's new to California.'

The conversation had meandered over several inconsequential topics when Cohen abruptly turned to Michael.

'Well, Stanton, and what did you see of the war?'

Michael searched for words. 'Yes... I was in France... We were among the first Americans to arrive... and well...'

There was an uneasy silence as Michael fidgeted with his drink and stared to the side. He was enveloped by a hot wave of embarrassment, when he realized that his awkwardness with his unrehearsed fabrication was being read as a reluctance to revisit unsettling memories.

'I guess you'd rather not. I've a cousin who was there. Mention the War and he just clams up,' said Mrs George Talbot, helpfully. 'Must have been pretty bad.'

'Pretty bad,' Michael agreed. 'It's not something I like to talk about.'

'Well, I think you're right!' cut in Cohen. 'Can't see any point wallowing about in the past. Anyway, you wouldn't know who saw any action and who was on a long furlough. Some grocer's clerk puts on a uniform and spends his war behind the lines guarding the quartermaster's bully beef. Next thing you know, he's back home again, strutting around like the conquering hero!'

Michael eyed him coolly.

'Where did you serve, Mr Cohen?'

'Right here on the Hollywood front! Making movies to keep up the nation's fighting spirit. Wouldn't catch me slopping around in the mud when there was something useful to do!'

'Must have been profitable for you,' commented Michael.

'Well, as a matter of fact, yes,' smirked Cohen. 'Why, Gavin, you've an empty glass! Who's for another horse's neck?'

While Mrs Kasselman instructed the drinks waiter on the recipe for an exotic cocktail, Michael excused himself and sought out Louise.

'Thanks for leaving me with Mr Cohen,' he chided her.

'Sorry, I just couldn't bear to be near him. He's the producer I was telling you about. The one who propositioned me, remember?'

'God! What an arrogant, utterly repulsive bastard!' replied Michael softly.

'The trouble is,' continued Louise, 'I've heard the Gilbertinis have also invited him to the restaurant tonight. In fact, he's just set out for the place. Michael, if that's so, I don't want to come. Period.'

'I understand. I'm not keen to see any more of him, either.'

Michael thought a moment and added: 'But we did accept their invitation. I was talking to them just before they left half an hour ago and I said we'd see them there. Tell you what, let's go anyway and if Cohen is seated too close, you can develop a headache. What do you say? Let's not disappoint Fran Gilbertini. She said she's bringing her daughter so she can meet a real movie star.'

'But we leave immediately I give the sign?'

'Of course,' said Michael. 'All we...'

At that instant there was a tremendous crash.

'My God! What was that?' yelped Louise.

The shattering sound of the thunderclap, so close it seemed the house itself had been struck by lightning, jolted everyone in the room.

Several guests rushed to the window to see if one of the tall trees in the garden had been hit. After a brief interval of nervous laughter, the band picked up its tune again.

Michael smiled, hardly able to keep his joke to himself.

* * *

Half an hour later, the rain was still sheeting down as the Stutz pushed its way along the winding path towards Rustavelli's Restaurant. From time to time, a sudden squall overcame the windscreen wipers, forcing Michael to slow down to a walking pace. Then, turning around a corner, they saw an open tourer stopped by the grass verge. It was empty.

'Look, Michael! There's someone down the road waving at us! We've just got to pick him up — he must be half-drowned!'

Michael stopped the car and, with no sound except the clacking wipers and the rain drumming on the car roof, they waited for the sodden figure running towards them through curtains of rain.

'Good grief!' cried Louise in astonishment. 'Michael, you won't believe this! It's our very own Mr Phil Cohen!'

Her face was contorted by the effort not to burst out laughing when the back door opened.

'Thank you... Thank you!' mumbled Cohen. 'It's unbelievable out there. Blue skies all day and then all hell breaks loose. The carburetor got flooded. Then I find I couldn't get the tonneau hood up. Completely jammed. To cap it all, I slipped and... sorry about the mud.'

'Don't worry,' said Michael. 'I take it you'll be coming with us to join Dick and Fran Gilbertini at Rustavelli's?'

Hearing that, Cohen wiped the rain from his eyes — and was startled to recognize his rescuers.

'Oh... its you! Some coincidence, eh? Well, I don't have a choice but to come along — even if its only to get a dry change...'

* * *

In the event, Michael and Louise were the last of their party to leave Rustavelli's that night. Amid much fussing and pantomime, the drenched and begrimed Cohen fought to maintain a vestigial dignity as he was bundled by a flurry of waiters into a backroom. He reappeared some ten minutes later in one of the maitre d's spare coat-tail suits. In this preposterously baggy attire, the mortified Cohen presented such a ludicrous figure that the whole restaurant broke into spontaneous laughter. Louise's guffaws were conspicuously loud and Michael had to pinch her knee.

'Shall we go now, Brooksie?' he whispered.

'No fear!' was the expected reply. 'I'm not going to miss one second of this!'

With such a raucous start, the party stayed on a boisterous note throughout the evening. At one stage, Fran Gilbertini called her daughter over to be introduced to Louise and young Suzette remained wedged between her and Michael for the remainder of the dinner. At first Michael felt a little piqued that this plain little 12-year-old should monopolize his consort's attention, but even he was won over by her wide-eyed awe at being in the presence of a Real Hollywood Movie Star. Louise played the role to the hilt and when she discovered that Suzette was studying ballet, she insisted on giving her some lessons — and even (to Michael's mild embarrassment) demonstrated one of the more awkward pieces.

As the applause in the restaurant died down, Mama Gilbertini stroked the hair of her blushing child.

'Now, Suzette,' she said. 'You can tell people that you received a dancing lesson from Louise Brooks — *the Hollywood movie star!*' She turned to Louise. 'This will be something she'll remember even when she's an old woman!'

Not long after, a waiter informed Phil Cohen that his suit had been cleaned and pressed and was ready to wear again. This prompted the Gilbertinis to offer to take him back to his car to see if he could get it going now that the rain had stopped. Glad of an opportunity to be alone with Louise, Michael bade them all goodbye, saying they would stay on for another coffee.

After several more drinks, Michael noticed that Louise was now noticeably tipsy.

'You drink too much, Louise. Why do you do it?' he asked.

'Gives me the courage of my convictions,' she breathed and planted a wet kiss on his lips. 'I can be me and not care about those...'

She languidly swept her arm around.

'Those bastards.'

She drained her glass which she then twirled around.

'And other times, when I'm behaving myself. When I'm being a nice, d-e-m-u-r-e lady, a little hooch helps me smile my way through the whole, live-long, boring night. All that, and, yeah, if you must know, I also like it anyway. So fill her up, Buster. There's a sport.'

'You've finished the bottle, Louise,' stated Michael firmly. 'You've really had enough.'

Louise caught sight of a waiter who was in the middle of writing down an order at the next table. She spun around and tugged violently at his elbow.

'Another bottle of champagne — just as fast as you like.'

She briefly contemplated the circle of raised eyebrows.

'My friend here is dying of thirst,' she said.

Louise leaned forward and lowered her voice to a confidential stage whisper.

'He suffers from acute hydrophobia — s'why he can only drink champagne. Dr Brooks' orders...'

She turned back to Michael.

'Did I ever tell you, my late Grand-daddy was a doctor? Never made any money. Too patient with his patients, y'know! Where's that fellow gone?'

With that, Louise suddenly wheeled around and knocked a tray full of glasses out of a passing waiter's hands. There was a cry from a thin lady at an adjoining table as something splashed over her shoulder.

Michael stood up.

'My apologies... Sorry. Actually, we're just leaving. Come on, Louise...' He pressed a fistful of money into the waiter's hand. 'Don't bother with the bill. This should cover everything. Including that lady's dress.'

Furious, Michael steered Louise towards the door. He pushed her into the backseat of the car and revved up the motor. He was already moving when their waiter ran out, just in time to throw a hat and stole through the open window.

23. YOU KNEW, DIDN'T YOU?

As arranged, Michael met Louise in the coffee shop. He rose as she joined his table and after she had taken her seat, he took a step back.

'Well, my Louise, tell me — how do I look. Do I strike you as a stylish sort of man-about-town?

'Oh, absolutely. Now what is it you want me to notice... Christ, Michael where DID you get those cufflinks? They must have cost a fortune.' Louise's frown turned to an awkward smile. 'Aren't they just a little too big... perhaps even somewhat...?'

Michael cut in with a roar of laughter.

'How dare you impugn the aesthetic sensibilities of Toby Ferris, Esquire!' he rebuked her. 'These handcrafted cufflinks are a token of his inestimable esteem for me — not to mention his deepest gratitude. Didn't you know that I helped him with his investment in Rosario Canning Company stock. Did very well, it seems. Quite a windfall.'

Louise suddenly looked serious.

'Michael. I just don't know how you can always keep coming up with the right forecasts all the time. You never seem to put a foot wrong. It's weird, almost uncanny. Where do you get the information?'

'Louise, I study the stock market very carefully. Where others ride on hunches or marketplace sentiment, I go on logic and facts. I even quantify the illogicality of the market and factor it in. I don't gamble, Louise — I practice a carefully disciplined science that identifies clear probabilities under the light of cool analysis. That's what makes the difference.'

She reflected on this explanation for a moment.

'You know, Michael, the other strange thing about you is that every other big-time speculator I know is always edgy. Some try to bottle it up and others openly fret about their play. But not you. You act as if there's not the least chance of something not turning out right. That's amazing.'

'I've just explained to you, Louise, I have no place in my business affairs for emotion or feelings. That's precisely why I'm good at it. And of course, I have an infallible adviser...'

'Anyone I've heard of?' she asked.

'Madame Rosa. Every movement of the Dow Jones index is revealed in her tea leaves in precise detail. I can't miss!'

Louise arched an eyebrow.

'Now I don't find this line of conversation at all entertaining,' said Michael impatiently. 'So, why don't we get onto something else.'

Then, he moved close behind Louise and draped his arms over her shoulders and around her neck.

'You now I'm no cold fish, Louise. Why, I'm so crazy about you I just don't have any emotional energy to spare for anything else. Not even the stock market...! Now tell me, what's this about a train excursion down to the border?'

'Darling, Madie Gregory and I have always promised ourselves to see Tijuana. I said I'd talk to you about the four of us going down by train to San Diego and hopping over the border. There's some pretty wild nightlife. You'll love it! Tequila and genuine imported scotch — I've just had enough of all this bathtub gin!'

'Wait a minute. The four of us?'

'Yes. With Madie's beau. He's a land salesman.'

'Oh, no. Holed up in a Mexican hotel with a guy who's selling me parcels of desert all the time. I can just see it!'

'No, Michael. You'll like him. He's actually a bit on he quiet side. Anyway, I've booked us on the 11 am train on Friday morning. I told them you'd pick us up in your car and we'd all go to the station together about half an hour before.' Still in his embrace, she squirmed around, threw her arms about his neck and pouted. 'Go on, just say yes...'

Michael nodded and ushered her into the bedroom.

* * *

Louise and her two companions stood silently outside her apartment. Henry was a man in his early thirties with light sandy hair sitting atop a large, round face. From time to time, he paused from fanning himself with his straw boater hat to pull a handkerchief out of his pocket and wipe the perspiration from his brow. While he appeared a slightly comic figure at first glance, his eyes suggested an alert, yet patient, intelligence. His companion, Madie, was a tall, thin woman with slightly rounded shoulders and lively, dark eyes. A liberal application of fire-engine-red lipstick made her mouth seem even more spectacularly wide. She fidgeted and hummed to herself.

Louise looked up at the clock in the drugstore window and sighed.

'Henry, I just don't what's happened to him. He said he'd be here at 10.15 sharp. This isn't at all like him. He's a real stickler about punctuality, isn't he, Madie?'

'Well,' said Henry looking at his own watch. 'Whatever the reason for the hold-up. We've no chance of making that train now.'

Several minutes passed and at last Michael's car drew up.

'Sorry, folks. Had a flat. I raced here as fast as I could, but I guess we'll just have to wait for the one o'clock train. Let's find a coffee and I'll buy you lunch to show my deep contrition.'

They walked off and Henry good-naturedly shrugged off Michael's apologies while Louise and Madie chatted amiably. Michael found Henry to be quite as agreeable as Louise had promised and she couldn't help kicking Michael under the table when, without any prompting, he himself initiated a discussion about likely demand for residential real estate developments in Southern California.

An hour and a half later, they appeared at the station which they found thronged by a strangely agitated crowd. Henry approached the ticket clerk's window.

'We have four tickets booked on the eleven am, to San Diego, but we had car trouble and we'd like to take the one o'clock...'

The clerk looked at the tickets and slowly shook his head. He surveyed Henry and, standing behind him, Michael, Louise and Madie.

'That won't be possible, I'm afraid, sir. You see, this morning's train ran right into the back of a goods train. I got a wire here that says there's at least fifteen dead and quite a few badly injured. You should thank God for whatever made you miss that train...'

Louise turned pale, turned around and looked at Michael.

'You knew, didn't you,' she whispered softly.

* * *

As Michael drove back that afternoon, Louise said little. She was not so much cool as intensely preoccupied in thought. When his car drew up outside her apartment, she declined Michael's invitation to have dinner, saying she was auditioning in the morning.

'Well, what about another evening this week' Michael asked her.

'I don't know. Look, Michael, I would like to wait a little while before we see each other again.'

'Louise, what's wrong? Did I say something?'

'I don't know how to put it, but I've been feeling very uncomfortable with you lately. It's not you, yourself — I meant what I said before and I still do care for you very much.'

Louise leaned forward and held his hands in her lap.

'There is something very strange going on. I just can't explain it.'

'What... tell me what?'

'Michael, I think you know very well what I'm talking about. It's spooky... and it frightens me.'

'Missing the train? Why that's perfectly...'

'You never had a flat. The spare wheel hasn't been touched — it's still brand new and the dust marks show the strap hasn't been touched for days: I checked. And your shirt cuffs. They were still immaculate when you arrived.'

Louise stared hard at Michael.

'Michael, you deliberately stalled... I *know* you did.'

She began to catalog a long list of incidents that, said Louise, went far beyond the possibilities of coincidence or astute perspicacity. And these inexplicable absences — and equally disconcerting appearances — always seemed timed to coincide with the most telling moment. And why did Michael always disappear before daybreak after they had made love? Why was it there was not one person who could verify anything he said about his past life? Though her reason rebelled against the notion, she could not help thinking that he was employing supernatural powers. She did not know. She was confused.

'I'm sorry, Michael. I need time to think, perhaps a few weeks or a month or two. Please don't call me for a while.'

She kissed him on the cheek and left the car. Without a word, Michael watched her walk through the doorway of her building and straight into a waiting lift. Then, suddenly, she was gone.

24. THE BREACH

In quick succession, four large, black cars drew up in the back parking lot of the country motel. Exchanging no more than a few perfunctory words, the passengers climbed out and were directed by the motel manager into a small conference room. The drivers looked at one other and, upon a silent signal, climbed back into their vehicles and drove off down the road.

Inside, six people gathered around the table: General O'Keefe and Captain Mackenzie (both wearing civilian suits), Dr Havas, Ericsson, Vince Fadowsky and a quiet man with thin, sandy hair who was obviously unknown to most of the others. General O'Keefe spoke first.

'Dr Havas, gentlemen. I'll start by introducing Jim Holyoake. He's from Internal Electronic Systems and Communications... heads up their security section. I've asked him to come here for reasons that will be all too clear to you over the next half hour or so.'

Holyoake half-raised himself from his chair and nodded curtly to the others in the room.

O'Keefe looked up from his notes and continued.

'I apologize for all the cloak and dagger security arrangements and my insistence on meeting at this somewhat inconvenient venue. I ask you to trust me that this degree of precaution is fully warranted.

The fact is that we have the strongest reason to believe there has been a gross, continuing incursion into our CyberProfile system.'

He paused to gauge the effect this announcement would have on the group. Their faces wore a look of stunned disbelief and the only sounds were an audible exhalation from Ericsson and a half-muffled 'My God!' from Captain Mackenzie.

'I have to tell you we know very little,' said O'Keefe. 'We don't know who he is, where he's getting in or how. All we can tell at this point is that no less than 37 separate breaches into our system have been effected since October 8 last year, with the most recent detection being in the early hours of this morning. Altogether that adds up to a total of 168 hours illegally logged on in that period. Before we look at the very serious implications of this security breach, I call upon Mr Vince Fadowsky. He is a programmer in the CyberProfile Group and it was he who discovered the breach and advised me of it. You should note that at this time no-one outside this room is aware of what has happened. Mr Fadowsky, please recount what you came across.'

Vince stood up and walked over to the white board and began to describe what had prompted his telephone call to General O'Keefe three very long nights ago.

25. COUNTDOWN

Michael sat up in bed and turned on the light. It was three-thirty-seven in the morning and for several hours he had been drifting in and out of an uneasy half-sleep. Now he had finally relinquished any hope of slipping into a restful escape from the feverish and unhappy thoughts playing tag in his brain.

Where was she? What was she doing right now? Who was she seeing? And, above all, had Louise even once given him a single thought since they were last together?

Through the long, dark hours, Michael had pursued all sorts of troubling scenarios. Some were the constructions of strange, twisting dreams, which left him baffled and betrayed. In one, he found himself frantically following Louise in a mad chase through endless parties and crowded confusion. Every time he came close she would give him a sad, wistful smile and once more disappear again into the throng, leaving Michael's path closed off by a group of men in evening suits who looked his way with mock pity and smiled knowingly within their conspiracy. And always Michael's mute anguish was smothered by the merriment and noise all around him.

In this nightmare world he was powerless and passive, stripped of all the confident powers that accompanied him during his previous incursions into Louise's domain.

Walking through his apartment, Michael turned on the TV and flicked across the channels with faint interest. Then he riffled through a magazine on his tablet. As the slow hours dragged by, he retraced his time with Louise. Flippant remarks were dredged out of his memory to be invested with sinister new meaning; lighthearted and spontaneous gestures were now seen to be coldly dismissive. Relentlessly, he raked back and forth through their time together and the best moments became indistinct and ambiguous, while trifling incidents — a show of irritation or an impatient inflection or a sly teasing — were now recognized as dark portents.

It was eleven days since Michael last talked to Louise. At first, his dismay at her request for time to herself had been tempered by a certain relief. Now he could concentrate on the demanding tasks so neglected while he moved in and out of her world. He badly needed this break.

But as the days passed, Michael was overwhelmed by a great emptiness. Despite being so immersed by work, there was now scarcely a moment when Louise was not the centre of his thoughts. The smallest thing would entice him into a daydream in which he was amusing her with clever anecdotes, listening to her confidences and smiling at her careless laughter. With equal and undiminished conviction, he moved from one conflicting mood to another. In one moment he was seized with a sad-sweet nostalgia — and only a little interval later, he was buoyed by the confident hope that all would turn out well, that she must miss him as he missed her. At other times he would rage against the ingratitude of a creature who owed her entire existence to him, yet would repay him so with such callousness. Then he would be enshrouded by empty despair, when he could see nothing that was not bleak and melancholy.

Walking pensively into his lounge room, Michael paused at each of the large portraits of Louise and looked into the face whose beauty, after all this time, still astonished him. He reflected on their last conversation and tried to imagine how things might seem through Louise's own eyes. Yes, it had been all too easy for him to play the master of the universe. Winnowing through their days together, he was astonished at how rarely he had resisted the temptation to orchestrate events to make things easier for him, to impress Louise and her friends, to play little games.

Yes, it was unutterably intoxicating to deploy powers that he could never call upon in his real world. And yes, he had been too careless about how it might seem to Louise and others in his cyberworld. But all the time, when he had been trying so hard to impress her, it might have sufficed if he had been no more than a mere, fallible mortal, just like everyone else. After all, how else could anyone have reacted to his flagrant over-manipulation of events?

From now on he would let things fall naturally in their own way and cope with them, as might any other normal being. But, again, no matter how carefully he measured his steps, could he really mask some sort of dissonance in his behavior? Was he mad to think that he could slip back and forth from one world to another, so effortlessly?

And there was something else which made Michael uneasy.

It was hard to pin down any one thing, but he had begun to notice some anomalies in the way the system was operating, particularly when he was entering the closed sector. Log-on security checks were taking unusually long and he noticed that traffic was being re-routed to different servers, ostensibly for maintenance work, even though he knew that no such activities were scheduled to take place. On top of that, Vince — normally the most garrulous of his colleagues had become noticeably withdrawn and was spending time outside the office or having lengthy telephone calls behind a closed door.

At last he deliberately confronted Vince. What was going on? Why these unaccountable delays in security clearance? Had he heard anything? Vince looked uncomfortable and gave an evasive shrug that hinted that he knew something, but did not want to, or could not, say.

Later that day, when the office was almost empty, Vince knocked quietly on Michael's door. He ushered him outside to the empty carpark.

'Look man, about what you said. You're right — there *is* something happening, OK? Mike, swear you'll keep this to yourself...'

'Sure. Of course, Vince. What is it?.'

'No, I mean, *swear*. Your solemn oath, man.'

'I swear on my honor, Vince. My word. Now what is it, for Christ's sake! You're making this seem like the end of the world!'

'Mike, there's an intruder. Someone's broken into our sector.'

Mike showed unfeigned shock. So, they were on to him!

'No, I don't believe it,' he whispered slowly. 'Have we any idea who? How'd he get in?'

'This is more than I should have told you,' replied Vince, looking around the carpark anxiously. 'I'm the only one here who knows about it — and that was only by accident. But they've got some big guns in on it. It's only a matter of time before they nail this son-of-a-bitch. But, Mike, don't breathe a word to anyone. If any of your people notice anything, just tell them it's routine maintenance and testing, some new gear our people are working on. Smokescreen.'

Vince slipped into the shadows, impressed by the look of devastation on his friend's face.

For Michael, this was an intestinal shock, of course, but not a surprise. As he drove home, he recalled that, right from the very beginning, he had known that, no matter how well he covered his movements, the time would come when someone would uncover the breach. From now on, he had to be even more alert and cautious. At the slightest hint of anything unusual he would back off and try later. Especially, he would meticulously avoid being seen to be operating to any predictable pattern. Once inside the system he was undetectable, but great care had to be taken when entering and leaving it, then was the biggest danger of detection.

If Louise agreed to see him again, it would be wise to leave longer intervals between his visits. This need not affect her, for if he had to, he could arrange it so that an interval of days in his own time need span no more than a few hours for her. Nonetheless, he accepted that he could not count on moving freely across to her world.

And when he was finally unmasked — what then? He would be in serious trouble, of course. Far worse, they would force him to open up the world he had created — and would then shut it down.

And kill Louise.

Michael numbly contemplated this awful possibility. Whatever it took, he could not, ever, let this calamity happen. To lose Louise now would be unbearable, unthinkable. He returned again and again to the thought of this danger, and all the while aware that each passing day revealed another hint of unseen forces relentlessly building up and closing in on him.

With cold intent, he constructed new detours, false trails and elaborate mazes that might buy just a little more time, a few more days. All the while, an oppressive litany kept drumming away in his mind, over and over again: I'm safe when I'm outside the sector, I'm unsafe when entering it, I'm safe inside, I'm unsafe when leaving it!

Only when he closed this vulnerable entry point for the last time would Louise be sheltered, forever beyond the reach of anyone from this loveless world. The trails now being followed so avidly would have come to an abrupt, tantalizing end — he would see to that! Then his domain would be invisible to outsiders until the end of time. As the global network evolved, Michael's cyberworld would continuously absorb and adapt the new technologies to remain forever in perfect and secure symbiosis within the system that sustained it. In time, his secret realm would be diffused across a network reaching beyond the Earth and linking up with orbiting stations and colonies on the Moon, on Mars and beyond.

But now Michael faced a simple, stark choice. He could decide to never again re-enter this cyberworld, never again see or talk to Louise. Or he could enter her world completely and cut all links with his 'real' existence — and any memory of it. There were no other options. But if he did not act quickly, Louise, his precious, lovely Lulu, was doomed.

It was a choice Michael made instinctively and decisively. He knew there could be no life for him, anywhere, without her.

Perhaps leaving this world forever might be a welcome release. Michael recalled all the complexities of his existence, the grinding demands of his work and the strain of sustaining Louise's world. He thought wryly of how little there would be to miss in the meandering and empty trail that his private life had followed. So, what was there worth staying for? What out of all this could hold up against the promise of a refuge in a simpler sphere in which he would have, he already knew, some chance of independence and the freedom — and the power — to follow his real impulses? And to be with Louise.

One thought, above all others, had flitted in and out his mind ever since he first contemplated crossing to the other world. With no conscious link to *this* Michael, would he still be the same person? Would not this other Michael Stanton, identical to the last detail in appearance and psychology, still be a 'self' as different and as separate to him as any other being? Was it a complete illusion to imagine that his very soul, whatever that was, could be excised intact from this flesh and reincarnated within immaterial streams of code shimmering across the system's fragile web?

He could not know. But, he mused, there was little to show that those inhabiting our own reality are blessed with fixed qualities. The child is not the adult it becomes. And morning finds one subtly different, ever so slightly reworked by those hours of dreaming. To be alive is to be in unquiet motion, he mused, with our very essence in transition from one condition to the next, impelled by the events of each crowded hour.

All that I have in common with the 'me' of yesterday, he realized, was a continuity of self-awareness and shared memories, reactions, dreams, fears and impulses.

Look at Louise, Michael thought. Knowing nothing of the real provenance of her own being or the world around her, the life she experiences seems to her to be as real as mine is to me. Surely, then, when finally untethered from this self, he would awake in her world with the very same, unquestioning trust in his own authenticity?

But this could only be, he knew, if he brought nothing with him from this world: no memories or narratives, no inexplicable powers. He would be marooned forever and no longer in control of his — or everyone else's — destiny. No longer an all-knowing, all-powerful avatar, he would be as vulnerable, weak and uncertain as anyone else. And, so, no different to his condition in *this* world!

To find himself marooned in the early twentieth century knowing what he had left behind, so aware of the inescapable travails ahead, would be the worst kind of hell. If not, then the time would come, he knew, when he would yearn to end his self-imposed exile. The craving would grow and gnaw at him; he would blame Louise for his banishment in her netherworld.

That was not all. By retaining his present consciousness and memories, he would be condemned to know the every unfolding detail of the future. Good things would be robbed of surprise and devalued by anticipation; the countless evils and outrages of a half century would hang over him, magnified and extended by the leisurely contemplation of all that lay ahead, certain and inescapable, with unknowing victims already marked by their predestination.

No, instead he must be re-born completely. And so Michael began to make his plans to this end.

He wondered how Louise would think of him if she could only know that not only was he forfeiting his 'real' world, but also the vast powers that he had enjoyed until now in her universe. Could this fickle creature even begin to understand the depth of love that might prompt such a sacrifice?

Surely, Michael worried, Louise must somehow sense his loss of self-assurance as he struggled with a world which he, too, would now find capricious, unyielding and, often, incomprehensible? And what if she found that this mere groundling was no longer mysterious and interesting or in any way different from the other wealthy young men she played with — and then threw aside?

But his purpose was now set and all the anxieties and indecision resolved into a sudden clarity. He was lifted by the elation that comes from reclaiming control of one's actions, even in a sea of peril. At last, he knew what he had to do — and from now every moment would count to its success. First, his cyberworld must be made an impregnable fortress that would forever protect Louise and himself. An inviolable sanctuary as remote and unreachable as the farthest star.

Earlier, when he drew up the plans for his cyberworld, Michael had designed a complex lattice-work of ingenious tricks and devices that would render it almost invisible to any chance discovery. On top of that, he had woven a skein of electronic tripwires around the point of entry. And if an ingenious — and tirelessly persistent — interloper managed to navigate their way past these daunting barriers, a 'slingshot device' would send them directly to another closed system: a top-secret site dedicated to submarine detection systems and surrounded by its own warning-alert devices.

These were all measures to eliminate the risk of a chance discovery. The difference now was that Michael had become the quarry in a concerted hunt driven by some of the country's ablest electronic security brains, with vast resources pitted against him. Whatever cunning and ingenuity he employed, he knew it would be in an unequal contest with an almost certain outcome.

If he could not outsmart his opponents, his answer would lie in a much less subtle response. He would create a doomsday device that would threaten catastrophic destruction if anyone attempted to enter or interfere with his cyberworld. Naturally, he would have to design this so that its warnings would be reinforced by a series of graduated responses certain to ward off even the most skeptical or foolhardy. Anyone who came close to the entry point of his cyberworld would be confronted by a threat to completely paralyze vital systems.

If they ignored that first warning (as he assumed they would), the next response would be a salutary shot across the bows: a temporary shut-down of a major power grid. Next, he would disable the satellite meteorological data processing network. If they still persisted, he would strike into the nation's very vitals: he would obliterate the New York Stock Exchange's links with other financial centers in America and around the world. Further incursions would prompt ever more crippling waves of havoc that would rapidly dismantle global communications systems and engulf every nation in economic and social chaos. Encircling Louise and his new world would be a protective wall that could be breached only after an electronic apocalypse had been unleashed. In this way, he could feel safe at last.

As Michael looked at the list of targets, he recalled a half-forgotten scene in an old movie. A cornered desperado with a pistol and several sticks of dynamite standing atop a giant gasometer and taunting the police surrounding him: 'One step closer — and we'll all go up together!'

He smiled briefly and then quickly turned his thoughts to the great task ahead. He had to work quickly. He had bought himself little time, but enough for his final enterprise: to upload himself into cyberspace.

26. MR SCOOTER

Still in her robe, Melissa joined Vince in their dining room and placed a fresh pot of coffee on the table beside some unopened packages. Unacknowledged, she sat down beside Vince, who absent-mindedly stared out the window. Melissa regarded him for several moments and then spoke quietly, with a slow and deliberate delivery that barely hid her irritation.

'Vince, it's mother's birthday today. Remember I said I'd like her over for dinner tonight? It's just eight months since Dad died and I thought it would be best if she had company, so I...'

She waved her hand in front of his eyes.

'Vince, for God's sake, could I please have your attention for just one minute at least?'

'Oh, sure, honey. Sorry. Yes, she's coming tonight. I know. We talked about it.'

'Good. All I want to know is that you'll be sure to come home early this once. Seven o'clock latest. But it would be nice if you got here sooner, so you could help me get things ready.'

He stood up, gave her a perfunctory kiss and made for the door.

'Right. Seven.'

'That's right. Don't worry about the card or present OR the cake. I'll look after that... as usual,' Melissa called out wearily.

* * *

The tires squealed as Vince swung his car up the ramp of the parking station. He braked heavily at the check-out gate, right behind a maintenance truck. Drumming his fingers on the wheel, he waited while the driver conversed with the boom operator. By the time a whole minute had ticked by, Vince was beginning to seethe.

'Hey, what's the hold-up? I'm in a hurry! Just move it, will you!' he yelled.

'What's your goddamn' hurry, ya jerk!' was the predictable reply.

Leaning out the window, the driver stabbed his single digit skyward and the truck moved off. Moments later, Vince was through and he shot out onto the road. As he turned around, he heard the loud blast of an airhorn and, almost immediately after, the loud shriek of brakes and gasps from air-hoses. There was a loud clang as his car was bounced forward by a large truck's front fender. Vince immediately accelerated away to angry hoots and flashing headlights.

'What in God's name am I doing?' he shouted to himself as he hammered the wheel in frustration. 'I've almost killed myself... just to watch an old duck blow out the candles on a cake!'

Breathing deeply, he slowed down and continued his journey until, about fifteen minutes later, he finally pulled into his compound's car park. Inside the apartment, he found Melissa seated by the air-conditioner, leafing rapidly through a magazine. She did not look up.

'I'm sorry, Melissa. Really, I am.'

'That's quite alright, Vince. Mother left forty minutes ago. She'd have waited longer, but I said not to bother — you often worked right through the night without even a phone call.'

'Look, if you just listen to me...'

'Vince, no. For a change, I want you to listen to me. I'm through with all this. Never seeing you from one day to the next. When you are home, your mind's still back there. You don't give a shit about me or anything else.'

She stood up and faced him.

'Remember, I have a career, too. I get stressed and tired. I've got a project that's so far behind schedule I can't sleep nights. The contractors keep letting us down. I can't even get any help from you. So, tell me, what's so special about you that I have to put up with being alone all the time, your moods and every other damned thing?'

'Melissa...'

'Vince, I asked you, I begged you, just tonight. It was my mother's birthday...'

Vince buried his head in his hands and sighed deeply. Silent moments passed before he spoke in a quiet and weary voice.

'Sweetheart, we've a really bad problem. It's just not like anything I've ever been involved in before. I shouldn't be telling you..'

Several seconds passed before he continued.

'There's been a major security breach. A foreign agent — or some sort of spook is walking all around in our cyberprofile space.'

She jerked her head up.

'I'm the patsy who clicked to it' Vince continued, punching his fist into his hand. 'And guess what, I'm the patsy they're expecting to flush him out!'

'Vince, can't you cut him out? What have you tried?'

'Everything. Just everything. We've got teams monitoring the site twenty four hours a day.'

'OK. Tell me what you've done,' said Melissa in a voice that had suddenly softened. 'There's got to be a something you haven't tried.'

* * *

The clock in the dimly-lit computer room showed seventeen past two in the morning. Two young men in light-blue shirts stared at their screens while another, older, man looked over their shoulders. The phone rang, startling the two seated men.

'Jim Holyoake — Intelscom. Sorry... that's Internal Electronic Systems and Communications. Yeah, we're OK.'

He looked down at the other two.

'Names of Smith and Clark. We'll be here till seven. Yeah... Ring me when our relief arrives. That'll be Pallister? Got it... Right.'

Hanging up the telephone, he turned to the others.

'OK, boys. How're we doing?'

Clark gave a non-committal grunt and settled down for what was sure to be another long, fruitless night's wait. At regular intervals he looked up at the analogue clock and sighed at how grudgingly slowly it traced each tedious minute of their quiet vigil.

Suddenly Smith called out: 'Hey, Jim, there's something here! It's him... We've got him! It's Mr Code-Name Scooter!'

Holyoake leaned intently over the backs of their chairs.

'Easy, guys. Just keep close. Move there. Quick.... quick... now copy it. Now run it back again. Wait, baby, wait... wait. Hot shit, we're through! The gate's closed behind us. OK, now let's just wait a second... Hold it, what the hell's this?'

A message slowly faded up on the screen: 'Do not try to proceed any further. If you attempt to do so, your action will cause the disablement of a major communications utility. Exit this sector immediately!'

'Shouldn't we call Henderson? Or General O'Keefe?' asked Smith anxiously.

Holyoake looked at the screen disdainfully.

'Typical hacker trick. They always put up crap like that when you get close. Like to see him try. Ignore it.'

Smith still hesitated. 'Ignore it,' repeated Holyoake.

Clark leaned forward and decisively punched a key on his colleague's keyboard.

'There you are, just a lot of bullshit,' said Holyoake. 'Now, let's try and pick up the trail again...'

At that instant, the screen froze. A caption slowly faded up and disappeared a moment later. 'Congratulations!' it read. 'You have just turned out the lights for three hours.'

* * *

O'Keefe grabbed the telephone by his bed and grunted a reply. Picking up the handset, he got up quietly so as not to further disturb his sleeping wife and closed the bedroom door behind him. All the while, he gravely nodded as he took in the full impact of the caller's message.

'When exactly did it happen...? Three hours? Jesus! OK, now tell me, is the rest of the grid working normally? Good. What are the immediate implications for us...? Uh-huh... I'll be there in thirty minutes maximum. No, leave it to me — I'll call him myself.'

O'Keefe called up the telephone memory and pushed several buttons.

'Jesus!' he intoned to himself quietly. 'Why the hell does all this shit only ever happen in the depths of the night...? Henderson? O'Keefe here.. You've heard...? Yeah... Yeah... Unfortunately, a great deal more than you'd guess. Our Intelscom surveillance crew seemed to have come close to our friend Scooter's entry point. Up jumped a warning that if they went any further he'd knock out the grid. Well, that's just what they did... and that's just what *he* did!'

O'Keefe put his hand to his forehead.

'Listen carefully. Tell everyone to back off. No more probing. Nothing. No, I don't want to hear...'

He cut across the voice on the other end of the line and spoke in a firm, measured tone.

'Henderson, we're dealing with a madman. He's shown he can cause real damage, if his back's to the wall — and, believe me, this is probably just for openers... We just have to think... OK, I'll see you there.'

He walked straight into the bathroom and turned on the shower.

'Well, Mr Scooter,' he said to himself. 'Now we all know the game's out in the open. From here on we slug it out, your move against ours!'

27. GETTING THE FIX

General O'Keefe was at his desk, immersed in a report. His secretary's voice came through on the intercom.

'Mr Fadowsky to see you, General,' she said. 'I've sent him in.'

'Ah, Fadowsky... sit down. So, what's the situation? Exactly where are we?'

Vince shrugged his shoulders unhelpfully.

'Well, sir, we've tried everything in the book — and a few other tricks besides. Nothing. Every time we get anywhere close, he just loses us. I think he's buried some dynamic encryption routine into our system, so whenever he logs on our server recognizes him and immediately switches over to this special code that only his computer can read.'

'Well, can't we crack it?' asked O'Keefe impatiently.

'No chance. It must re-encrypt every few seconds. There's no predictability, completely random. Some quantum tool, I'm sure.'

They both fell silent for a moment. 'I'd sure like to meet this dude,' added Vince softly. 'He's one real mastermind...'

'I think we all would,' O'Keefe replied. 'So, what next?'

'Sir, we've been working on an idea. It's taking a very different tack, but it looks promising...'

'We? Who's *we*? Isn't there a security blackout on this?'

'Melissa Schneider, sir. She's waiting outside. She's a friend... er, actually, we live together. But the thing is that she has the knowledge we need about network operations. All I've told her is we're having trouble with hacker probes, that's all.'

'Bring her in.'

O'Keefe stood up when she entered and shook her hand in a direct, down-to-business way. She looked at Vince, who motioned her to talk.

'General, I've been working on a way to target an unauthorized entry into a protected system. Basically, it comes up with a geographical fix on the intruder. I've tested it several times and we've come to within a couple of hundred meters of the hypothetical intruder. Of course, those were in ideal conditions...'

'And the beauty of this is that there's no way you will alert the intruder,' Vince interjected.

'Tell me more,' said O'Keefe.

Melissa drew a deep breath and began to explain. 'When our system opens to any connection, it exchanges a series of protocol messages between the outside computer and our nearest server hub. These never vary and the duration is exactly the same, measured down to a very precise figure.'

O'Keefe nodded.

'If we measure the intervals between exchanges, we can use the known speed of transmission down fiber cabling to measure how far away the intruding computer is located. Now, using that distance as a radius, I draw around our server knowing that our target must be somewhere on that circle. Like this...'

They watched Melissa draw a sketch on the immaculate pad on O'Keefe's desk.

'What we do next,' she continued, 'is temporarily relocate our system's entry point to another server, wait for another incoming call from that intruder and measure and repeat the exercise. The two points where the circles intersect give us the two possible locations of the intruder. Repeat the exercise using a third server and we've got a single, exact fix on him.'

O'Keefe's eyes lit up.

'Well, well! Triangulation. They used that back in the Second World War to locate clandestine transmitters.'

'And astronomers use it, too,' Vince added.

'What's involved?' demanded O'Keefe.

'No big deal,' replied Melissa. 'We often move around to different servers to test the system's ability to switch in an emergency — usually very late at night and at weekends. There's a break of just a fraction of a second during the switchover operation. No-one notices.'

'It's just that there'll be a lot of around-the-clock waiting until we catch the intruder make a move,' added Vince.

'OK, I've got some questions,' said O'Keefe. 'What if he's coming in on microwave relay on some part of his link?'

'No way, sir,' Vince interjected. 'That's too open. A guy this smart just wouldn't risk it. He'd check it out — and work around it if he had to.'

'Alright, here's another one. Wouldn't your calculations be thrown out every time his transmission hits a booster station?'

'We factor that in,' Melissa cut in. 'Every time a transmission is boosted there's a tell-tale string of code tagged on the end of the data — a tiny little squiggle. One squiggle, read one boost. Two squiggles, two boosts. We calculate for the known delays and then do our sums. We lose some accuracy in the process, but it still works out.'

O'Keefe stared hard at the sketch for so long that Vince turned to Melissa and raised his eyebrows quizzically.

'So, we get a fix on him... or her,' said the General, smiling at Melissa. 'What sort of area are we looking at? How close will we be?'

'Could be a couple of square kilometers, maybe less,' replied

Vince, with Melissa nodding in agreement.

'So far, so good. But now there's the problem of how we zero in on an individual hacker from there,' asked O'Keefe, tapping the sketch with his pen. 'We could be looking at hundreds — even thousands — of possible candidates. Everyone in that area who's on-line.'

'We had a look at that, too, sir,' replied Vince. 'Most amateur hackers are opportunists looking for an unlocked door. They keep applying the same limited combination of tricks until they get lucky.'

'This dude's different. He really knows how to work within a system. Picks the lock and leaves no evidence anywhere. That's why Ms Schneider and I are very sure that we're up against a professional.'

Melissa cut across Vince. 'If he's a pro, he's bound to be registered with FASDAP — and probably a few other groups as well.'

'FASDAP?'

'Federation of American Software Designers and Programmers — one of the professional groups. They provide industry-wide accreditation. You need their certification to get a job... outside the Defense forces, of course,' explained Vince.

'So what we do,' continued Schneider, 'is check their membership list against the postcodes in and around the area where we think the intruder is located. Most members are registered by their home addresses because they tend to change jobs more frequently than they move home...'

'Then we just sift through whatever names we are left with — and bingo!' added Vince.

'Seems right to me' O'Keefe grunted. 'Impressive...'

'OK, let's get this happening! Figure out what you need to do and who you have to bring in on this, but keep the team tight so we don't risk security. And we'll need a good cover. In the meantime, I'll set up a meeting with my brass to get their nod.'

As if talking only to himself, he added: 'We've got to choke this bastard real soon! And if this guy's a pro, who the hell is he working for? What's he after?'

There was a knock on the door. O'Keefe's secretary appeared.

'General, I'm very sorry to interrupt. I have an urgent message for you. I think you should see it immediately!'

'Come in, Helen,' he said and took a piece of paper from her. Looking to Vince and Melissa, he added, 'Excuse me one moment…'

Impassively, he scanned the paper — and then carefully and slowly read it again.

'Thank you, Helen, I'd like a word with you shortly.'

After his secretary had left the room, O'Keefe turned around and held up the message he had received.

'This... this is a declaration of war. Mr Scooter has just gone public. He's e-mailed all the news agencies and told them that if we don't back off he'll start knocking off other utilities.'

He looked at the paper again and read out aloud.

'I am operating a project which has no bearing whatsoever on any matter of concern regarding military or commercial security and in no way poses any threat to any national or community interests. However, it is important that it remains completely closed to outside scrutiny. Any further intrusions into this space will be met with immediate retaliation. Because these responses will impact upon the general community with progressive severity, it is my duty to advise the public of this situation so that pressure can be brought to bear to halt any further incursions.'

'Hell's teeth!' whispered Vince.

'But there's more,' said O'Keefe. 'This e-mail message was routed from within our Neptune submarine tracking system. The bastard's telling us that if he can get in there, he can be anywhere. The whole goddamned computer system's just become completely transparent!'

He placed his hands on his desk and leaned towards his visitors.

'We've got very little time. You know what you've got to do. Go do it!'

28. ALTER EGO

Michael was on two weeks' leave. He needed the time, he had explained, to redecorate his apartment.

In fact, he spent day after day at his home computer, preparing his profile which, at the right moment, he would upload to his hidden site on the network. He had gathered all the information he could find about himself: letters, school and college reports, articles he had penned while secretary of the college computer society, old photographs and all the other little scraps and mementos of his life's journey of ten thousand days.

He set up a camera to record images of himself moving in front of the camera, performing all sorts of movements, with and without clothes. He talked and talked, in the process mimicking anger, dismay, hurt, affection, confidence — all the tones and shades the voice can orchestrate. He troweled deep into his memory to describe the books he had read and how they had affected him, the films he had seen, the paintings, photographs and remembered images that had left an imprint of some sort in his mind, often impressionistic and evocative of a mood or sense so faint and intangible that it defied words.

In profiling himself, Michael had to deal with a challenge never encountered in any previous cyberprofiling exercise.

Of course, to create a faithful replica of his personality, he would have to feed in memories of the many events in his life that had shaped his character and attitudes, even fairly recent occurrences. But, he then had to filter out any knowledge of those actual events, while only retaining the mind-shaping imprint they had made. This was only to ensure that the other Michael would have no conscious recollections that would clash with his perception of himself as a citizen of the early twentieth century. He had to be reborn, emerging as unconscious of his true origins as Louise was of hers.

To help refine his emotional profile, Michael sat through an exhausting series of interrogations by his computer to gauge his attitudes on various subjects. Presented with real and hypothetical situations, he answered as honestly as he could and the computer faithfully noted his responses.

For these sessions, Michael wore a specially-adapted Sensator helmet which read brain signals, including evoked responses, and fed them into a computer for profile-building.

The interrogations ran for one or two hours at a time and, because they seemed to Michael so like a session with a psychotherapist, he amused himself by lying full length on the couch — one of the few items of furniture now left in his apartment.

'What do you remember of your sister?' the computer asked.

'Very little. I was six years old when she died. Wendy was 14. But what I do recall is very clear, although nothing seems to have a particular beginning or end to it or any apparent reason why it should have stuck in my memory. Just images, little vignettes. But because they are all I can recall about her — or us — they have a very strong emotional charge to them. When I was younger, just thinking about these images started me crying. I guess, even the particularly happy things made me pretty sad. I'm sure that if Wendy were still alive — and my mother too — all those recollections would just seem pleasant scenes from a normal, happy childhood,' said Michael.

'Describe these memories.'

Michael thought for a minute and his mind drifted back thirty years or more.

'It was summer, I remember Wendy wearing a cotton frock with these flowers printed on it and it had short, ruffled sleeves. We were in the back seat of the car with Mom and Pop up front and we'd been driving for some time, probably a Sunday outing. I think I was dreaming or dozing off when the car suddenly swerved and braked. It gave me a real shock, especially the way that Wendy grabbed my arm, hurting me.'

'What happened?' asked the computer.

'A small dog had run out in front of us. We just missed it, I'm sure we didn't hit it. But there was a car coming in the opposite direction and the dog went right under it. I didn't see that, luckily. Anyway we stopped and Pop walked over to see what could be done. There was a lot of yelping and a woman was screaming. I just put my hands over my ears. Pop came back and opened the trunk and went back again. Wendy got out of the car and ran after him, although Mom told her to stay put. Then everything went still except for the woman on the other side of the road who was crying quietly. I looked out and saw Dad and Wendy had returned to the car and he put a tire lever back into the trunk and we drove off. Wendy didn't say anything all this while but I remembered seeing her crying. I reached over and I think I was trying to touch her hand, but I saw blood on her fingers... and held back. I was scared. I was scared that Wendy had held something that was dying. And scared that my own father had just killed that little dog.'

'How did this affect you?'

'I'm not sure. But when I looked back on this it always seemed somehow that Wendy was... somehow she was linked with death. That she had a strange familiarity with death that I didn't have.'

'How do you feel about death?'

'My own death has never worried me,' said Michael. 'After Wendy and then my mother, I never felt I had much else to lose. When I was a kid I often dreamed about when I would be joining them. I was pretty religious in those days. Pop... well, we were never too close and he's lived out a pretty full span, I suppose... You want to know how I feel about... about crossing over?'

'Yes,' replied the computer.

'I'm ready for it, that's all. I'm ready.'

'Do you see it as dying?'

'Yes, I do. And as a rebirth...'

Michael slowly sat up and looked directly into the camera sitting on top of the computer.

'How do you feel about...' it began.

'Sorry. Let's finish here', said Michael quietly. 'We'll pick it up later.'

'I am sorry to have tired you,' said the computer a little too solicitously. 'I suggest we recommence at seven-thirty this evening. I would like to talk to you about Louise and your feelings for her. Perhaps you might think about this in the meantime. Closing now until 1930 hours. Thank you.'

Michael lay back on the couch and stared bleakly up at the ceiling.

He was exhausted by the days and nights of unrelieved fear of facing his pursuers. Yet, with each hour, he was inching closer to when he need no longer move in and out of his cyberworld. This was an enticing prospect, for the burden of two existences left him soul-weary. It was hard enough coping with just one life, he observed, whichever one it was.

But was he really prepared for what lay ahead? Exchanging his own natural, here-now, life for a mirror existence, entombed forever within the electronic circuits and synapses of a giant computer system. What was that but suicide? The extinction of this, his *authentic* self! Yet, he had firmly resolved that it was impossible to live without Louise. Yes. He had to die. For if he stayed on in this world, he would be tormented, not consoled, to know that his doppelganger, his self-fashioned avatar, was with her, talking to her, loving her.

* * *

By the tenth day Michael could see an end to all the profiling routines and interrogations. Lately, the computer's questions seemed less open-ended and general and now focused almost entirely on points to be clarified or details confirmed. To gauge its profiling progress, the computer presented Michael with questionnaires and then compared his responses with the replies of the other Michael. The initial score of 88.7% accuracy had inched up to an impressive 99.2% — as good as the best scores achieved by the CyberProfile Group's own experiments.

As the computer itself reminded him, this was as high a correlation as could be achieved with the technology being employed — and was, in any case, close to the theoretical limit.

So, now the new Michael Stanton was poised ready for the strange journey to Louise's world! There, he would inhabit a place where events would unfold in their own way from a starting point identical to where the 'real' world had once been on the fifth day of August in 1929. In all respects, everything and everyone would be in place just as they had been once before, a century ago. Or almost the same. For Michael had decided to interpose just one change...

29. STAY A MOMENT

It was time for Michael to make his only farewell.

He had seen little of his father over the years. They had never been close, but nonetheless, Michael had always admired him and thought warmly of him. The old man had been a good, occasionally indulgent, parent, but from the earliest years, there had always been a certain emotional distance. As an adult, on the infrequent occasions when they were together, they had (with almost comic awkwardness) talked of closeness, affection even. But, more than ever, Michael felt the same old discomfort.

Was it the quiet, self-containment that had been refuge for both father and son after Michael's mother died, when neither could bear to burden the other with their own grief? Or was it Michael's certainty that Pop, in his heart, would have preferred that he, and not Wendy, had died? Or had his own survivor's guilt pushed his father away? And what had his father ever understood — or wondered — about Michael's life or goals?

He rang the nursing home and said he would be calling over at the weekend, but that he would like to surprise his father, so please do not mention this to him.

Michael set out while it was still dark and drove till the early afternoon. He paused in a small town not far from his destination to buy a present. The only likely store was a little bookshop where the owner — a small, middle-aged woman with half-rim glasses approached him. I am looking for a book — a gift for my father, he said. And what sort of things would he be interested in?, she asked. Michael searched his mind and looked blankly at her. He rescued himself from this dilemma by spotting an illustrated book on National Parks. There, this would be ideal, he thought, recalling that once when he was about ten or eleven his father had taken him hiking in a forest where they had shared a barbecue with some campers they encountered. The book might prompt a retelling of that experience.

At the nursing home, Michael was met by a nurse who led him to his father's room.

'We'd no idea that Mr Stanton had any relatives,' she said, reproachfully. 'There was nothing in his files about any next of kin. Perhaps you would be so kind as to fill in a form before you go, so that we can contact you if — when — we need to. He's very frail, you know.'

Left at his father's doorway, Michael saw an elderly man in a dressing gown, dozing in a chair by the bed. He leaned over and gently shook him.

'Pop, wake up. It's me, Michael. Pop, can you hear me? It's Michael!'

Still befuddled with sleep, Mr Stanton Senior opened his eyes. 'Michael? Where is he?'

'It's me, Pop,' Michael acknowledged, smiling indulgently. 'I'm Michael.'

The old man slowly nodded.

'How are you, Pop? How are things going for you? Health not too good, they tell me.'

Awkwardly trying to straighten his wispy white hair, Mr Stanton counted off a long chronicle of ailments, in the way the old and lonely do, with each tribulation listed without comment or description. With tired resignation, he said he was tormented with aches and discomfort and hated his loss of freedom. It was the way things had been pretty much since Michael's mother had died.

'Son, she was the only woman I ever loved. The only one. I miss her so much that... that I'm looking forward to being with her again. Apart from you, there's nothing here for me. And I don't see too much of you anyways.'

'I'm sorry, Dad. I'm always too busy. I know that's no excuse...'

The old man looked at his son for a while and smiled.

'Tell me, you're still doing well?'

'I guess, I am, Pop.'

'That's good. You were always clever. Trouble is, when they ask, I don't know what to tell them you're up to. It's all beyond me.' He chuckled and then coughed wheezily. 'Give me the mask... there, that's better. I don't go too far without my oxygen.'

They talked for an hour. But with only a distant shared past to trawl through, they labored to punctuate long, reflective pauses with stories of half-forgotten people and incidents. Finally, Michael took his father's hand.

'Pop, you're tired. I should let you rest...'

'Son, rest is just about all I do here. Stay a moment. Tell me, do you have time for any girlfriends? I mean, anyone special?'

'Well, yes, I do.'

'I'd like to meet her one day. I'd like to see you with some kids, Michael. They'd be good for you. Your mother always wanted grandchildren, but that's too late now... A good woman...'

Mr Stanton's eyes filled with tears and he settled back, clutching his son's hand tightly. After several silent minutes, the old man was asleep and Michael kissed his forehead then quietly left the room.

His throat tight with emotion, Michael made his way out of the nursing home, pretending to forget to fill out the next-of-kin form the nurse had left out for him. He walked past his car and slowly made his way through the large garden surrounding the nursing home. It had just rained and the damp earth was releasing a rich, loamy smell that mingled with the pine-needle fragrance of the nearby wood.

Michael paused and inhaled deeply. I must be mad, he thought. To even think of taking a one-way trip to a world where I may never enjoy these scents again. Never see my father again.

For the briefest moment, Michael thought he would stay — and leave Louise in her own world. Or what if he uploaded his replica and remained in this world just as he was? Would it be enough for him to know that, somewhere, there was a world, forever unreachable, where another Michael Stanton was sharing his life with Louise? Despite his earlier misgivings, perhaps this might work, after all. Michael shook his head violently at the idea. No, no, no... He wanted no existence that was separate from hers. How could he even *think* of it!

* * *

Michael arrived home just after eight that evening. There were some personal matters to attend to, things to tidy up before he... Michael searched for the right word... departed. For once he started the uploading process, he would be most exposed and conspicuous — and every minute longer he spent in this condition would put him at even greater risk. This would certainly be no time to break away from the uploading and focus on less critical matters.

He made a snack from some leftovers in the refrigerator and, as he ate, drew up a schedule of tasks so he could leave his affairs in some sort of order.

This was certainly less complicated than it might have been for most people. A fastidious orderliness had always governed his private and working lives (a habit remarkably rare among his colleagues). Besides that, his disregard for possessions meant that the effects of a lifetime could be brought together and sorted out in one room: a single weekend's work.

He composed a list on his computer tablet and then arranged and re-arranged entries, adding and deleting as he went.

Personal Effects	*- To be Destroyed*
	- To be Given Away/Recycled
Car	*- Lodge spare set of keys with Apartment Manager*
Financial	*- Payments to be made*
	- Bank accounts
	- Shares and Superannuation
	- Insurances Cancellation
Personal Instructions	*- Will (lodged with lawyer, address details)*
	- Work (keys, security cards, return items kept at home)
Letters	*- (Several)*

Moving from room to room, Michael gathered up his various articles and heaped them up into two piles on the lounge floor. One for the items he would give away: clothes, his sound system, the TV and other appliances, tinned food, selected recordings, videos and books. Some had notes on them, naming friends who were to receive them. Most went to Vince, recognizing several shared enthusiasms, such as old films, blues recordings, philosophy books, zen, and so on.

The other pile was made up of personal effects he did not want to be poked through by strangers, including photo albums, school and college certificates, old cards and other sentimental bric-a-brac. Here also went anything which might point to Louise and his cyberworld, especially his notes, logbooks and diary. He removed the portraits of Louise from the walls and shelves and added these to the large heap.

By about one in the morning he had finished. In front of him were neatly-arranged parcels of what he had gathered over a lifetime. It struck him as pitifully scant. Yet, after tomorrow, there would be even less to remind people that he had ever existed.

The sorting finished, he sat on the bed and leafed through an old photo-album. There he was as a child, wearing the odd little hat his mother made him wear when there was the faintest glimmer of sun. She worried that he might get a melanoma on his fair skin.

A premonition, perhaps, of the cancer that took her away in her middle years.

Michael gazed at a favorite picture of his mother. It was easy to see why Pop always treasured it and kept its framed enlargement by his nursing home bedside. She looked so pretty and so vital and, as Michael contemplated the old print in his hand, he saw in it the transience of all things. Here was an instant, frozen long ago, when this young woman looked ahead to an unknown future with hope and optimism.

Yet what of all those dreams — and fears — now? Swallowed up in the night. Very soon he, too, would be no more and he found it remarkable that he was not afraid. From the first moment the decision had been forced upon him, he had moved towards his own departure with deliberate and orderly calm. There was no possibility of letting Louise go — and there never had been. His life was where she was.

Michael closed the photo-album and returned it to its pile. He lay on his bed and his mind drifted to a conversation with Louise many months ago. She had speculated earnestly on what lay beyond death, about the possibility of another existence. Hearing her sometimes shifting fancies, he was struck by the paradox that Louise was quite unaware that she — or her other self — had already made that journey... and returned again.

With that thought in mind, Michael took the opportunity to impress her with his recent reading of Schopenhauer.

'You know,' he had said, 'Our friend Arthur believed that at death the individual intellect disappears, but one's will still remains. He said it hangs around in what he called a cognitionless, but not unconscious, state.'

Noticing Louise's encouraging nod, Michael continued, 'Now what's interesting in Schopenhauer's thinking is that in this condition, the antithesis of subject and object — that is, the opposition of the me and the world outside me — has now disappeared. When we are born, we emerge from this condition and, when we die, we merely return to it once more.'

'Everyone? Sinners and saints alike?' asked Louise.

'He said every single existence is on loan from this source,' explained Michael. 'Nothing that dies, dies for ever, and no being that comes into existence is fundamentally new. We all carry within us a germ of a previous being, even though we know nothing of its existence. We are all of us — the dead, the living and the yet-to-be-born — giving way, the one to the other, and yet still remaining linked by this eternal chain. This recycling of the will, endlessly taking on new forms and minds, Schopenhauer described as "palingenesis".'

'Isn't this what you meant when you said Schopenhauer was close to Buddhist thinking?' asked Louise. 'I should really do a bit more reading on Buddhism.'

'Certainly,' he replied. 'There's the Buddhist concept of Karma in which craving or desire — what he calls will — can move from existence to existence. There's the ego-less state of Nirvana in which the distinctions between self and all else disappears. And other, similar concepts, too.'

'Well, now! Doesn't that all sound... well, I'm not quite sure why, but somewhat reassuring,' answered Louise brightly. 'We all go back into the melting pot and get served up for another go later on! I quite like that...'

* * *

Michael awoke just after daybreak the next morning, which was Sunday. As discreetly and as quietly as possible, he ferried material from the 'give away' pile down to his car and made several trips to a nearby charity recycling center. Three or four selected items were handed over to people he knew only vaguely. More often, Michael simply left an anonymous little bundle at a doorstep, rang the bell and slipped away.

Destroying things, he found, called for a degree more caution. Less important possessions he took to a waste tip and buried them deep under layers of old trash. The critical items — the books and notes — he burnt over a small fire he lit beside the wall of a derelict building in the middle of a wasteground, the site of a recently demolished factory.

As the last of these critical pages turned to ash, Michael added his portraits of Louise. One by one, each beautiful image blackened and disappeared. Michael tried to imagine how many times he had looked upon each photograph with love and yearning over the years. Holding up his favorite portrait — a profile of Louise looking upwards, innocent and serene — Michael gazed at her for several moments. It seemed impious to destroy her images in such a way. But more powerful was the fear of leaving behind the least thing which would point towards her.

Through it all, the consolation was that he would soon be with her, his real Louise. Very soon.

Michael returned to his apartment. Empty apart from some essential furniture and clothes, it looked stark and cold. He sat down at his desk and began several handwritten letters. As each one was completed, sealed within its envelope and addressed, he walked over to the list on the kitchen wall and drew a neat line through one more entry.

He continued in this fashion deep into the night. He was exhausted, yet also refreshed by a welcome respite from the stress of being connected to the system. But he knew what his adversaries knew: that he must soon again re-enter their domain, and come under their vigilant watch. And he also knew that they were already preparing themselves with all speed and resources to be ready for that moment.

30. THERE'S NO OTHER WAY

Turning away from his computer monitor, Vince leaned back in his swivel chair and stretched his arms high above his head. Simultaneously, the phone rang and he answered with the sing-song inflection that always signaled he was in a buoyant mood.

'Hello-o-o! Fadowsky.... Oh, hi, baby. What's new?'

'Quite a bit, Vince,' Melissa replied. 'Mr Scooter obligingly came on line last night, so we were able to complete the triangulation fix. We can forget the southern sector, he's definitely in the northern sector. Right, bang in the middle!'

'Holy smoke, that's great! Got him!' he shouted, punching the air with his fist. 'Just when they'd all run out of ideas — breakthrough! Oh shit, will I be the golden haired boy or what!'

'Vince, you may just recall that I...' Melissa began testily.

'Sure, Mel, sure. I didn't mean that. I meant me bringing you in on it, that's all. You know you're *brilliant!* Now, what about the FASDAP membership list? How do their addresses run against that location? Have we checked that out yet?' asked Vince.

'That's why I'm calling, Vince,' Melissa replied. 'We've identified 17 possible people.'

'17? Shouldn't be hard for the security folk. What'd O'Keefe say? Bet he was a-hootin' and a-hollerin'!'

'I haven't told him, Vince. You're the first to know.'

'I'm flattered. But, baby, you people should've told him first. Ring him right now, really. Or do you want me to call him?'

There was a long pause at the other end.

'Hey, Melissa — do you hear me?'

'Vince,' said Melissa quietly. 'I called you first because you should know... I *think* you should know... about one of the people who's on the list. It's Michael, Vince. Michael Stanton's on the list!'

'Mike? Oh my God...'

* * *

Henderson threw a folder down on the table. Out of it spilled two security photographs of Michael and various printed sheets, including his employment and security clearance records. General O'Keefe spread them out and scrutinized them carefully.

'Well, Dr Havas. What do you think?'

'The other 16 have checked out as consultants or low-level operatives, mainly in small or medium-sized firms,' she replied, looking in Henderson's direction. 'I agree, Stanton's our number one suspect.'

'He has to be,' Henderson cut in. 'Look, no mere hacker could slide through our security systems the way this guy has. We tightened things up — and what difference did it make? None! Because the bastard was on the inside all the time. Right inside the CyberProfile Group, for Christ's sake!'

Henderson stabbed his finger at the photograph on the table and held it there.

'General, he's our Mr Scooter... I'll bet a month's salary that he's the one!'

Dr Havas interrupted: 'General, we can't afford to take any risks. We should be putting taps on all 17 of them — but starting with him.'

'Too damn' right,' said O'Keefe. 'And total surveillance. I don't want him to go to the can without a camera on him. The works!'

Dr Havas nodded in agreement.

'General,' she said. 'Identifying the intruder — Mr Scooter — is only part of our mission...'

'Right! We've got to find out who he's working with. And what he's passing them,' said O'Keefe.

'And, General, how he got into that sector. There's a hole in the system — and we have to plug it before others discover it,' commented Havas patiently.

The other two waited for her to continue.

'Gentlemen, the only way to pin something on him is to actually catch him in the act of unauthorized intrusion.' She paused to let her point settle in. 'More than that, we have to immobilize him before he can exit, otherwise we lose his open screen as evidence. That's one thing. But what's most important is that if we lose his open screen, we'll have missed any chance of finding out where he's been and how he got there. Without his pass protocols — which he might never reveal — we're stuck right where we are now!'

Henderson rose from his seat.

'Dr Havas is absolutely right, General. By the time we grab him, he'll have Loony Toons on his screen and a bill for the door we've just axed busting into his apartment! It'll be a lot easier if we can winkle him out of there. Somehow get him to... I've got it! We'll find a way to get him to try it from within the CyberProfile Group's own building. We'll have our people in place, sneak up at the right moment — and grab him before he can even raise his finger.'

'Could that be done?' asked O'Keefe.

'Sure. General, there's no other way — like Dr Havas said, we've got to keep his terminal open and on-line so we can get in ourselves and find out what chicanery he's been up to. But we've just got to think of a way to persuade him to access that sector from inside the CPG building.'

Dr Havas waited until he finished.

'Supposing we advise net users in his immediate area that transmissions are about to be temporarily swung over to include a microwave link — and suggest they take security precautions,' she said. 'He'll avoid that risk of exposure and will be desperate to find a more secure, alternative access.'

'OK,' said Henderson. 'That's the push. Now for the pull. Why don't we give him an urgent project calling for some heavy time out of hours? This will give him perfect cover to walk in and out of the CPG building at nights and weekends — and sneak in a few hours of non-authorized slinking around.'

O'Keefe stood up and walked over to the window. He looked out, his hands clasped behind his back.

'It's too critical,' he said. 'We'll barely have a second to get him. As soon as you open the door, he's gone. And there won't be another chance if something goes even slightly wrong. What we need is just a few moments' leeway.'

The three fell silent and for several minutes the only sound was Henderson cracking his knuckles. Dr Havas winced and Henderson gruffly apologized.

'Gentlemen,' Dr Havas said. 'Perhaps this approach might help. We set up a special intrusion monitoring system to screen all Defense Department sectors. We wait until Mr Stanton is operating, shall we say, suspiciously. Then we significantly reduce the bandwidth and speed of all the sectors we think he could be using. That should slow any attempt by him to make a quick exit — and give us time to catch him in the act,' she explained.

'Dr Havas, let me get this straight. Are you suggesting we put critical elements of our nation's entire defense and security system into slow-motion — again?' queried O'Keefe incredulously.

'Only for 100 seconds or so,' she replied.

'No! No!' he waved his hands. 'There'll be hell to pay. The last time that happened — and that was less than a minute — the inquiry went on for weeks...'

'General,' said Havas coldly. 'There is no choice. We're dealing with a gross security breach. Don't you think there would be an even bigger inquiry if we don't kill it — right now?'

O'Keefe shook his head.

'Dammit, we keep turning off the system, switching traffic for so-called repairs — people must think the whole frigging set-up is falling apart at the seams! Er, apologies, Dr Havas, but you appreciate my position.'

'Well, sir, the system's currently had an unusually high rate of difficulties, in any case. I'm sure the users won't find these interruptions too far out of the ordinary,' said Dr Havas looking meaningfully in Henderson's direction.

O'Keefe picked up the folder and walked towards the door.

'OK. let's do it,' he said. 'Just remember, we can't afford to take the least chance of alerting him. Nothing at all. So let's forget about putting a tap on him — or any sort of cover at all. Better put any investigations on the other 16 possibilities on hold, too. Just in case something leaks out. We're gambling on Stanton, being the one. And by God, we'd better be right!'

'Don't worry — he's the one, General. Just wait,' replied Henderson. 'I'll talk to Fadowsky. He'll keep an eye on him.'

* * *

Quietly locking his garage from the inside, Michael took some materials from the back seat of the car.

When he had finished taping the flexible hose to his Jaguar's exhaust pipe, he led the other end to the passenger's side window. He inserted the hose through a hole in a plastic panel that fit snugly into the window frame and then sealed it into place with more tape. Confident that everything was secure, Michael got into the car and closed the door.

He started the motor and, after revving the motor a few times, he let it settle down into a gentle tickover. Next, Michael placed a disc of his favorite music, the Adagio from Mahler's 5th, into the player and turned it up loud enough to mask the low rumble of the idling motor. For several minutes he lay back with his eyes closed, lost in gentle, sad-sweet music, while the heavy, warm fumes built up around him.

Suddenly, he leaned forward and turned the ignition off and opened the door, gasping for air. Yes, he thought to himself, a nice piece of handiwork. It would work perfectly!

* * *

Vince paced up and down his apartment in high agitation.

'Melissa, listen to me! I just don't want to get involved. I've done everything I should have done. Jesus! It was *me* who sprang him in the first place. They wouldn't have known a thing even now if I hadn't cottoned on to him.'

'Vince,' interrupted Melissa coolly, 'They think highly of you. I know they do. What you did made a good impression. Paul Henderson told me that...'

He spun around.

'Henderson told you? You know, the thought of him working on you behind my back, now *that* makes my skin creep! I just told him I wasn't interested.'

Melissa beckoned Vince over.

'Honey,' she said soothingly, 'I know how you must feel. But just look at it from their point of view. Think what's really at stake here. You know that we're just about the only people who can talk to him without making him suspicious.'

'Look, I know Mike. I really do,' said Vince in a low tone. 'He wouldn't be doing anything too bad. He's a hacker. Just playing games with them — and he let it get out of hand...'

'Well, just answer me this, Vince,' cut in Melissa. 'If he's not up to his neck in something sinister, tell me why did he shut down a big part of the national power grid?'

'Well, that's their problem. I'm no Judas,' shouted Vince. 'I'm just not going to get involved in it. Period.'

'Then,' said Melissa in a matter-of-fact tone, 'I'll do it. You sit right there and nurse that picky conscience of yours. I'll be back in about an hour — and don't try to ring me, I'm turning my phone off.'

'You really enjoy this game, don't you?' Vince sneered.

'Go to hell,' she retorted and slammed the door behind her.

* * *

Michael had just stepped out of the shower when the doorbell rang. He paused, thinking that he would ignore it. Then he heard a woman's voice.

'Hi! Michael! It's Melissa here!'

He threw a robe over himself and tentatively opened the apartment door.

'Hi… Just having a shower…'

Melissa smiled and, after an awkward pause, she asked him if she could come in. Unable to find a plausible excuse to keep her out, Michael looked down the corridor and motioned her inside.

'Why, Michael! It's almost empty… and what have you done with those lovely big photographs you had — they were over there on that wall, I remember.' Melissa leaned forward and whispered conspiratorially, 'Michael, you're not going to suddenly leave town, are you? You can tell me!'

He laughed nervously.

'No, I'm not.' With barely a pause, he ran through his rehearsed story, 'Actually, I saw my father recently and I've agreed to take some of his furniture in here. I thought this would be the time to repaint the place, before it arrives next week. I put most of my own stuff in storage in the meantime. It's just hopeless having to move furniture from one room to the next when throwing paint around and...'

Melissa cut across him. 'Well, seems I came at just the right time. You see, Vince and I'd like to invite you over for dinner this weekend.'

'Thanks, I...'

'I've got this girlfriend in town. She's from back home and we've been like this since high school.' She crossed the fingers on one hand and with exaggerated coyness continued. 'Anyway, Carol's divorced about a year — and I thought, you know...'

'Well, Melissa, I'd like to, but I'm really busy at work. I've been going in almost every night — and the painting...'

'Oh, don't let me down. I told her about you and she's really keen. It would be a big favor for me. We can make it any evening that suits you. Carol's much more your type than the date we lined up for you the last time. Say yes, Michael!'

'It's nice of you, really, but... Oh well, Friday. OK?'

'Why, Michael, that's great! Look, you're dripping water all over. You go inside and get changed and I'll put on the water for a quick coffee — and then I'll be gone! Go on, off you go!'

As soon as Michael disappeared, Melissa flipped open her phone and slowly scanned the room. Only seconds after she had sat down on the edge of his divan and opened up a technical magazine, Michael reappeared.

'Oh my gosh, I was going to make coffee. I just got immersed in this. You know, Michael, there are times when I'm such a butterfly brain!' she said sweetly.

* * *

'That's the situation to date, gentlemen. Now here's what we're going to do about it!'

Henderson's gaze slowly scanned around the briefing room. Before him were a dozen men wearing close-fitting blue uniforms and forage caps. Their lean and taut look and the intense attention they focused on him pleased Henderson. Certainly a cut above the average military product, he thought. If anyone could do the job, this was the crew.

'We want to catch Mr Scooter with his guard down. We'll jump him just when he's strolling though our top-security classified sectors. It seems we can do that in one of two places — either in his apartment or while he's operating at work in the CyberProfile Group. Let's start with the apartment scenario. Slide show, Henry...'

He stepped back as the lights dimmed and an image came up on the screen.

'One of our operatives gained access to his apartment and took these pictures. This is the living room and you can see the kitchen area over to the far right... A better view of the kitchen... Reverse angle from the kitchen back to the living room — and in the right side you see a sort of recess or alcove... Here it is: the computer and the focal point of the exercise... Since these photographs were taken we have arranged for Mr Scooter to be lured out of his den for an evening so an agent can effect an entry and load one of these into his computer.'

He held up a small piece of circuitry the size of his thumbnail.

'This invisibly records and diarizes every function his computer will perform over the next couple of weeks. Why am I telling you this? Because I do *not* want you to be shooting the crap out of his computer under any circumstances. We need to get this back intact. It may not tell us much — or anything — but it could be very useful. Understand?'

He tilted around as a new image appeared on the screen.

'A view up the corridor leading to two bedrooms, a bathroom and storage cupboard. That's the apartment. Now, gentlemen, let me introduce... Mr Scooter — and we'll give you his real name just before the raid. As you can see, dark hair, slightly above-average height, lean build and reasonably fit. What these pictures don't show you is his intelligence. Take my word for it, a very smart operator. IQ of 157. Not just smart, but cunning, street-wise, too. You need to be on your tippy-toes. And, what's more, he knows we're coming after him.'

Without further words, Henderson flicked through a bracket of images of Michael outside his apartment block... in his car... walking from the work car park... a slide of him with Vince and Melissa in which she was pointing towards something in the direction of the unseen camera so that Michael could be seen full-face. Finally, Henderson went back through the photos of the apartment again and then turned around to his audience.

'Now, I want to ask you something. What do you notice about this apartment? What's different? Anyone? Yes?'

'It's virtually empty' observed one of the uniformed men.

'Got it in one!' snapped Henderson. 'This apartment was full of effects and furniture. They've gone. See those light-colored squares on the wall — just here — and here? Well, up to very recently he had framed pictures there. Now, suddenly, they're not there any more. OK, gentlemen, what does that suggest to you?'

A forest of hands shot into the air.

'Right!' Henderson called out loudly without calling for a reply. 'Right! Our Mr Scooter has got himself all ready to... scoot!'

As the laughter abated, he then motioned for the screen to be switched off.

'That means we have very, very little time to nab him. He's obviously close to finishing whatever he's doing. He's ready to run. We could pick him up within 15 minutes, but it's very important we get him in the act of intruding into the system. That's precisely why the apartment raid is not our preferred option. It's really a fall-back plan — and I'll get back to it later. What we are really trying to do is entice Mr Scooter onto our own turf where we have more control over things and can respond faster.'

In very precise detail he outlined exactly how they planned to catch Michael at the CyberProfile building. He stressed the absolute importance of surprising Mr Scooter and immobilizing him before he could exit whatever sector he was in.

A raised hand caught his eye. He looked over to the squad leader, Lieutenant Pete Barker.

'Sir, we were told this would be an LW 2 mission. Is he likely to be armed?'

Henderson picked up the cue immediately. 'No, he won't, Lieutenant. So why will you all carry light weapons? Because we have to keep his computer line open — at any cost. Remember, the success or failure of your mission ultimately hangs on that above all else.'

Several squad members looked uneasy.

'Of course, we want to capture him alive *and* with the computer line still open. But if it's a choice between the two, you've got to know he's expendable. What I'm telling you is that if this guy makes the slightest move when we call him to freeze, you're to shoot him. And I don't mean a warning shot or winging him. Immobilize him instantly.'

'Kill him, sir?'

'If that's what it takes, kill him! Gentlemen, this advice carries authorization directly from the Network Executive, cleared through the highest national security levels.'

31. THE LURE

When Michael entered O'Keefe's office he found him in an unusually friendly, almost avuncular, frame of mind.

'Come in,' the General said, leaning over his desk, as if he wanted no-one else to hear what he was about to say.

'Now, Stanton, I know how busy you guys are over there in CPG. But I've a problem — and I'm going to have to ask your help on this one. The psych boys have been looking at the age-adjustment factors we apply to our earlier profile subjects. So, they've come up with new data that suggest a revision — or that's what they say. Anyway, they've worked out some new formulae, which I'll give you now.'

He placed a folder on the desk.

'What I need to know is roughly what sort of budget I've got to ask for to convert all our profile subjects to these new numbers.'

'How can I help?' asked Michael.

'Since we've no idea how these will ripple through all the second and third generational suppositions, the only way is to take a cross-sample of profiles — say, six in all — and check them out. Don't worry about keeping an individual log on each one, because you're bound to pick up speed as you go along. Just give me the aggregate hours for the whole parcel, then we'll average things out. I need this by the end of next week. Sooner, if any way possible. Can do?'

Michael opened the folder and scanned its contents. 'It doesn't look too complex, but it'll be a ball-breaker of an exercise, General. A real slog. What about the other deadlines?'

'What can I say? You heard me tell the Secretary of State's people we'd have those three profile scenarios by month's end.'

He raised his hands in a gesture of powerlessness.

Michael smiled bleakly. 'Well, if it has to be done...'

'Whatever hours you put in over the top doesn't matter. Just go for it. I'll make sure you get the time off when we're through. Maybe a little cash, too, if we put it down as an away-from-home assignment — and I can tell that you won't be seeing too much home life for the next few weeks! That way you can take a break when it's finished. Believe me you'll have deserved it!'

As he ushered Michael to the door, O'Keefe slapped his hand on his shoulder. 'Appreciate your help,' he said, winking at him.

What a lucky break, thought Michael as he walked over to the CyberProfile Group Building. Just the night before, a message had come up on his screen warning about his local server being switched to a microwave link for an indefinite period — and that users should not count on traffic being secure. And there he was, just about to start the protracted uploading that would take him into Luluworld! Now, at least, he had the cover to spend all the time he wanted right beside the CyberProfile main computer, with all the resources and power to speed the job through. True, O'Keefe's project would burn up a great many hours, but it would give him an ideal opportunity to do a lot of his own work at the same time.

* * *

That night, hunched up in front of the computer, Michael entered his secret zone. Holding the microphone close to his lips he whispered his instructions.

'I have a letter to be written and delivered in my handwriting to Miss Brooks at her home address. It reads:

"My Dearest Louise,

Since I saw you last — it seems an eternity ago — I have done a lot of thinking about what you said and other things that have been on my mind. There was something very important I must tell you... Something I am confident will answer all your questions, remove all your doubts.

I will call on you very soon.

All my love

Michael"

* * *

Michael rushed from the CPG building to his car. He wanted to arrive exactly on time for Melissa's dinner. In that way, he should have no excuse not to leave at the earliest moment.

That night the conversation opened with a desultory exchange about work, cheerlessly retracing an inconsequential discussion they had earlier in the day. After some conspiratorial whispering with an unseen female in the kitchen, Melissa appeared in the doorway.

'This is my very good friend, Carol Hernandez. Carol, I'd like you to meet Michael Stanton.'

She shook Michael's hand and smiled awkwardly.

'You work with Vince, I hear?'

Michael nodded. She was a tall, slim blonde and stood with her shoulders rounded and hips thrust forward. The posture of a fashion model, Michael guessed and, after some pleasantries, he enquired if that were so.

'Why, yes, I am — or at least I was,' she said and turned to Melissa, who shook her head. 'She didn't tell you? My, how did you know?'

'Someone with your looks would have to be a model — or an actor,' was Michael's gallant reply.

'Carol, don't let him flatter you. You're a lost cause. He's only interested in dark-haired ladies — aren't you, Michael?' said Melissa, mischievously.

Michael furrowed his brows, quizzically.

'Louise... Louise Brooks, hair as black as a crow's wing. Cut in a very short bob. She was a movie star in the old silent era — and Michael's in love with her!'

Melissa turned away from Carol, who clearly had no idea what was behind the conversation, and looked at Vince.

'Do you remember all those lovely portraits Michael had in his apartment, Vince? He's removed them — every single one!'

'They'll go back once I've repainted the place,' replied Michael blankly. 'Or perhaps I might put something else up in their place.'

They moved to the table. Melissa had prepared an interesting dinner: a Moroccan dish, she said. To Michael's annoyance, Vince spirited away the claret he had chosen so carefully and it was not seen again for an hour. Instead, the guests were plied with several bottles of a rather oaky red from a local vineyard. (Well, thought Michael, I've lost my chance. Where I'm headed I'll never again taste a 2023 Frère Ambrose!)

The conversation drifted around, lightly and wantonly. Michael heard how far back Carol and Melissa went, they exchanged star signs, how clever Michael must be — and Vince, of course, too, and Melissa — and here was Carol just pottering about in marketing. Well, sales really. No, she didn't miss modeling and all that glamor. She believed that you have to look forward to each new challenge. After all, people, she confided deeply, people are what's important, don't you think, Michael? She shook his knee in a vain attempt to elicit an enthusiastic response.

'Tell me, Carol,' asked Michael, sensing the tedious dead end to which her monologue was steering her. 'Your surname, Hernandez — and you look so... Nordic?'

She explained that it was her husband's, sorry, correction — ex-husband's — name. She was a liberated woman, she wanted everyone to know, and she only carried his name because she had established her professional credentials under that name — and what would be served by changing the brand of a successful and established product?

Through all this, Vince said little. Michael sensed a growing irritation directed, oddly, not at Carol, but at Melissa. When he spoke to Michael, which was not very often, he was surprisingly friendly and considerate. (Strangely, it reminded him of O'Keefe's recent, somewhat uncharacteristic, affability.)

From time to time, he and Melissa went to the kitchen and, without picking up what they said, Michael sensed that all was not well between them. Twice during the evening, Vince glowered when Melissa, without any explanation, rose from the table and disappeared into their bedroom. Hearing the click of the phone in the living room, Michael guessed she was making a series of very brief calls.

Carol started recounting the saga of her failed marriage and this exhumation, which led her in quick succession from brave acceptance to anger, then remorse and finally to self-pitying tears, accounted for the remainder of the evening until Melissa led Carol into the spare bedroom. Although it was only about 10 pm, Michael saw this as a cue to leave early and he rose from the table.

'Oh, no, Michael, please don't go just yet. I'd feel so bad. Carol's still a bit upset. Normally, she's much more together. Look, the coffee's ready to be poured. It's still early. Vince, Michael's glass!'

As he dutifully sat and drank coffee, Michael could only reflect on what this miserable evening had cost him. Already he would have been well into the uploading — and, instead of enduring the inanities of Melissa's friend, he would have been so much closer to the rendezvous with his own, precious Louise!

* * *

A slightly-built man wearing a dark roll-neck sweater and jacket briskly walked out of the apartment block and strode up to the large car parked in the unlit lane just around the corner. He looked carefully around him and placed a small briefcase in the hands that eagerly reached out from the open window.

'No problems?' asked a large man from the back of the car.

'No problems.'

'Get in. OK, Stevens, turn on the receiver.'

'Signal's as clear as a bell, sir.'

The large man picked up his cellphone and tapped out a number with his stubby fingers.

'We're at Scooter's residence. We've just opened the window — and the view's fine.... Thank you, sir. On our way.'

He clicked off the phone and tapped the driver on the shoulder. The car glided quietly onto the road and disappeared into the night.

* * *

As soon as he arrived the next morning, Michael called Vince and several others together and explained what had come up. They agreed to re-allocate some of Michael's existing commitments among themselves and limit his involvement in the South African project to overall strategy design and review, with much of the direct supervision handled by Vince.

Michael then worked on O'Keefe's project throughout the rest of the day. He made a point of talking to Vince about the re-profiling and half-way through the afternoon they discussed his idea of combining several re-profiling routines into a single algorithm.

At about six-thirty, Vince popped his head around the door.

'Calling it quits, Mike. Apart from you, there's no-one else around. Ring me if you need anything.'

Michael looked up and nodded at Vince, who gave him his usual military-style salute and disappeared. He worked on until eight-fifteen. Other than the nod from the security guard an hour earlier, he remained quite undisturbed. He got a cup of coffee from the dispenser bar in the corridor and looked out the window. The car park was completely empty, apart from his own car standing forlornly under one of the tall light towers. He had the place to himself.

Michael hurled the empty coffee cup into the trash bin and sat down at his computer again. He would not exit O'Keefe's project completely, but for safety's sake he would leave an active screen in the background. If anyone did appear, a tap on a key would bring it forward to mask the uploading.

He cleared his throat several times. With a slow, firm voice he commanded the computer to open up.

'Access the CyberProfile secured zone. Voice I.D. clearance... CyberProfile Group... Stanton, Michael...'

As he went through the various security clearances, Michael noticed that his hands were shaking — then, suddenly, he was surprised to find himself in his familiar domain. He hit the spoken command toggle switch: from this point on, all interaction with the computer would be carried out through keyboard responses to text requests on the screen.

For almost an hour, he set parameters, responded to dialogue boxes, checked and adjusted. Finally, all was ready and he instructed the computer to ready itself to receive all the data he had so laboriously recorded over the previous weeks.

It was time to start! Michael booted up the first of the four solid memory cartridges he had brought with him from his home computer. Now he was about to invest his personality and attributes, his intelligence and mind, everything, apart from flesh and bone, that made him who he was, into the new 'self' that would soon live forever in Louise's world. He was so scared that he could feel his intestines knotting. And, yet, so elated that he could almost fly!

But, first, there was something important he had to do...

32. NO PROMISES

A long, cream-colored limousine drew up under the pool of light illuminating the entrance to Bellevue Court. A doorman stepped out and waited dutifully beside the car. At a nod from within, he opened the door on the front passenger side.

'Good evening, Miss Brooks,' he said as he extended an arm to steady her as she disembarked.

'Thank you, Gordon,' Louise replied. She turned to look inside to the driver.

'Lovely night, Boris. Really lovely. Thank you very much for everything...'

There was an indistinct reply.

'I will. I promise. Now off you go,' said Louise, leaning back into the car and kissing the driver on the cheek. 'I'm not the only one who needs to catch up on some sleep! 'Bye!'

The doorman closed the car door and escorted her up the steps and into the apartment building's lobby. The car waited until she was inside and well out of sight and then purred away into the night.

Inside the lift, the doorman smiled at Louise, who shivered a little, despite wearing a fur-collared coat.

'I do believe we are now well and truly into fall, Miss Brooks. It's been so mild till now that this chill's taken us a little by surprise.'

'You're right,' Louise replied affably. 'You'd never think I came from Kansas. Now *that* can be cold!'

'Kansas, Miss Brooks?'

'Wichita.'

'I've been there. I was a recruiting sergeant in '17. Our train went through the Mid-West and we stopped in Wichita...'

'So, now you know why I live in California!'

He smiled diplomatically and opened the door as the lift stopped.

'Home at last! Good night, Gordon,' said Louise.

Swinging her cocktail bag, she hummed to herself as she walked up to her door. She fumbled around for her key and then inserted it into the lock.

'Hello, Louise!'

She let out a startled yelp and peered anxiously into the dark alcove on the other side of the corridor.

'Jesus! *Michael!* What the devil are you doing here? You can't just sneak into my place like this. You gave me the shock of my life!'

'Do you mind if I come in for a moment?'

'Of course.'

Just inside the door, Michael suddenly froze and clutched her arm tightly, 'Listen! Listen!'

Again Michael heard it, from the shadowy recesses of the long corridor — that familiar sound, half way between a throat-clearing cough and a grunt. Henderson was through his protective barriers and was here — right here inside Louise's world! It was all over...

'Michael, Michael!' whispered Louise as she shook her arm free. 'It's only the doorman... Gordon? Is that you?'

'Yes, Miss Louise, came the voice from down the corridor. 'Just checking everything before I lock up the front door. Good night now.'

As Gordon continued walking down the corridor and around the corner at the end, Louise looked searchingly into Michael's eyes.

'It's nothing. Sorry. He sounded just like someone I know,' he explained.

'Obviously a character you're not too keen to meet again,' she observed.

'Especially not here,' Michael replied, still looking apprehensively down the corridor.

Louise pulled him inside and quickly closed her door.

'I leave one beau at the front door — and then there's another waiting inside! It's enough to give a girl a bad reputation!' she laughed. 'Well, Mr Stanton, how are you?'

'Not so bad. And you?'

'Pretty good. Anyway, I want to climb out of this, so why don't you set up a drink for us both and I'll join you shortly. That's today's paper beside you.'

She tweaked his cheek affectionately.

'Back in a moment!'

Michael poured out two large whisky sodas and sat down. The sound of Louise gaily singing to herself in her bedroom seemed a good omen and, as the warming draught of whisky began to loosen the taut muscles of his stomach, he sank deep into the armchair. Scanning through the newspaper with slight interest, his eye was suddenly caught by a headline.

Curfew After Berlin Riots
Nationalist Leader Assassinated

The report described a serious disturbance which had left 11 dead from gunfire, with an unknown number wounded, and had only been quelled after heavy police and army intervention. The violence had erupted during a crowded political rally in Munich after a member of the communist *Rotfrontkampferbund* militia had assassinated Herr Adolf Hitler, the leader of an extreme right-wing group called the National Socialist German Workers' Party.

Michael stared at the newspaper as the implications of that headline resonated within his mind. Would anyone ever guess what unimaginable horrors he had averted by engineering this apparently unimportant incident so far away? And yet, what train of other possibilities had he now set in motion? Surely nothing could be so bad as the catastrophe that had disfigured his own world in that era.

He looked up to see Louise in front of him, casually elegant in a black, silk pajama suit.

'Thanks. Would you believe that this is the first drink I've had today? True! That was Boris Wahlstein I was out with. An up-and-coming young producer at Galaxy Studios. I don't think he's aware of my bad reputation — or maybe he's chosen not to believe it. Anyway, I wanted to make a good impression.'

Louise sat on the arm of Michael's chair.

'With you it's different. You know all about my wicked ways,' she smiled naughtily as they clinked glasses.

'Alas, I do!' replied Michael, shaking his head with a feigned resignation. He looked at Louise over the top of his glass for several moments, watching a knowing smile play around her lips. He grinned in a boyish, embarrassed way.

'Good to see you, Michael. I missed you a little.'

'I missed you, too, Louise.'

'I got your letter.' She playfully tipped her drink from side to side. 'You said there was something you wanted to tell me...'

Michael took her hand in his.

'I've had time to think over the past few weeks... You were right, there were some things happening which weren't... may not have seemed... quite regular.'

'Well, that was the way I read them, Michael...'

'Fact is, Louise, I haven't been quite straight down the line with you. There are some things I haven't told you. And I think you ought to know — or at least I'd feel better if you did.'

Over the next thirty or forty minutes, Michael explained that he had deliberately tried to conceal his background. To begin with, he was not (as he let people assume) the scion of a patrician Eastern family. His wealth was real, yes, but this was not old money, the graceful, comfortable bequest that slipped so effortlessly from one genteel generation to the next. No, he had been launched with dollars that had been grasped for with the hunger of narrow and desperate ambition; it had been earned through stunting toil and cunning.

Louise gazed intently at Michael, but said nothing, as he quietly described how his father had arrived from a Warsaw ghetto, penniless, with almost no English. All he had was the vision that, through his efforts and their efforts, his two sons — Jerzy and Michael — would one day have the education and the wealth that would earn them the world's respect. As one hard year followed another, his father had clawed and inched his way ever closer to that dream. Unstintingly, schoolbooks, even when secondhand, were purchased with the money that could have covered his mother's thin shoulders with a decent coat or resoled the old man's boots. Even as the family's fortunes eased, every spare dollar was invested in propelling Michael and Jerzy from the shabbiness and meanness of the slum. And so it was that, one day, Mr Stanislowski decreed that the boys would henceforth be known by the name of Stanton.

Driven by their father's unrelenting ambition, the boys had studied hard. One day, Jerzy, the elder brother, arrived home with a letter and quietly told the family that he had won a university scholarship. Michael remembered that his father was infinitely more pleased by the honor and the promise of a dream soon to be fulfilled than by the prospect of his financial burden being eased.

When Michael returned home from the War, he was greeted by his parents at the railway station. He was shocked at how suddenly they had grown old. Their subdued welcome prepared Michael for the dreadful news. Jerzy had been killed, not as much as two weeks before the armistice. Now he, Michael, was the sole repository of the family's hopes — and he went on to fulfill them through untiring work. High school, university, his first job — all way-stations that for others also provided diversion, entertainment and the means to indulge a casual curiosity — were for Michael the focus of deadly intent which left no room for frivolity.

Faithful to his father's strategy, Michael moved from one employment to another, in a bank, a securities house, a bond dealer's and on the stock exchange floor. With each move, he burrowed deep to acquire the knowledge, the insights and the contacts to serve the greater design.

Then, on his twenty-fifth birthday, his father deposited a sum of money into Michael's bank account. It was little enough that it could be lost through one thoughtless mistake, the old man had warned him. But it might be enough, if husbanded carefully in the years ahead, to seed a great fortune.

'And that,' said Michael, 'was what I have done. When my father died six years ago, I was already worth more than one hundred thousand. Before my mother died just over two years ago, she had lived to see her son a millionaire — in fact, eight times over. I don't really know my realizable assets now, but they must come close to double that figure.'

'So, what brought you here to California?' asked Louise.

'Boredom. I have an investment house in New York. It's run by some of the best brains in the business — which is why we held out after the Crash. They're managing fine without me.'

He drained the glass.

'No, I needed a change and I thought I'd have a look at the movie business. Well, I've seen enough to know that I'd get chewed alive. Still, there are other things I think could happen here and I'm not sure too many others have woken up to them yet!'

'But, you were going to say something about...'

'The coincidences? Funny happenings?' Michael cut in. 'Well, the hot tips were cabled in code by my financial researchers in New York. And — I'm not really proud to admit this — I had a couple of private investigators trailing some people around so I could set myself up to best advantage. You know, always in the right place at the right time...'

'They followed me, Michael?' asked Louise incredulously. 'Did they really follow *me?*'

Michael looked down and did not answer. He slowly shook his head, appalled that he could ravel this skein of deception. (But, he consoled himself, in this world, his world, whatever he stated he could also make real.)

'You remember when I was late arriving to pick up you and Madie and... that real estate guy?'

'Henry.'

'We were going to catch the train that ended up crashing. You're right, I didn't have a flat tire. On the way, a car ran over a dog. It was in agony and past help. Anyway, I went to my car and got a tire lever and killed it. A kid came along — she owned it. I couldn't leave her there. I took her home and came back for the dog. I thought it would upset you and Madie if I told you. Anyway, I guess that dog saved our lives.'

'Oh, Michael,' sighed Louise. 'Why didn't you just tell me?'

'I'm sorry. I was desperate to be the person I thought would impress you. With my background I just didn't think I would have stood a chance. All I had was money — but less than a good many other men have around here. I could care less about the others. I contrived things so I could impress *you*. Nothing more. Because I wanted you so desperately.'

He stroked her neck.

'And I still do...'

Louise looked at Michael and softly brushed a light, lingering kiss across his lips.

'Michael, I was so pleased to get your letter. I really had thought you'd gone for good. I missed you more than a little.' She paused reflectively. 'I missed you... a lot, I guess. In fact, I'm really very taken with you. But I think you know that.'

For several wordless minutes, they sat together. Michael softly brushed the back of his hand against Louise's cheek.

'Louise,' he began. 'There's something else. I have to go away for a short while. East. Some bad business I want to get out of. I can't say any more and please don't ask, but there's a chance that something may go wrong. If you don't hear from me again, I want you to know that I will always love you.'

'Michael...'

'Sounds impossibly melodramatic, doesn't it?' Michael laughed. 'Don't worry, I fully intend seeing you again very soon. I mentioned it, just in case.'

Louise rose from the armchair rest and, holding Michael's hand, led him towards her bedroom door. She paused at the doorway and smiled, with her mouth pursing into a mischievous pout.

'Of course, Michael, I want you to remember that I'll still always be a free spirit. I can't make binding promises for the future, but...'

Michael placed his finger on her lips — and smiled.

33. GIVE HER MY LOVE…

'You don't have to be here,' said Henderson quietly.

'I know,' replied Vince, taking the coffee passed to him.

It was the first spoken exchange for an eternity. Yet it aroused no interest among the dozen uniformed men crouched at the back of the dimly-lit room. Until now, the only sound had been a barely-audible squeak as someone adjusted the strap on his automatic pistol.

'Known him for long?' asked Henderson, not looking at Vince.

'A few years. Since college.'

'Mmmm… Well, there you are. Seems there was a lot about him you never even suspected,' replied Henderson, giving one of his grunts. There was scarcely a pause before he added, 'That lady of yours. Now, there's one very smart cookie…'

Vince fixed his eyes on Henderson's smirking face.

Henderson turned and whispered, 'Lieutenant Barker, how are they going with the video surveillance?'

'Nothing new, sir. OK, men, settle down. Could be an hour…'

* * *

Michael took a deep breath and pressed the key that would begin incarnating himself in Louise's far-distant world.

The transfer reading bar moved almost imperceptibly from start to finish, telling Michael that each of the four cartridges would take at least forty or fifty minutes to configure for uploading. This left him with nothing to do but wait. After so many restless nights agonizing over this very undertaking, he was surprised that he now felt so remarkably detached and unemotional.

At last, the screen flashed that the first cartridge was successfully uploaded. Do you wish to exit? No... Do you wish to continue uploading?... Yes... Please load cartridge... Click...

Just to be on the safe side, Michael had set up the sequence to ensure that the most critical information was uploaded first, with decreasingly important data following. That way, if anything went wrong and he had to exit quickly or terminate the transfer, it would be easier to pick things up later. Anyway, he always preferred to get the more difficult or risky tasks out of the way first. It was his way of doing things.

Well after ten, the last cartridge had finally disgorged its information. Assured that everything was safely transferred, Michael secure-wiped the memory of each of the four cartridges. From now on, Michael simply had to monitor the profile compositing taking place within the Luluworld site. This was an automatic, background operation and Michael began tidying up around his computer.

This completed, he rose from his chair to get another coffee. As he dialed the dispenser in the corridor, he thought he heard a noise from down the passage. A squeak and a slight knock... then silence. He stood completely still for a full half-minute and, hearing nothing more, returned to his computer. His imagination — or perhaps an echo from his own footfall, Michael thought. He was becoming easily spooked.

A screen message told him the compositing was now finished. Before closing down, he just had to see for himself that Michael Stanton — his other self — had journeyed safely from one universe to the other. Very slowly and nervously, he moved over to Luluworld, choosing to view things on the screen rather than by means of the VR headpiece he had with him. It would be confronting enough to see his separate and independent self at this remove: he did not relish any additional realism!

In the usual way, the screen flickered and the soft picture took on a sharper resolution. The view was from behind a desk or bureau which was heaped up with newspapers. Towards the edge of the screen a hand could be seen, holding a fountain pen and writing on bond paper which carried an address printed in black:

Michael Stanton
Alhambra Hotel
1023 Granville Street
Los Angeles, California

Michael looked down again at the moving pen which, he could just make out, was jotting down details about share parcels. He was electrified to discover that the handwriting was his own. Identical!

He moved the toggle to get a side view of the profile subject. And there he was, a faithful facsimile of himself, seated at a bureau in his hotel suite. Despite the high, starched collar and the closely-groomed hair, Michael saw his exact mirror image. Fascinated, he watched for several minutes as the figure on the screen finished the letter and meticulously folded and inserted it into an already-addressed envelope. There was a knock on the door and Michael heard an eerily familiar voice call out.

'Yes? Who is it?'

'Room service, Mr Stanton.'

'Come in.'

A black man in the hotel's livery entered and placed a silver tray with a coffee pot, cup and cruet on a low coffee table in the middle of the room.

'Will there be anything else, Mr Stanton?'

'No, Barney, thank you very much... On second thoughts, take this letter to the front desk and ask them to send it by messenger.'

Barney thanked him for the tip, took the letter and left the room. The solitary figure then walked over to the window and stood there, motionless, looking down onto the street below.

Michael gave the toggle switch another light touch and the screen filled with an eye-view picture of the street outside the Alhambra. No-one could be seen, apart from a newspaper vendor across the road; and he could just make out an automobile in the distance, turning a corner and disappearing...

Suddenly there was a loud crash.

'Freeze!'

Michael spun around from the computer to see four men in blue uniforms filling the splintered doorway. Two of them were aiming handguns directly at him.

'I said freeze! Don't move or we'll shoot.'

Here it was at last — the dreadful moment Michael had spooled through his imagination over countless days and nights. Caught — and so agonizingly close to his destination!

Clenching his gun with both hands, Lieutenant Barker took a half pace forward.

'Now, very slowly, raise both hands in the air,' he said in a quiet, firm voice. 'Up in the air. Slowly swivel your chair around to face us. And no sudden moves... Right, just stay exactly like that. Piggott, the cuffs... Mr Henderson? We've got him.'

Seeing Henderson squeeze his way into the room, Michael felt a nauseous surge of panic.

Oh, Christ! he thought. The computer's still open — and Louise is unprotected. Louise! Suddenly, with a cry he spun around and punched the computer keyboard.

'Stop him! Shoot him! SHOOT him!!' Henderson shouted.

Two deafening shots cracked out, so closely spaced that most present thought only one gun had fired.

Michael's back arched and he half-raised himself from the seat. He paused for what seemed like seconds, looking as if he were faintly puzzled. Then, indecisively, almost absent-mindedly, he slowly subsided into the chair back and his tense body relaxed. He fell forward and his head banged sharply against the computer monitor. In all this time, Michael had uttered not a sound.

Lieutenant Barker stepped forward and after a peremptory look at Michael, shifted his inert form to one side. Henderson lunged at the computer, completely ignoring the body slumped in the chair. His face close to the empty screen, he furiously tapped on the blood-spattered keyboard. All the screen revealed was the familiar CYPROSIM master index page.

'Damnation! Damnation!' Henderson shrieked, pounding his fist on the computer desk. He sprang to his feet and rolled his head back in despair, clenched fists raised high. 'We've lost it!'

The silence was broken by Lieutenant Barker.

'I'm sorry, Mr Henderson, we had to fire without hitting the computer. We....'

His eyes wide and staring, Henderson looked at him, almost uncomprehendingly.

'OK, Lieutenant, it's OK,' he whispered at last. 'Your men did exactly what they had to do. Let's get out. The others can take over.'

A medical orderly entered the room and, without moving Michael, checked his pulse and examined his head wound. He stepped to one side and nodded to a uniformed man who photographed Michael from various angles. Vince Fadowsky appeared at the doorway and peered into the smoke-filled room. When the photographer finished, Vince walked over to Michael's side. He could see that his eyes were still open. They stared straight at the screen, as if transfixed by some indescribable epiphany.

'Ah, Jesus,' Vince sighed. 'Mike...'

At that moment the computer went blank and its screensaver came on. Against a background of changing colors, a pixilated image resolved itself into a cartoon. It was the face of a beautiful young woman with wide-set eyes and a short, black bob cut that Vince instantly recognized. A balloon caption carried the words: 'What a Lulu!' — then she pouted and winked seductively.

Vince looked hard at the screen. His brows furrowed as if waking to some strange revelation.

'Mike,' he said to himself so softly, 'Mike, wherever you are, be sure to give her my love...'

ABOUT THE AUTHOR

A former newspaper journalist and television producer-scriptwriter, Anthony Eames' varied career also includes roles as a book publishing editor, advertising creative director and public relations consultant.

With a partner, he operated a successful TV production company for many years and has seven international film and video awards to his credit.

An Anglo-Irishman who has lived in Sydney, Australia for many years, he is trying to escape the demands of his communications consultancy and invest more time in his writing projects.

Anthony is married to a Japanese molecular biologist.

Printed in Great Britain
by Amazon.co.uk, Ltd.,
Marston Gate.